THE LONG TRAIL

In the last months before the end of the Civil War, Cole Thomason's grandfather had been one of many to contribute gold to a fund to help the army. The disappearance of the messenger, Adna Fenn, who was to deliver it to the Treasury, had never been satisfactorily explained, and Cole had reason to believe that he was still alive. Arriving at the isolated ranch house of the lovely Jane Bowman and her father, Cole learns that Jane's grandfather and father had also been contributors to this same pool of gold. They join forces in what proves to be a violent manhunt for the man once known as Adna Fenn. But when Belle Dacey, the lush, high-spirited daughter of a neighbouring rancher, attracts Cole's attention, she causes Jane some uneasy moments . . .

SPECIAL MESSAGE TO READERS

THE ULVERSCROFT FOUNDATION
(registered UK charity number 264873)
was established in 1972 to provide funds for research, diagnosis and treatment of eye diseases. Examples of major projects funded by the Ulverscroft Foundation are:-

- The Children's Eye Unit at Moorfields Eye Hospital, London
- The Ulverscroft Children's Eye Unit at Great Ormond Street Hospital for Sick Children
- Funding research into eye diseases and treatment at the Department of Ophthalmology, University of Leicester
- The Ulverscroft Vision Research Group, Institute of Child Health
- Twin operating theatres at the Western Ophthalmic Hospital, London
- The Chair of Ophthalmology at the Royal Australian College of Ophthalmologists

You can help further the work of the Foundation by making a donation or leaving a legacy. Every contribution is gratefully received. If you would like to help support the Foundation or require further information, please contact:

THE ULVERSCROFT FOUNDATION
The Green, Bradgate Road, Anstey
Leicester LE7 7FU, England
Tel: (0116) 236 4325

website: www.foundation.ulverscroft.com

The Long Trail

Arthur Henry Gooden

First published in Great Britain by Hodder & Stoughton
First published in the United States by Dutton

First Isis Edition
published 2015
by arrangement with
Golden West Literary Agency

A catalogue record for this book is available from the British Library.

ISBN 978–1–78541–004–8 (pb)

Published by
F. A. Thorpe (Publishing)
Anstey, Leicestershire

Set by Words & Graphics Ltd.
Anstey, Leicestershire
Printed and bound in Great Britain by
T. J. International Ltd., Padstow, Cornwall

This book is printed on acid-free paper

Affectionately inscribed to
my young namesake
ARTHUR MAHLON PERKINS

CHAPTER ONE

The house was hardly more than a gray blur of adobe walls in the deepening twilight and looked as if it had not been lived in for years. The always encroaching chaparral was again in possession of what had once been a garden, and branches lay rotting where they had fallen from the surrounding trees. Deserted or not, a house usually meant water in the vicinity, and Cole Thomason was grimly aware that he could not keep going much longer without water.

He sank down on a boulder, exhausted by the stiff climb from the sandy wash of the arroyo, and conscious too of a strange giddiness that made him wonder if the whole thing was only a mirage — the distorted imaginings of a thirst-crazed brain.

His quivering nerves steadied as he continued to look, taking note of certain telltale signs his first surprised glance had failed to see. It was obvious that the place was no longer deserted. Some attempt had been made to clear the brush from the yard and garden. Horses drowsed in the corral of barbed wire strung on freshly-cut juniper posts. A ranch wagon and a buckboard stood under a cottonwood tree near the new barn.

Something else he now saw jerked Cole upright from the boulder, a flume of six inch boards that spilled water into a big barrel set on a platform near the kitchen door.

His thirsty gaze traced the course of the flume up the slope behind the house to a spring-fed pond under high red cliffs. The surplus run-off made a little stream, hardly visible in the thick undergrowth, and formed another pool below the house before meandering on its way to drop down to the insatiable sands of the arroyo. Another flume carried water to a horse trough that poked under the barbed wires of the corral.

He studied the old house with growing interest. Some Mexican *ranchero* had settled here long before General Kearney's march to Santa Fé had made the province of New Mexico a territory of the United States. It was easy to understand why he had chosen to make his home on this peninsula-like bit of mesa in the hook of the great arroyo. Water was precious in this land of little rain, and here was water in abundance, guaranteed by the big, ever-flowing natural well. The place was ideal for the headquarters of a sizeable cattle ranch. Ample water and plenty of range back in the hills.

Despite his maddening thirst, Cole continued to hesitate. This remote corner of the territory was only a short jump from the Mexican border and it was quite possible that the long-abandoned old rancho was now a secret hide-out for desperados. It might be fatal to show himself. He would not be allowed to get away alive with their secret.

The continued deep stillness began to raise the hope that nobody was at home. Wishful thinking, he realized with a wry grimace. The sound that broke the twilight stillness was the unmistakable clatter of a stovelid, and more convincing was the voice that reached to him from the old house, a girl's fresh young voice singing a song he had not heard in years, a favorite of his mother's.

My love is like a red, red rose
That's newly sprung in June —

A relieved grin wiped the anxiety from Cole's dusty, unshaved face. He took a quick step, halted, drew back into the concealing bushes. A lone rider had appeared with startling suddenness from a ravine beyond the corral. He slid out of his saddle, a bearded, middle-aged man with the erect bearing of a one-time cavalry officer.

He stripped off the saddle and bridle, turned the horse into the corral, closed the gate and stood watching while the horse nosed the water in the trough.

The girl's father, Cole guessed, and again he took a step, froze in his tracks, with his startled gaze on a second man who crouched in the chaparral a hundred yards up the arroyo and perhaps some fifty yards behind the unsuspecting owner of the horse in the corral.

The thing happened with horrifying suddenness. Before Cole could shout a warning, flame spurted from the rifle in the ambusher's hands. The crashing report of the gun smothered Cole's frantic yell as the bearded man staggered and fell.

The song stopped abruptly, and there was a momentary deep stillness, broken by the slam of a hastily-opened door — a scream. The killer slid stealthily into the chaparral. He was too far away for Cole to get a look at his face.

The girl was pushing and stumbling through the brush to the limp body sprawled against the corral fence, and Cole began to run, or tried to run. His legs were unsteady, his knees like rubber. He was weaker than he had suspected, and he was again conscious of the disturbing giddiness. The fear that he might collapse horrified him.

The quick thud of hoofs, drew his look, in time to glimpse the ambusher spurring a white-maned pinto down the trail that dipped into the arroyo. He would recognize that pinto if he ever saw the horse again, Cole promised himself savagely as he clawed through the bushes.

The girl heard his approach, hastily snatched the gun from the stricken man's holster and sprang to her feet. Cole was aware of dark, blazing eyes in a white face. Her voice lashed at him, and he sensed that he was very close to instant death.

He halted, forced slow, painful words from swollen lips.

"I only want to help —"

"You fiend!" Her knuckles showed white over the butt of the long-barrelled Colt in her hand.

"I didn't shoot him," protested Cole in his slow, whispering voice. "Can't you see? I'm unarmed — nearly dead for water!"

She hesitated, quick comprehension of his exhausted condition wiping the hot anger from her eyes. She motioned with the gun to the water-trough, and he staggered to the little flume, put his mouth to the cool water that spilled from it.

When he turned from the trough she was again on her knees by the side of the prostrate man. Her face lifted, and the wordless appeal in her look did more than the water to steady Cole. He stooped quickly, eyes keen again as he studied the bearded face, fingered the limp wrist. He muttered a surprised ejaculation, gave the girl a relieved look.

"He's not dead! I can feel a pulse!"

Her eyes closed, and he felt that she was praying, and after a moment he spoke again. "Bring water, and something for a bandage. We must stop the bleeding."

The gun dropped from her hand and she sped away. Cole's look followed her briefly, returned to the wounded man. The bullet had torn a gash through the upper arm, below the shoulder and furrowed across the ribs, leaving an ugly red smear. Apparently no bone had been touched.

The girl was soon back with strips of fresh, clean linen and a tin pail that she stopped to fill with water from the flume. Cole guessed that the linen bandages had come from a freshly-laundered bed sheet.

He wasted no time with talk, sponged away the blood and deftly adjusted a bandage. The girl was on her knees, anxious eyes on the wounded man's face.

"It's not a fatal wound," reassured Cole. "The impact of a heavy rifle bullet can knock a man senseless. He'll soon recover consciousness and then we'll get him to the house."

Her tension relaxed, and she sat very still, one of her father's hands clasped in hers. His eyes were suddenly wide open, met her relieved look.

"I reckon something happened," he said feebly. "Don't seem to remember —"

She touched his face gently. "Don't try to talk —"

"I'm all right." His eyes focussed waveringly on Cole. "What's going on here, Jane? Who's this man?"

She hesitated, realized it was best to tell him. "You've been shot and he came along in time to save your life. I don't know his name." She turned her head in time to see Cole suddenly snatch up the fallen gun. He shook his head at her, finger on lips warning her not to speak, and crawled into the brush.

Amazement, fright, held her speechless. She heard her father's feeble whisper.

"What scared him away?"

She heard something else now, the sound of horses, and in another moment she saw the riders, four of them, rounding the arroyo bend. New fears constricted her heart, and then she recognized the pair in the lead. Jasper Dacey and his redheaded foreman, Lute Soler.

"It's Mr. Dacey," she whispered, and something made her add, "Don't say anything about the — the man who's been helping us."

His puzzled eyes held hers. "I reckon you've some good reason."

"He's been good to us," Jane said simply. An understatement, she thought to herself. Her father might have bled to death despite her own efforts if it had not been for their unknown good Samaritan. She must say nothing that might betray his whereabouts, place him in possible jeopardy.

From where she knelt by her father she could see the little ravine without turning her head. The stranger was hiding there to avoid being seen, perhaps recognized, by the approaching horsemen. It was odd that he would fear Dacey. She and her father both disliked the arrogant cattleman, but his reputation was good and his JD outfit the biggest in the Boca Grande country. No honest man had need to fear Jasper Dacey.

The thought that the stranger was possibly not an honest man hurt, and then she recalled his fine, rugged face, his clean, unafraid eyes. His flight into the brushchoked ravine had nothing to do with lawless occasions, nor could he have known who the approaching horsemen were. He had disappeared into the ravine while they were still hidden from view around the bend.

A voice, loud, demanding, broke into the maelstrom of her wild conjecturing. "Anybody home?"

Jane's quick look told her the horsemen had halted close to the house.

"Over here," she called.

She heard a surprised exclamation, the scrape of saddle leather in the brush, the crunch of shod hoofs. She was busy now, dabbing her father's brow with a piece of cloth hastily dipped in the tin bucket.

The riders pulled to a standstill behind her. She turned her head in a look at them. The momentary silence was broke by Dacey, a tall, dark man with a touch of frost in his hair and drooping mustache.

"Didn't see you back here in the brush, the light gettin' poor," he said, and then, his gaze fastening on the still form of the wounded man, "What's happened here?" He was out of his saddle, stood on wide-spread feet opposite her, his face grim as he stared down at her father. "My God — it's Bowman!" he added in a dismayed voice. "Looks like somebody has used a gun on him."

"You've said it, Dacey," groaned Jane's father. His eyes closed, and Jane guessed he was taking the best way out to avoid questions.

"He's been shot," she informed Dacey. "Somebody shot him from over there in the chaparral." She gestured at the arroyo.

"Did you see the skunk who did the shootin'?" Dacey asked.

Jane shook her head. "I was in the house, starting supper. Father had just ridden into the yard and turned the horse in the corral when I heard the shot."

"I'm sure mighty sorry," commiserated the tall cowman. He stared hard at the dark head bent over the wounded man. "Are you sure you didn't get a look at the scoundrel you say was back in the chaparral?"

Her face lifted in an impatient look at him. "Instead of asking questions you could help get him to the house. Questions can wait."

Dacey's sunburned face reddened and he gestured at the group of silently-attentive riders. "Climb down, boys, and help get Mr. Bowman over to the house."

They followed Jane through the dusk, her father cradled in their arms, gently lowered him on his bed. Dacey stared worriedly at the wounded man.

"Climb your saddle, Cherokee," he said to one of the cowboys. "Get Doc Johnson out here on the run."

"I don't want a doctor," protested Jane's father. "Jane has fixed me up fine. She's all the doctor I need."

"I'm sending for the doc," insisted Dacey. "You're in no shape to savvy what is best for you, Bowman." He gestured at the long, lean man hesitating in the doorway. "Get going, Cherokee. Make dust for town." He smiled at the girl. "You did a mighty good job, tying him up. He could have bled to death if you hadn't got that bandage on him in time."

"I'm glad you happened by." Jane was wishing they would go, and wondering what purpose had brought them riding up to the house through the shadowed twilight. The JD home ranch was fifteen miles away. "Thank you so much for your help, Mr. Dacey. I couldn't have got him to the house by myself."

"We didn't just *happen* by," Dacey said. "We're looking for a fellow who got lost back in the hills. He might have come by your place."

Jane was conscious of their intent eyes and was glad the growing darkness shadowed her face. "Nobody has come here to the house," she said.

"He'd likely be looking for water," rumbled Dacey.

"He could have come and gone and I wouldn't know," Jane pointed out. "He wouldn't need to come to the house for water. He could have gone to the corral flume, or up to the pond." She paused. Dacey might wonder if she showed no natural curiosity. "Why do you think he is lost?"

"One of the boys found a horse and pack-mule lying dead in the chaparral, up in the Big Hatchets," Dacey explained. "Both of them shot. Looked like an ambush."

"We found his empty canteen, a bullet hole in it." added Lute Soler. "Mighty tough for a tenderfoot to be lost in these hills if he don't know where to look for water."

Jane said again, a bit impatiently, "He could have come and gone without my seeing him. I haven't been watching the yard."

"I sure would like to pick up his trail," grumbled Dacey. "He's likely a friend I've been expecting from Santa Fé. He failed to show up at the ranch yesterday and I'm mighty worried."

"If he happens to come here I'll tell him you're searching for him," Jane offered. "What's his name?"

"Well —" The cowman hesitated, reddened. "His visit is kind of secret and he wouldn't want his name spread 'round."

"I see." Jane kept her voice casual. "Anyway, if he does come I can tell him you were here."

"No chance now, to pick up his trail," grumbled Dacey. "Getting too dark. Might as well start for home." He stared thoughtfully at Bowman, lying on the bed, eyes closed. "Maybe one of us should stay till the doc gets here. Kind of hate to leave you alone with your sick dad."

Jane saw the quick gleam in Lute Soler's eyes. The thought of being alone with the redheaded foreman appalled her. She said hurriedly, "You're very kind, but I'm sure I can manage."

Her father spoke from the bed. "I'll get along fine, Dacey." Irritation rasped his weak voice. "All I want is to be left alone and if you meet Doc you can send him back to town. When I want a doctor I'll send for one myself."

Dacey started an impatient rejoinder, saw the silent appeal in the girl's eyes and turned away with a gesture at his companions. Jane followed them from the bedroom and across the low-ceilinged living room to the outside door. Dacey halted, looked back at her.

"Your dad is too bullheaded for his own good," he said harshly. "I don't give a damn what he says. Doc Johnson is going to have a look at him."

Jane had no answer. She wanted to be rid of them, stood watching from the doorway while they got their horses and rode away.

She continued to stand there, peering into the dark night and listening to the fading hoofbeats. Satisfied at last that they were really gone, she closed the door, lit a lamp and carried it into her father's bedroom.

His head turned on the pillow in a look at her as she placed the lamp on a table. "He was lying, Jane."

"Yes," agreed Jane. "He was lying." She studied her father with anxious eyes. "You must keep quiet — rest."

"I'm all right." Bowman fingered the bandage, his expression thoughtful. "I'm wondering about that young man."

"He didn't even wait to see who was coming," puzzled Jane.

"Proves he was afraid of being recognized by somebody who intended harm," grimly surmised Bowman.

Jane nodded. "It was still light enough for him to get a look at them. He wouldn't have been afraid if Mr. Dacey *is* his friend."

"Which means Dacey lied," her father said again, and added worriedly, "I don't trust that man."

"He's been very kind." reminded the girl. "He could have made things difficult for us." She hesitated. "It must have been a shock for him when he learned this place belonged to us."

"He couldn't deny our legal claim to the ranch."

"He didn't try —" Jane hesitated again, feeling for the right words. "After all, Father, Mr. Dacey could have made us a lot of trouble. He's been grazing his cattle on this land for years and years. It would be natural for him to think this place belonged to his JD ranch."

"I'm thinking he *does* have that notion." Mr. Bowman stared up at his daughter, an odd gleam in his eyes. "Perhaps it explains this business." He again fingered his bandage.

"Oh, *Father!*"

"Somebody sent a killer to shoot me in the back."

"I can't believe it." Her tone was incredulous, touched with alarm. "Not Mr. *Dacey*, Father!"

He was silent for a long moment, evidently regretting his words, and when he spoke his voice was gentle. "No need for you to get frightened," he reassured. "I shouldn't say foolish things just because I happen not to like Dacey." He gave her a faint smile. "Forget it, child."

His concern made her instantly all tenderness. She bent and kissed him. "Don't think about it now. The main thing is for you to rest and get well fast."

"I sometimes wonder if I did right, letting you come to this wild country with me."

"You couldn't have stopped me!" She kissed him again, went swiftly to the bedroom door, glanced back at him. "I'm going to leave you for a few minutes."

He understood what was in her mind. "That's right, Jane," he said. "We've got to help him — if he's still somewhere close."

She nodded, hurried through the living room to the kitchen and lit a lantern that hung from a hook near the stove. The fire was low. She took a chunk of wood from the box and dropped it on the red coals, and after a moment's thought, took the lantern from the hook and went to the door. The lighted lantern intensified the darkness outside. She wanted to signal with it, was suddenly fearful that Dacey might have left a man to spy on the place. She could only dare stand there, the lantern motionless in her hand. Perhaps Cole Thomason would see her in the lighted doorway and would understand. She hoped he would.

CHAPTER TWO

She heard a stealthy movement in the brush, and suddenly his voice came to her from the darkness. "I'm afraid of the light," Cole said. "Somebody might be watching."

He saw from her brief gesture that she understood. The door closed and the kitchen windows went dark.

He waited a few moments. The only sound that broke the stillness was the sharp bark of a coyote down in the wash of the arroyo. Reassured, he went swiftly to the door. It was not fastened, opened to his touch. He slipped inside, closed the door, stood motionless in the dark kitchen. Another door opened and he saw Jane, framed against dim lamplight.

"I hoped you would come." She turned away with a gesture for him to follow her. "My father wants to see you."

She led the way into the bedroom. "Here he is, Father."

"Well, young man —" Bowman's tone was a bit grim. "Why did you hide when your friends came looking for you?"

"I didn't know they were my friends, Mr. Bowman."

"You seem to know my name," Bowman commented.

"I couldn't help hearing it."

"Didn't you recognize Jasper Dacey's voice?" asked Bowman, his own voice touched with suspicion.

"I don't know Jasper Dacey." Cole looked at the gun still in his hand, laid it on the bed. "I believe I ran off with your gun, sir."

Bowman shook his head impatiently. "Dacey thinks you're a friend he was expecting from Santa Fé. Your dead horse was found with signs of an ambush. He's searching the hills for you."

Cole shrugged. "It's true about the ambush," he admitted. "I've been just one jump ahead of the men who shot up my camp."

Bowman gave his daughter a grim look. "Tell him what Dacey said."

"Mr. Dacey refused to give us the name of the man he is searching for," Jane told Cole. "He said his friend's visit was secret and he didn't want his name known around here."

Cole's eyes narrowed thoughtfully. "It's quite true that I'm from Santa Fé, but as Mr. Dacey can't possibly know my name it seems obvious that I'm not the friend he's expecting." A smile warmed Cole's tired face. "I don't mind telling you that my name is Thomason — Cole Thomason, and that I was on my way to Boca Grande when attacked."

"It's mighty queer business," Bowman frowned. "Do you think it was Dacey who shot up your camp?"

"I don't know what to think," answered Cole. "I only know that somebody apparently doesn't want me in Boca Grande. Perhaps that *somebody* is Dacey. Anyway, I couldn't take a chance when those men rode into the yard." His voice warmed. "I owe you a big debt. I might have been a dead man now if you had told them how close they were on my heels."

"The shoe is on the other foot," smiled Bowman. "I'd likely have bled to death if you hadn't happened along when you did."

Cole moved closer to the bedside. "You're making a good recovery, Mr. Bowman."

"I reckon that bullet wasn't wearing my name," chuckled Jane's father.

Cole looked at him steadily. "Do you know anybody who wants to kill you, sir?"

"I'm like you, Thomason. I don't know what to think, except conjure up fool suspicions."

"The man was riding a black and white pinto with a white mane and tail," Cole told him. "I wasn't able to get a look at his face."

Bowman shook his head regretfully. "Pinto horses are common in this country." He sank back on the pillow, closed his eyes wearily. "I reckon we're in the same boat, Thomason, and we don't know what to use for oars."

"No more talk for the present," commanded Jane. She looked at Cole. "You must be starving for food."

"I haven't eaten for over twenty-four hours," he admitted.

"Jane will fix you up," murmured Bowman drowsily. His eyes opened. "Keep that gun of mine handy, Thomason."

"Thanks." Cole reached for the gun still lying on the bed. "I left mine back at the camp, along with the rest of my outfit." He grinned. "At that I'm lucky."

"You keep that gun handy," repeated Bowman. "I don't much like this business."

"I'll do my best, sir," Cole assured him. He was again aware of the disturbing giddiness. Lack of sleep, an empty stomach and sheer fatigue, were getting him down.

"You don't look so good yourself," worried Bowman. "You go along with Jane and fill up on that beef stew she's been fixing for supper. You'll feel better." He grinned. "I could eat some of that stew myself."

"Do you think you should?" Jane looked doubtful. "I think we should get you undressed and properly in bed, Father."

"No hurry," demurred Bowman. "I can wait until Thomason gets some food and hot drink into him. Your stew is just the medicine for him." He was suddenly frowning. "Talking of medicine reminds me that Dacey is sending Doc Johnson to look me over."

"He can't possibly get here before midnight," Jane said. She looked at her father thoughtfully. "Mr. Dacey is quite right and I'm glad he is sending the doctor."

"I'm thinking about Thomason." Bowman's frown deepened. "It won't do for Doc Johnson to know he's here, not after what we told Dacey."

"I can be a long way from here before midnight," Cole said stiffly. "I have no wish to add to your troubles, Mr. Bowman."

"Don't be a fool." Something like a twinkle in Bowman's eyes softened the words. "We want you to stay as long as we can keep you. Jane needs a man here, now that I'm laid up with this bullet hole in my shoulder."

Cole grinned back at him, followed Jane into the living room. The lamplight showed a low ceiling supported by *vigas* of time-mellowed pine. It was a long room, much in need of repair, and Cole guessed that the several pieces of massive furniture had been laboriously hauled on oxcarts from Santa Fé by the Mexican *ranchero* who had built the house a century or more earlier.

"We've been here less than a month," Jane said. "You must forgive the mess." She reached for the lantern on the floor. "We had an old Mexican, Father found in Boca Grande, but he disappeared a few days ago with one of our horses. It was a real blow. He seemed so nice and trustworthy." Jane paused, added in a troubled voice, "After what happened to Father tonight I'm beginning to think we may have misjudged poor Benito. It's quite possible he's lying dead in the brush somewhere."

"It is also possible he stole the horse and fled because something frightened him," suggested Cole.

"He seemed so trustworthy," Jane said again. "I can hardly believe that Benito would be a thief."

Cole made no reply, stood gazing intently at a small portrait above the fireplace. It was obviously the work of an amateur, but the bold splashes of color had somehow managed to make the girl's face luminously alive. He turned a wondering look on Jane.

"I could almost think it was you," he said. "The resemblance is startling."

"My grandmother," Jane told him. "I'm named after her."

"Juana?" Cole was staring at the portrait, an odd excitement in his eyes.

"Yes, only they called her Juanita. Her father, Don Francisco Rivera, owned this rancho before the war with Mexico. She married a young American adventurer who carried her off to Mississippi."

"Tell me some more," Cole urged. "What was the name of the young American?"

"Carter Ruffin. He was with those Texans who attempted to march on Santa Fé several years before the war. Governor Armijo's soldiers captured them and Carter Ruffin was one of the survivors imprisoned at San Miguel where Don Francisco and Juanita were visiting relatives." Jane paused. "Why are you so curious about him?" she asked.

"For a very good reason." Cole tore his gaze from the portrait and looked at her. "Please tell me more!"

"Well —" Jane gave him a puzzled smile, "It seems the soldiers were going to shoot the young American but Juanita persuaded Don Francisco to help him escape. They brought him here to the rancho." She smiled tenderly at the lovely face glowing from the canvas. “He painted this picture, and they gave it to Don Francisco when they married and went to live in Mississippi.” Jane turned to the hall door. “You must be starving —”

Cole’s look held her back. “Has the portrait been hanging here all these years?” he asked. “It’s my impression nobody has lived in this house for a long time.”

“Don Francisco abandoned the rancho when Mexico lost the war,” Jane explained. “He fled across the border with his cattle and died in Chihuahua soon after. Juanita was his only child, and her daughter married my father. It is only recently we learned that I am the legal owner of the rancho.” A hint of distress shadowed her eyes. “It seemed like a gift from heaven, but now I’m not so sure. You see, Jasper Dacey has been grazing his cattle on the land for years and Father thinks there may be trouble.” She shook her head, as if impatient at her fears. “Yes, we found the portrait lying under a lot of junk in a storeroom. Of course I’d heard about it and knew it was the one Grandfather Ruffin painted.”

“You’re the living proof of it,” Cole said.

He followed her to the kitchen. She gestured at a door. “You’ll find a basin and water — and clean towels.” Her smile was rueful. “This old house is a dreadful ruin and there has been so little time to make it even decently livable.”

“I’ll be glad to get rid of some of this dust,” Cole said.

"You'll need a light." Jane took a candle down from a shelf. "I'll have supper on the table by the time you are ready."

Cole was looking doubtfully at the curtainless windows. "I think they should be covered," he said. "Any prowler can look in."

"It never occurred to me!" Jane set the lighted candle on the table and gazed around helplessly. "I've been intending to make curtains —"

"Anything will do — for the moment."

"I saw some old blankets in the storeroom —" Jane snatched the lantern from its hook and lighted the way down the hall. She indicated a door. "In there —"

A brief search uncovered several moth-eaten Navajo blankets. Cole gathered them over an arm and they returned to the kitchen.

"They're dreadful old things," Jane said. "Look at the dust!"

"They've been lying there for a lot of years," grinned Cole.

"Ever since Don Francisco died and that is nearly forty years ago," Jane said.

"I'll give them a shake outside." Cole started for the door. Jane's exclamation halted him.

"You might be seen, with all this light in the room." She led the way back into the hall, the lantern in her hand. "There's an empty room down there where you can shake them. I'll wait here with the light."

He was back in a few moments and between them they soon had the blankets draped over the three windows. Satisfied, Cole picked up the candle and went to the washroom.

Jane was hurrying in from the hall when he finally reappeared. She had a cartridge-filled gun belt in her hand. “I took Father a cup of coffee,” she explained. “He said you might need this.” She held out the gun belt.

Cole buckled it on and pushed the Colt .45 into the holster. “I’m hoping it won’t be needed, but we never know.”

“No,” Jane said. “We never know, but we *do* know that somebody has just tried to kill my father, and you have good cause to believe your own life is in peril. It would be silly for us not to realize that death lurks unpleasantly close.” Her smile came. “Sit down, Mr. Thomason. I’ll have supper on the table in a jiffy.”

Cole drew up a chair, watched in silence while she deftly served the stew and poured coffee.

“It smells good,” he said, when she finally took the chair opposite him. “Just the medicine I need.”

“I have an apple pie keeping warm in the oven.” She gazed at him over her coffee cup. “You look better already.”

“Thanks to soap and water I got rid of a wagon-load of dust.” Cole rubbed a bristly cheek. “I still feel like a tramp.”

“Father will lend you his razor,” Jane promised, “and tomorrow morning you can have a real bathe in the pond down by the arroyo.” Her eyes danced. “It’s the only bathtub we have, but the bushes make it very private.”

"I'll be using it before sunup." Cole grinned. "I'm still wondering at the good luck that guided me here."

"It was good luck for all of us," Jane told him soberly. "I felt so dreadfully frightened — and helpless when I saw Father lying there."

Cole was conscious of a quickening pulse as he met her grave look. She wore her dark hair in the manner of the Juanita of the portrait, parted in the middle and drawn back over her ears, and she had the same delicately-raised cheek bones and straight little nose and warm coloring.

Jane, too, was aware of an odd stirring in her as their eyes locked in that brief exchange. She felt instinctively drawn to this man who had so strangely and dramatically appeared from the wilderness. It was a curious coincidence that like her father he had miraculously escaped death from ambush. Or was it a coincidence? She found herself wondering, and wishing she knew what purpose could have brought Cole Thomason to this remote corner of the Territory of New Mexico.

Cole broke the silence. "You are wondering about me," he said.

"You must be a mind reader." Jane looked at him steadily. "Yes — I am wondering why somebody would rather see you dead than in Boca Grande."

"I'm wondering, too," Cole said. "I'm wondering why somebody should want to kill your father." He paused, his expression grim. "Perhaps it is the *same* somebody who wants us both dead."

"I don't see the connection," puzzled Jane. "You and Father had never met until this evening. Why should the attempt on his life have anything to do with the ambush of your camp yesterday?"

"It's possible somebody in Boca Grande doesn't want us to meet." Cole spoke slowly, as if thinking aloud. "I'm afraid the failure of that ambush explains the attack on Mr. Bowman."

Jane gazed at him worriedly. "You must know something that I don't."

Cole put down his empty coffee cup. "I've learned a lot from your grandmother Ruffin's portrait," he said.

"The portrait?" exclaimed Jane. "Why, what in the world has that old portrait got to do with it?"

"It explains why our unknown *somebody* has marked your father and me for death." Cole was silent for a moment, his eyes full of concern as he looked at the girl opposite him. "I don't want to frighten you, but I think you were more than right when you said that death lurks unpleasantly close."

"I can't help feeling frightened." Jane made an effort to steady her voice. "I still don't understand what Juanita Rivera's portrait has to do with it."

"You are the living proof that she is your grandmother, and that means your father is the Lewis Bowman who with several of his friends was deeply wronged by the most treacherous scoundrel unhung." Cole's face hardened. "It's been a long trail to this corner of New Mexico."

CHAPTER THREE

Jane could only gaze at him, too amazed for words, her eyes big with sudden excitement.

"I think you know the story." Cole's tone was grim.

"Yes," Jane said. "I was a very small child, then, but Father told me all about it when I was old enough to understand."

She sat still, recalling the story of that meeting in her grandfather Carter Ruffin's home in Natchez on the banks of the Mississippi. The little group of grave-faced men in her grandfather's study. Some of them old, like her grandfather Ruffin, some of them young and in uniform, like her father, Captain Lewis Bowman of the Confederate cavalry. Planters and sons of planters. None very rich, but ready that dark day to give their gold to help General Lee continue his desperate struggle to save the already doomed Confederacy.

The sum collected in gold was not large, a little over five hundred thousand dollars, but it was the entire cash wealth of those ten or twelve men who met that day in old Carter Ruffin's study. Judge Spottisford was selected as custodian, with instructions to hurry the money to Jefferson Davis, and that night saw him start on the long journey, accompanied by his clerk. They were never seen or heard of again, and with them vanished the five hundred thousand dollars in gold.

Jane broke the silence. "Father thinks they must have been waylaid and murdered by guerrillas." She shook her head sadly. "It was a useless sacrifice at best, with the surrender at Appomattox only a few weeks away."

"It was a fiendish act of treachery that ruined Carter Ruffin and his friends, including your own father," Cole said.

Jane looked at him curiously. "You seem to know a lot about it."

"My mother's father was one of the men in your grandfather Ruffin's house that night."

"Let me think!" Excitement made Jane's eyes very bright. "I know all their names, and — and your grandfather must have been Cole Sims."

"That's right," smiled Cole.

"But that makes Marian Sims your mother, and she was my mother's best friend when they were young girls in Natchez."

"She left Natchez before you were born, married a Texan." Cole grinned, added laconically, "His name was Thomason."

"I must tell Father!" Jane stood up from her chair, was suddenly very still, her startled gaze on the gun Cole slid from his holster.

"Listen —" He got up quietly, faced the door. "That coyote — began a bark and then stopped. Something scared it."

"The doctor —" Jane frowned. "No, he wouldn't have had time to come from Boca Grande."

"*Somebody* is coming," Cole said. "Riding down from the arroyo."

Jane spoke uneasily. "Whoever it is, mustn't see you here."

"I'm not leaving you alone," Cole told her.

The approaching hoofbeats hushed. They heard the scrape of saddle leather, the crunch of boots approaching the door.

Jane gave Cole a frantic look. "You mustn't be seen," she repeated in a whisper. "Quick — in the hall!"

Cole nodded, went swiftly into the dark hall, gun in hand.

Knuckles rapped on the door. Jane snatched Cole's plate and coffee cup from the table, hastily pushed them from sight in the cupboard near the stove. The knock was repeated, louder this time.

"Who is it?" she called.

"It's me, ma'am, Lute Soler."

Jane was conscious of a disturbing prickle of fear. She asked sharply, "What do you want?"

"The boss sent me back to keep an eye on things," answered the JD foreman. "He got to worryin' about the skunk as shot your dad. Figgers the feller will mebbe sneak back for another try."

It was a plausible explanation. Jane hesitated. She disliked the JD man and his crude attentions, but it was possible he was telling the truth and she was reluctant to incur Jasper Dacey's resentment.

"It's very kind of you, Mr. Soler, but we don't mind being alone." She kept her voice pleasant. "There was no need for Mr. Dacey to worry."

There was a brief silence, and then Soler's voice, gruffly apologetic, "I sure hate to be botherin' you, ma'am, but mebbe you could fix me a cup of coffee before I head back to the ranch."

"Why — of course —" Jane went to the door and slid the bolt. Soler stepped inside, and his wide grin, the sly gleam in his eyes, made her instantly realize her mistake. She moved swiftly, put the table between them.

Soler tossed his hat on a chair, fingered tobacco sack and papers from his shirt pocket. "You act like you was scared," he drawled.

Jane gazed at him. "You lied when you told me Mr. Dacey had sent you back."

Soler lit his cigarette, insolent eyes covering her from head to foot. "I had to figger out *some* way to get better acquainted. I been thinkin' about you a lot ever since the first time I seen you at the Stockmen's dance."

Jane's head lifted scornfully. "What I saw of you at the dance doesn't make me want to know you better. Getting drunk and brawling the way you did."

"You sure look pretty when you get mad," grinned the man. His narrowed eyes were suddenly hot. "I reckon breakin' you would be right good sport."

"You wouldn't dare force yourself into this house if my father could get off his bed," Jane said. "I advise you to go, Mr. Soler."

"Too bad about your dad." Soler looked at his cigarette, flipped it across the table onto the stove and was suddenly between her and the hall door. "I'm handin' out advice, too," he said huskily. "I'm advisin' you to act plenty nice, Jane."

She backed away, picked up a chair and held it in front of her. Soler turned as she turned, hands outstretched, a wide grin on his face. The half turn presented his broad back to the hall.

"When folks find you and your dad they'll figger it was that feller we're trailin' done it." Soler's words ended in a groan and he was suddenly down on the floor.

Cole stared at the senseless man, wondering if he had laid the gun barrel a trifle too hard on the carroty-thatched skull. His eyes lifted in a look at the white-faced girl.

"It was the only thing I could do." He spoke regretfully.

Jane lowered the chair to the floor. Her hands were trembling. "You couldn't do anything else," she said. Anger darkened her eyes. "Except kill him."

"It wouldn't have been murder," Cole told her grimly. "The man came back, knowing your father was unable to protect you."

"You heard what he said?" asked Jane in a low voice.

Cole nodded, a sick look in his eyes.

"He was going to put the blame on you, the stranger lost in the hills. You could never have proved your innocence."

Cole nodded again. "The story would have made me the ambusher who shot down your father at the corral. The whole thing would have beautifully suited the *somebody* who doesn't want me in Boca Grande."

Jane said, a bit unsteadily, "I'm glad you were here. It would have been dreadful for all of us — if you had not been here." Her eyes closed. "I was so horribly frightened."

"Forget it," he advised, his voice gentle. He stared speculatively at the senseless foreman. "I've got to get rid of him before he recovers consciousness."

"Do you think he saw you?" Jane asked worriedly.

Cole shook his head. "For all he'll ever know he was hit by a bolt of lightning."

Jane stifled an hysterical giggle. "He'll more likely think Father wasn't as helpless as he imagined." She paused, looked at Cole searchingly. "Why did you say that Father was involved in the business that brought you from Santa Fé?"

Cole hesitated, watchful gaze on the unconscious JD man. "It's been a long trail and goes back to the murder of Judge Spottisford which was *not* the work of guerrillas."

Jane's eyes widened. "But everybody said it was guerrillas!"

"The murderer and thief was Judge Spottisford's clerk," Cole told her. "The man knew the Confederacy was doomed and saw his chance to acquire a fortune. He killed the judge and fled to Texas with more than five hundred thousand dollars in gold." Bitterness edged Cole's quiet voice. "The money your grandfather Ruffin and his friends ruined themselves to raise."

"They were patriots," Jane said simply.

"The treachery was all the more base," continued Cole. "My grandfather was not satisfied with the guerrilla story and did some private investigating that led to Santa Fé. He died before he was able to definitely pick up the clerk's trail." Cole frowned. "A lot of years passed before I was old enough to get the story from my mother and do some scouting on my own account."

Jane broke the silence. "And now the trail leads to Boca Grande?" she asked.

"That's right." Cole's look lifted from the unconscious foreman. "We mustn't waste time getting this man away from here."

"What in the world can we do with him?"

"Only one thing we can do." Cole was already dragging Soler across the floor. "Bring his hat and open the door."

She grabbed up the Stetson and ran to the door, held it open for him. Lamplight flowed out, showed Soler's horse under a nearby chinaberry tree. Cole hauled the foreman down the steps.

"Get the rope off his saddle." He took the foreman in his arms and with some difficulty got him across the saddle. Jane handed him the rawhide lariat, held the snorting horse while he bound the unconscious man to the saddle. She noticed that he handled the rope with the skill of an experienced range man.

"I think that will hold him safe." Cole eyed the knots critically. "He'll be a long way from here by the time he comes out of it."

"A long way towards where?" Jane wondered.

"The JD ranch," replied Cole. "A horse always heads back for his home ranch."

"I'm afraid Mr. Dacey will be terribly suspicious," worried Jane. "He'll want to know how it all happened."

"It's going to be up to Soler to do the explaining," Cole said. "I doubt if he'll admit he came back here on the sly."

They watched in silence while the horse vanished into the blanketing darkness, both of them uneasy, wondering about the story JD's foreman would tell his boss.

"I'm afraid." The lamplight from the open door showed Jane's troubled face. "It's — it's only the beginning, and I'm afraid."

"The beginning of the end," Cole said grimly. "The end of a long trail that began with treachery and murder."

A coyote called from somewhere down in the wash of the arroyo and suddenly the yipping bark became a wailing chorus that seemed to come from all directions.

Jane repressed a shiver.

CHAPTER FOUR

Jane's father gave them a grim, questioning look when they entered the bedroom. "Heard a commotion back in the kitchen," he said. "Woke me up."

"We had a visitor," Jane told him. "He didn't stay long." Her shoulder lifted disdainfully. "Lute Soler."

Bowman frowned. "A bad hombre." He gave Cole a glimmer of a smile. "You threw him out, judging from the noise."

"Something like that," Cole admitted.

"Too bad he had to see you," fretted Bowman.

"He didn't," reassured Jane. She gave her father a brief account of the affair. He listened in grim silence, the deep anger in him darkening his face.

"I'm afraid Soler will think it was you." Jane shook her head worriedly. "He won't know what else to think."

"I'd have killed him," Bowman said. He looked at Cole. "Our debt to you grows, Thomason."

Cole grinned. "The pleasure was all mine, sir." He paused, keen gaze on the bearded face. "How are you feeling, Mr. Bowman?"

"Not too badly, thanks to your bandaging." Bowman looked at him curiously. "You seem to know about such things."

"I grew up on a cow ranch," Cole said laconically. "We learn to be handy on a cow ranch."

"Father!" Jane's eyes were very bright, her voice breathless. "He — he's Cole Sims' grandson."

"I'm not much surprised," Bowman said. "I've been digging back in the past while you two were in the kitchen, got to remembering that Marian Sims married a westerner named Thomason."

"That's right," Cole said.

"Your name began to make sense," continued Bowman. "You *had* to be old Cole Sims' grandson. Cole Sims was a diehard and surrender was a word never found in his dictionary. I reckon that's why he pulled stakes after the war, headed west to Santa Fé and went into the cattle business with your dad."

Cole hesitated. "That was only one of the reasons why he headed west to Santa Fé."

"I hadn't heard of any other reason," puzzled Bowman.

"He was following the trail of a thief and murderer," Cole said.

"It's a long time ago since Cole Sims left Natchez," reminded Jane's father. "News was hard to get in those days and I wouldn't know what he was doing. Just what do you mean, Thomason?"

"I'm referring to the five hundred thousand dollars in gold that disappeared with Judge Spottisford."

Bowman frowned. "The guerrillas got that money, and the judge, too. We all agreed there could be no other answer to the mystery."

"Grandfather Sims didn't agree."

Jane's father nodded. "I recall that Cole Sims was dissatisfied with the generally accepted solution. Nothing we could do about it. Not a jot of evidence against the clerk. I don't even remember the man's name. He disappeared as completely as the judge."

"Disappeared with the gold," Cole said grimly. "His name was Adna Fenn," he added, "and his trail led to Santa Fé."

"Fenn," muttered Bowman, wrinkling his brows. "Yes — the name comes back to me." He frowned up from his pillow. "Too bad Cole Sims let the scoundrel get away."

"He died before he could do anything about it," explained Cole.

"Couldn't *you* have done something?"

Cole shrugged. "You're forgetting that I was still only a kid, mixing school with learning how to run a cow ranch."

Jane was watching him sympathetically. "What made you take up the trail again, after all these years?" she asked. "Something must have happened."

"That's right." Cole's eyes narrowed thoughtfully. "It was a story I heard a few months ago at the annual meeting of the Stockmen's Association in Silver City. I met an old-timer there who had known Grandfather Sims. He knew about the Adna Fenn affair and told me that one of his riders was sure he had seen Fenn in Boca Grande. He was an old Natchez man and used to know Fenn."

"Have you been in touch with this rider?" Bowman asked.

Cole shook his head. “My old-timer friend hasn’t seen him for years, doesn’t even know if he’s still alive. He does know that he went to Silver City to see grandfather because grandfather wrote and told him the man had furnished proof that would bring Adna Fenn to justice.” Cole shook his head again. “Grandfather hadn’t told me anything about it.”

“How about the letter he wrote to your old-timer friend?” queried Bowman.

“He couldn’t remember the details,” Cole said. “It was a long time ago. He remembers putting the letter in some safe place because of its importance and promised to make a search for it.”

“We’ve got to hope he’ll find it,” muttered Bowman.

“I told him to let me know if he does,” Cole said. “He knows I planned to head for Boca Grande and will write me at the post office there.”

Bowman gazed up at him speculatively. “Is it in your mind that Dacey is Adna Fenn?”

Cole shrugged. “He could be.”

“He’s likely back of the attempt to ambush you,” Bowman pointed out. “That story of his seems mighty thin to me.”

“I’m beginning to think myself it was lucky he didn’t find me.” Cole gave his new friends a grateful smile. “I probably owe you my life for not giving me away when he rode into the yard.”

“You can thank Jane for that,” Bowman told him.

“I couldn’t do less,” Jane said quickly. “Not after what you had just done for Father.”

Cole broke the brief silence. "The circumstances are suspicious, but we can't take it for granted that Jasper Dacey is Adna Fenn. I only know the trail leads to Boca Grande."

Bowman looked at him thoughtfully. "Don't forget that somebody tried to kill *me* this evening. The shooting points to Dacey. He's been grazing his cattle on this old Rivera rancho for years. He'd want to get rid of me." He nodded grimly. "In fact he would have a double motive for wanting me dead. Fear that I might eventually recognize him as Adna Fenn and fear of losing a valuable range."

"You make the evidence sound convincing," Cole admitted.

"I can't bear to think of Mr. Dacey doing such dreadful things." Jane looked at them with troubled eyes. "But he *did* seem very anxious to know if I saw the man who shot Father."

"I should never have let you come to this place," Bowman said gloomily. "I think there is only one thing we can do, Daughter, get you to Santa Fé."

"I'm not going to run away," Jane said in a low, hard voice. "This rancho belongs to us."

"It's leave this place or risk being shot in the back every time we set foot in the yard," worried her father. His hand lifted in a despairing gesture. "We're up against a sly devil."

Jane had no answer, could only look at him miserably. She knew that her father's blunt statement was too hideously true.

Cole's quiet voice broke the long silence. "What you need here is an outfit of tough fighting men."

"We made a start," Bowman said gloomily. "A Mexican I picked up in Boca Grande. He turned out a rascal, skipped with one of my best horses."

"Father —" Jane spoke defensively. "We can't be sure that Benito ran away — and is a horse thief, not after what has happened to you."

Bowman gave her a thunderstruck look, slowly nodded his head. "Maybe that's the answer, Jane." Again he gestured despairingly. "He's likely lying out in the chaparral some place for the buzzards to find."

Jane shivered. "I can't bear it!"

Cole's voice broke another painful silence. "I'd like to help, Mr. Bowman —" He hesitated. "I mean I'd like to stay here until you've had time to get an outfit together."

Bowman's face brightened, then he shook his head. "You have business in Boca Grande," he reminded.

"Boca Grande can wait."

"They're after your scalp, too," Bowman said gruffly.

Cole looked at Jane, saw the glow in her eyes. "Boca Grande can wait," he repeated. "And that means you've hired a man, Mr. Bowman." He grinned. "I was raised on a cattle ranch, you know."

An exclamation from Jane halted Bowman's feeble protest. "Somebody is coming," she said.

They listened, tense, apprehensive, heard the unmistakable rattle of approaching wheels.

"I reckon it's Doc Johnson," Bowman guessed. "A couple of hours ahead of time. Dacey probably met him on the road." He looked at Cole. "You better get out of here."

Cole nodded, followed Jane from the room. She halted in the dimly-lit hall, hand light on his arm, face lifted in a grateful look.

"It's wonderful — your offer to stay."

"I couldn't think of running away now," he said in a low voice. "Not after what you did for me."

"I was feeling frantic," Jane whispered. "Father so helpless, and — and —" Her voice choked.

"It's all right," he comforted. "You won't be alone much longer, not any longer than it will take to get word to my Diamond S ranch near Silver City. Bill Hobson, he's foreman, should have a bunch of his riders here inside of ten days. Tough fighting men."

Her hand tightened on his arm. "Quick — the room down the hall. I can hear him coming to the door."

Cole drew his gun, stood motionless while she hurried into the kitchen. He wanted to make sure the visitor *was* the expected doctor and that he was unaccompanied.

He heard a jovial voice. "Well, well, Miss Bowman . . . sorry to hear your dad's been shot up."

Satisfied, Cole slipped into the room, watched from the dark doorway. Jane appeared in the hall, followed by a short, paunchy man, who from the bag in his hand was obviously the doctor. He wore a wide-brimmed hat pushed back on graying hair, and a long linen dust coat that billowed behind him as he trotted briskly after the girl.

Bowman greeted him with a wry smile. "I told Dacey not to send you," he said. "Nothing much wrong with me."

Dr. Johnson tossed his hat on a chair and worked out of his dust coat. "Met Jasper down the road a piece . . . was on my way home from FlyingY . . . a bronco buster there took a bad tumble and broke a leg. Lucky I met Jasper so handy to *your* place."

"Too bad Dacey asked you to come," grumbled Bowman.

"All in the day's work," chuckled the doctor. "I'd have been here a lot sooner if I hadn't run into Lute Soler roped up like a papoose across his saddle."

Jane held her breath, darted a warning look at her father.

"Funniest sight I ever saw." Dr. Johnson's paunch shook with merriment. "Lute's horse was tangled up in the brush and Lute lying across the saddle, kickin' and cussin' like a wild man."

"Why, doctor!" exclaimed Jane, her voice properly astonished. "How very strange!" She wondered wildly if Lute Soler had explained the cause of his predicament.

"Seems Lute ran into the man who took that shot at you, Bowman," continued Dr. Johnson. "Lute got down from his bronc and tried to stalk him. The scoundrel jumped him from the brush and knocked him senseless. That's all Lute remembered, except that when he came to he found himself roped hand and foot to his saddle." The doctor chuckled again. "No harm done . . . only a cut head which I tied up for him."

Relief waved through the girl. Cole had prophesied correctly. JD's foreman was going to keep quiet about his brief visit to the house.

The doctor had the bandage off now and was examining the wound critically. "Not serious," he congratulated. "A close thing, though, Bowman."

In less than half an hour he had his patient freshly bandaged and in bed and was rattling away in his buckboard. Jane closed and bolted the door, and when she returned she saw Cole smiling at her from the hall. She smiled back, conscious of a lightness of heart she had not felt since the crashing report of the ambusher's rifle.

"Dr. Johnson says Father is doing splendidly," she told him, and laughed softly. "He complimented *me* on a perfect job of bandaging."

"I heard him," chuckled Cole. "He doesn't speak in a whisper."

"You heard what he said about Lute Soler?" she asked mirthfully.

Cole nodded. "It's obvious friend Soler doesn't want to talk about his little visit."

"I'm so relieved," Jane said. "I was afraid he'd come back — try to find out who hit him and sent him off tied to his saddle like a bundle of old clothes."

"He must be a very puzzled man." Cole grinned. "He thought up a good story at that."

Jane was suddenly practical. "I told you I had an apple pie in the oven. I think it is still warm." She placed fresh cups and plates on the table. "If you'll put a chunk of wood in the stove we'll have more coffee and I'll heat some broth for Father."

They were soon opposite each other at the table again, and Jane said, a bit shyly, "So you are a cattleman, Mr. Thomason."

"That's right. Lived on Diamond S about all my twenty-eight years, except when away at school in Santa Fé." His eyes twinkled. "You make an excellent pie, Miss Bowman."

Jane suddenly laughed. "It seems silly for us to be so formal, doesn't it? After all we are very, very distant cousins."

"Come to think of it, we are," smiled Cole. "I used to hear my mother speak of your grandmother as Cousin Juanita. Everybody in Natchez seemed to be some sort of cousin to her."

Jane's eyes danced. "All right, tell me about my pie again."

He grinned. "It's *delicious* pie, Jane."

"Thank you, Cole."

It seemed good to laugh, relax too taut nerves. Cole leaned back in his chair, felt in a pocket for tobacco sack and papers. "I'll take a look in the barn," he said. "Shake down some hay for the stock." His eyes narrowed thoughtfully. "I could sleep out there. Wouldn't be the first time I used hay for a mattress."

"No!" She shook her head. "I'd rather you slept in the house. I'd feel safer."

He shrugged. "Just as you say —"

"There's a small room off the patio. I cleaned it out the other day, and I can find you a cot and blankets."

"Fine." Cole put a match to his cigarette, stood up from his chair, was suddenly rigid.

Jane heard the distant drumming of hoofs too. "Horses!" she exclaimed. "A lot of them — and coming to the house!"

They gazed at each other, and the fright he saw in her eyes steadied Cole. His face took on the hardness of granite.

"Go to your Father, Jane. Leave this to me." His gun appeared in his hand and he moved on quick, soundless feet to the door, stood there, listening, grim, purposeful.

The trample of hoofs, the squeak of saddle leather drew up close and suddenly the night was very still. Jane had not moved and the only sound she could hear was the thump of her own heart.

A voice broke the frightening quiet. "Señor — Señorita, ees me, Benito. I breeng fr-riends."

Jane could hardly believe her ears. She stood there, dazed, unable to speak.

"Señor — Señorita, ees me, Benito," repeated the voice. "I 'ave breeng fr-riends."

She found herself at the door, hand reaching for the bolt. Cole stopped her. "Ask him who his friends are. It may be a trick."

"Who are your friends, Benito?" she asked in Spanish. "Where have you been and why have you brought friends?"

Another voice answered, a deep-throated rush of Spanish. "Señorita — I am Tranquilo Baca, son of him who was Don Francisco's chief of vaqueros. I was born here on this rancho, Señorita Juanita, and am come to serve you as my father served Don Francisco Rivera."

Cole nodded, and Jane slid the bolt, pulled the door wide. The moon was up, disclosed some half score horsemen grouped in front of the steps. Moonlight glinted from rifles in scabbards and guns in holsters. A startling picture, but one that put a satisfied gleam in Cole's eyes.

Jane, framed in the lamplit doorway, said falteringly, in Spanish, "You are welcome, Tranquilo Baca. It is an honored name I learned to know from my grandmother when I was a little child."

Baca slid with lithe grace from his saddle, a tall, powerful man in his early fifties, and the lamplight showed a swarthy face that hinted of a touch of Yaqui. He swept off his hat, bowed low over her hand. "My heart is full this night, señorita." His head lifted and he looked hard at Cole. "But I do not understand. Benito brought word you and your father were alone on the rancho."

"Mr. Thomason has only been here since sundown," Jane said. "My father has been shot, Tranquilo, and Mr. Thomason saved his life. We are in great trouble, Tranquilo, and were much worried when Benito disappeared. We thought he had run away, stolen our best horse."

Bowman's alarmed voice reached them from the bedroom. "Jane — what's wrong out there?"

"Benito has come back," she called.

"Bring the rascal in here," commanded her father.

Another rider scrambled from his saddle, a thin, elderly Mexican, a frightened look on his brown face as he approached the steps. "*Por Dios!*" he muttered. "Boss no like w'at I do."

The three men, Cole, Tranquilo Baca and the worried Benito, followed Jane into the bedroom. Bowman lifted his head in a startled look at the smiling big Mexican.

"Who is this man?" he asked Jane.

"He is Tranquilo Baca, the son of the Tranquilo Baca who was Don Francisco's chief of vaqueros." She smiled encouragingly at Benito. "We owe Benito a big debt, Father."

The happiness in her voice wiped the alarm from Bowman's face. He said, "All right, Benito, I'm wanting to know why you ran off with my horse."

The old Mexican, hat clutched in both hands, hesitated, burst into a torrent of Spanish. "When I came to work for you I did not know who you were." He motioned with his head at Jane. "I see her, and she is like the Señorita Juanita who lived here when I was a young vaquero. I see the picture and then I know who she is. I do not tell her I know who she is. I am unhappy — frightened, because I hear talk that bad men want the rancho and plan to kill you . . . I am afraid and ride fast to Chihuahua." Benito broke into his halting English. "I no ron away, señor! I no steal horse! I go breeng Tranquilo Baca for 'elp you and señorita."

Bowman gazed at him, and when he spoke his voice was husky with emotion. "Come here, Benito. I want to shake your hand."

A relieved smile wreathed the old Mexican's troubled face. He dropped on one knee by the bedside. Bowman clasped his hand. "You're a man — and a friend, Benito."

Tranquilo's deep-throated voice interrupted him. "Señor — with me have come more friends like Benito. Sons of vaqueros who were born on this old rancho and lived their lives in the service of Don Francisco Rivera." His voice lifted in thunderous command. "Ramon, Manuelo, Julio, Domingo — all of you come!"

There was a sudden stir outside, the hurried tramp of booted feet, the jingle of spurs as the Mexicans pushed into the bedroom. Tranquilo's uplifted hand brought them to a standstill, swarthy-faced men whose eyes rolled interested looks at Jane before fixing solemnly on their chief.

Tranquilo made a grand gesture. "They have come to serve you, señorita." He fastened a fierce look on the attentive vaqueros. "Swear to serve the señorita as your fathers served Don Francisco and his father's father."

The vaqueros held up hands, thumbs crossed over forefingers. "*Por esta cruz!*" they shouted. "*Viva La Señorita! Viva El Rancho!*"

"It is good!" declared Tranquilo. He was magnificent, and knew it. "Attend to your horses, and be on guard day and night, for death stalks this rancho of our fathers."

The swarthy riders jingled from the room, eyes sparkling, teeth flashing in smiles at the breathless *señorita* they had sworn to serve.

The room grew very still. Tranquilo stood watching Jane — a brooding eagle on his crag. His head turned in a slow look at her father.

"I am sorry, señor, that we came too late to prevent the attempt to kill you."

"The wound is not serious," Bowman assured him. He paused, added emotionally, "I can never thank you enough for coming."

The big Mexican laughed deep in his throat and his hand went out, seized Bowman's in a hard grip. "We beeg fr-riends, señor," he said in English.

"*Amigos*," chuckled Bowman.

Tranquilo's head lifted in another rumbling laugh, and then, soberly, "I have more news. Five hundred cattle are now on the trail from Chihuahua. Young cows, bulls, steers to fatten for the market, a *remuda*, and wagons with supplies." He beamed at their stunned, amazed faces. "Also the women of your vaqueros, and their little ones." Tranquilo nodded happily at the tongue-tied Jane. "You will be their mistress, señorita, and they your servants in this old house."

Jane came out of her trance. "It's only a wonderful dream." Her voice was not quite steady. "Even if it were true, it's quite impossible." She looked wildly at her father.

"She's right, Tranquilo," Bowman said regretfully. "We are poor and have no money for all these cattle and horses, and no money for such a big payroll."

"Señor — señorita —" Tranquilo spoke earnestly. "These cattle — these horses, all belong to this rancho. Before the Treaty of Hidalgo Guadalupe was signed, old Don Francisco drove his herds to Chihuahua. They belong to his heirs, so I bring only what is yours. The payroll?" He gestured. "It is nothing. These few vaqueros will live where their fathers lived and their wants are small." He nodded his head sagely. "You cannot run a cattle ranch without vaqueros."

Jane and her father looked at each other, looked at Cole, as if seeking from him some solution to the bewildering situation.

"Tranquilo Baca is right," Cole said. "The cattle and horses seem to be legally yours, Jane, and you *will* need an outfit to handle them. These vaqueros look like good men."

"Señor Thomason also speaks my language," beamed Tranquilo.

"I've lived in New Mexico all my life," Cole said laconically.

The two men measured each other and they liked what they saw.

Cole went on, his tone significant. "You heard Tranquilo tell the vaqueros to be on watch day and night. It means that Dacey or anybody else won't have an easy time running you off the ranch."

"That's right," muttered Bowman. The worry smoothed from his face. "Fine, Tranquilo, it's a deal, only I want you to stay, too."

"*Si, señor.*" The big Mexican smiled contentedly. "I will be chief of vaqueros like my father before me. We will raise much beef on this old rancho." He stood for a moment, prideful, competent. "I go now to see to my vaqueros."

They listened in silence until the jingle of his spurs faded into the night.

Cole was the first to speak. “I think your immediate problem is settled,” he said.

“I’ll wake up soon and find it’s all a dream.” Jane’s eyes were misty.

“It’s no dream,” Cole assured her. A faint smile touched his lips. “No reason now for me to stay, so tomorrow should see me in Boca Grande.”

Bowman nodded. “I wouldn’t want to hold you back, Cole.” And he added grimly, “You have unfinished business waiting for you in that town.”

Jane was conscious of a cold hand squeezing her heart as she looked at them. She wanted to cry out, tell Cole to abandon the trail that could only end in death. Somebody would die at that trail’s end, and she didn’t want it to be Cole Thomason.

CHAPTER FIVE

Cole signed the register, a dirty, thumbed copybook and after a glance at the freshly scrawled name, the man behind the desk fished a key from a drawer.

"A dollar a day, or six a week, mister," he wheezed.

Cole laid a five dollar gold piece on the desk, added a silver dollar. "Where's the nearest livery barn?" he asked.

"Only one feed barn in this town," answered the man. "Nat Murran's — down the street a piece, the other side of the blacksmith shop." He was fat, and the small eyes in his beefy face were hard bits of brown glass. "You passed it, if you come in from Hachita." He stared inquisitively at the hotel's new guest.

"I didn't come in from Hachita," Cole said.

"Wasn't meanin' to be nosy," grinned the man.

"I've heard that Boca Grande is a good town," Cole drawled. He gave the fat man a hard look, added softly, "A right good town if you want to take it easy for a while."

"Sure is." The clerk winked knowingly. "Right handy to the border."

Cole returned the wink. "That's what kind of interests me, mister."

"We get a lot of 'em like you," chuckled the man behind the desk. "You won't be lonesome." He leaned hairy forearms on the desk, friendly, confidential. "Plenty of good liquor and girls, and a feller can get into a game most any time day or night. Faro, roulette, stud poker —"

"I reckon I'm going to like your town right well," Cole said, enthusiastically. "I sure admire plenty excitement." The hotel clerk's mistake was natural enough, and Cole had no intention of putting him right. In fact he had purposely helped the fat man to the conclusion that he was on the dodge from the law. Here were gathered the bad men of the border west, the renegades, the cattle thieves — the killers. To be regarded as one of Boca Grande's lawless denizens could offer some immunity from dangerous speculations about his business in the town.

He stole a cautious look at the empty lobby, leaned closer to the man behind the desk. "What's the word on your town marshal?" he asked in a low voice.

"Sil Turlo's a good hombre," the clerk earnestly assured him. "He don't ask questions, and don't make no trouble for a feller that minds his manners while he's in this town." He thrust out a large moist hand. "Blackie Stenlo — that's me," he introduced. "Any time you want somethin', just ask for me, Mr. Thomason."

"*Gracias*." Cole withdrew a tingling hand. Blackie Stenlo's fat fingers were surprisingly strong. "I reckon I'll get my bronc headed for Murran's barn." He tossed a parting grin over his shoulder, slammed through the screen door.

He crossed the wide, unpainted porch and went thoughtfully down the steps. On either side of the shabby, two-story hotel were the twenty or thirty flimsy frame buildings and flat-roofed adobes that comprised the border town of Boca Grande. Several of the buildings sported pretentious false fronts from which desert sun and wind had peeled most of the paint. Over the board sidewalks were wooden awnings to break the merciless glare of the sun. At this noon hour the shaded sidewalks looked dark and cool in contrast with the fierce sunlight in the street. It was the time of day when little life stirred. Here and there screen doors slammed as men pushed in and out of some eating place, or through the swing doors of saloons where cow ponies drooped at hitchrails. Aside from the general merchandise store and a few other commercial establishments, most of the town seemed to be in the liquor and entertainment business.

Cole made a cigarette, meditative gaze on his buckskin horse, a loan from one of Tranquilo Baca's vaqueros. The Chihuahua horse was Tranquilo's idea. The Mexican had been told enough for him to realize the dangers that would confront Cole in Boca Grande. He had frowned on the idea of using one of Bowman's horses for the trip. "*A Bowman horse will be recognized, señor, and that will be bad trouble for you. Men will wonder why you ride a Bowman horse.*"

The argument was sound, and when Cole left the Bowman ranch he was riding the tough-looking buckskin now tied to the rail in front of the hotel. The horse had never before been north of the border, and was unknown in Boca Grande, a fact that lessened the chance of arousing dangerous speculations about the rider.

He reached for the tie-rope, aware now of inquisitive eyes peering from the hotel door. Blackie Stenlo was watching to see if he were *really* going to the livery barn.

Cole hid a grin as he swung into his saddle. His question about the nearest livery barn had been the usual inquiry expected from a stranger just arrived in town. Benito had already furnished interesting information about Nat Murran and his livery stable. He recalled the old Mexican's troubled words, before setting out from the ranch. "*Thees Nat Murran ees bad hombre. Cuidado!*" The warning was unmistakable. Benito was telling him to be careful and watch his step where Mr. Murran was concerned.

Benito had given him other helpful details. A friend of his worked as stableman in the livery barn. "*Show Mateo Cota this little silver cross, señor. It is a sign between us. Mateo will be your friend, too.*"

The thought of the little silver cross now in his pocket warmed Cole. It was the old Mexican's cherished good luck piece, a token of friendship. He hoped nothing would prevent him from returning it to Benito.

The livery yard was on the town's edge where the street became a narrow road that crawled through harsh cacti into the desert haze.

A man gazed up at him from a bench under the trees that shaded the water trough. He wore amber-tinted spectacles and held a long telescope across his knees. He said, amiably, “Howdy, Stranger. Looking for a place to stable your bronc?”

“That’s right.” Cole grinned down at the chubby-faced man on the bench. “Blackie Stenlo sent me here.”

“No other feed barn in town,” the man said. He flapped a limp hand. “Help yourself, mister. Mateo will fix up a stall for you.”

“I reckon you must be Nat Murran.” Cole got down from his saddle, let the buckskin nose the water. “I’m Cole Thomason.”

The liveryman smiled genially. “I saw you stop off at the hotel.”

“You can see a lot with that telescope,” Cole said.

“I like to watch things,” chuckled Murran. “I don’t miss much.”

Cole had an impression of sharp, scrutinizing eyes behind the amber spectacles as he led his horse off to the barn. He recalled Benito’s warning to be on his guard where Nat Murran was concerned.

The man puzzled him. Outwardly he seemed harmless enough, an amiable, plump little man with a chubby, beaming face and quiet-spoken voice. It was hard to picture this bald-headed, elderly liveryman as the sinister character Benito had described. Perhaps the physical exterior masked the evil in him. Cole found himself wondering about the amber spectacles that hid Nat Murran’s eyes. He would have liked to see behind those tinted glasses. A man's eyes were apt to betray him.

A wide-shouldered Mexican limped from a stall, pitchfork in hand. He had a thick thatch of graying hair and a high-boned face the color of old saddle leather. There was the look of a hawk in the keen, fierce eyes that instantly fastened on the buckskin's brand.

"Are you Mateo Cota?" asked Cole.

The Mexican's eyes lifted in a brief glance. "*Si, señor.*"

"The boss said you'd fix up a stall for my horse."

"*Si, señor.*" Mateo leaned his pitchfork against the wall, reached for the buckskin's bridle reins and led the horse into the stable.

Cole followed, fingers closed over the little silver cross. It was obvious that Mateo had recognized the Chihuahua brand, and was puzzled, inclined to be suspicious of the buckskin's owner.

The stall was at the far end of the runway, near the rear door which stood open, revealing a network of corrals. Beyond the corrals was a large field through which meandered a creek fringed with willows and alders. Cole guessed that Nat Murran had devised an irrigation system that kept the field attractively green against the background of bleak hills. Barbed wire enclosures protected long, low stacks of hay from the grazing horses and cattle.

The Mexican haltered the buckskin and stripped off saddle and bridle. His movements were slow, deliberate. It was plain that he was doing some troubled thinking.

Cole broke the silence. "I may be in town several days, Mateo. I want you to take good care of my horse."

"*Si, señor.*" The Mexican carefully hung the saddle on the peg behind the stall. He continued to stand there, his gaze fiercely intent on the silver *conchas* that decorated the saddle.

"You are wondering where I got that saddle — and the horse," Cole said.

"*Si, señor.*" Mateo turned his head, and Cole saw suspicion and hostility in the fierce, hawk eyes.

"They belong to Tranquilo Baca," Cole said in Spanish. "I see that you think I am a horse thief, perhaps a murderer, or else why would I be riding this Chihuahua horse that belongs to Tranquilo Baca."

A long knife was suddenly in the Mexican's hand. He said softly, in Spanish, "If harm has come to him, I will kill you."

"He is my friend," Cole said. "He has lent me this horse and saddle, the rifle in the boot, the gun you see in my belt."

"Why should I take your word?" asked the Mexican. "I do not know you."

"You know this?" Cole's fingers opened, revealed the silver cross in the palm of his hand. "Benito said it is a sacred sign between you."

Mateo gazed at it, slowly reached out and took the cross from Cole's extended hand. "It is Benito's," he said after a long silence. His brown fingers fumbled a similar cross hung from a chain inside his shirt. He placed the two crosses together, and Cole now realized that each was the half of a cross that had been carefully split. The two pieces were an exact fit when placed together. "It is Benito's," repeated the Mexican. "A sign that you are his friend."

Cole nodded. "Benito said you would be my friend, too." He gave the Mexican a grim smile. "I'm needing a friend in this town, Mateo Cota."

Mateo's hand lifted, the joined pieces of cross between thumb and forefinger. "*Por esta cruz*," he said solemnly, "I am your friend, too, as Benito promised."

"*Bueno!*" Cole held out his hand. "Benito will want his token back when I see him again."

"*Si*." Mateo's own piece of the cross vanished inside his shirt, and after a momentary hesitation he placed the other half in Cole's hand. "It brings good luck to the one who carries it, and that means you will surely see Benito again. Benito once saved me from the Apaches, and I in turn saved his life from a wild bull. It was then we split the silver cross and vowed friendship to the death."

"I will return it to him," Cole promised. "If I live."

Mateo nodded, his expression troubled. "I do not understand," he muttered. "If I am to help you I must know more about this business that may end in your death."

"Do you know where Benito works?" Cole asked.

"*Si*. He is with the *Americano* who plans to raise cattle on the old Rivera rancho." Mateo shook his head gloomily. "I warned Benito that bad trouble rides fast on his *Americano's* trail."

"Trouble has already arrived at the rancho," Cole told him. "Mr. Bowman was shot from ambush, but the wound is not serious."

"*Por Dios!*" The Mexican frowned. "Where was Benito when this happened?"

"He had ridden to Chihuahua for help." Cole grinned. "He got help in a big way. Tranquilo Baca and his vaqueros are now at the rancho."

Mateo's eyes gleamed. "That is good news. They will be bad medicine for the enemies of Benito's señor."

Cole stole a nervous glance down the long runway. "We must not talk here too long, or your boss will get suspicious."

"He is a devil, that one," muttered the Mexican. "Do not trust him, my friend. His smile masks a foul fiend. He will offer you friendship with one hand and knife you in the back with the other."

"We must talk again, soon," urged Cole. "Where can we meet, Mateo?"

The Mexican considered, wary gaze on the door at the other end of the runway. "I will be at the *cantina* of Ambrosio Garcia after six o'clock," he finally said. "I will wait there until midnight."

"I'll be there," promised Cole. "Just where is this *cantina?*"

"In Old Town." Mateo gestured nervously. "Please go, señor."

"Keep my rifle in a safe place," Cole said. "It's really Tranquilo's rifle and I don't want to lose it."

"I will keep it safe," promised the Mexican. He snatched the rifle from saddle boot and disappeared into the harness room.

Nat Murran was still on the bench under the trees. He lowered his brass telescope and readjusted the amber spectacles. "Looks like the stage coming, yonder," he said in a conversational tone as if Cole was an old crony who had just dropped in for a chat. "A couple hours late. Shouldn't wonder but what Sam Hanney met up with trouble some place." He wagged his bald head pessimistically. "Anything can happen these times, with Nana on the warpath again." His head turned in a smiling look at the younger man. "Mateo fix you up all right?"

Cole assured him that everything was all right. "Where's the best place to eat in this town?" he asked. "A big steak is what I'm craving."

"You could try the Chinaman's," suggested the liveryman. "You can't beat Chang when it comes to steaks." He went on in the same lazy drawl. "Took you a long time to get your bronc stalled."

Cole sought desperately for a satisfactory explanation. "I was interested in that alfalfa field of yours back of the corrals. Alfalfa isn't grown much in this part of the country."

"I put in irrigation ditches," Nat Murran said complacently. "Alfalfa needs a lot of water, and that's what I've got." His hand lifted in a contemptuous gesture. "These ranchers — they're too lazy to get water on their land, and that's why most of 'em go broke."

"I'm a cowman," Cole said. "Give me plenty of range and you can have your irrigated alfalfa land." He grinned. "Digging ditches just don't appeal to me."

"I figured you for a cowman," drawled Murran. His tone was thoughtful. "Lookin' for a spread, or a ridin' job?"

"Well —" Cole shrugged. "I heard that this town was a good place to rest up in."

The liveryman beamed. "The law don't bother us none, if that's what you mean, Mr. Thomason."

"I'm not one to talk too much," Cole said, coldly.

"No call for you to get on the prod," chuckled Murran. "A lot of 'em like you come and go and no questions asked." He paused, asked abruptly, "Would you like a job, young feller?"

"I might —" Cole's eyes narrowed speculatively. "Depends on the job."

"A friend of mine runs a big cow outfit," continued Murran. "He'll be in town this evening and I can speak to him if you say the word."

"I'd like to know more about him," Cole said. He shrugged again. "I wouldn't mind a job with a good outfit."

"Jasper Dacey's JD ranch is the biggest in the Boca Grande country," assured Murran. "He pays top hands top wages."

Cole appeared to hesitate, not wanting to betray his secret elation. The chance was too good to lose. As a member of JD's outfit he could learn a lot about Jasper Dacey.

"Well?" Murran's placid voice was edged with impatience. "Do you want me to put in a word for you?"

"I reckon so." Cole gave the liveryman a wry smile. "It was in my mind to kind of lazy around a few days, have me some fun in this town, before huntin' up a job."

"You'll have plenty chances for fun," smiled Murran. "We get a bunch of JD boys in town every Saturday." He chuckled. "They sure play hard. You'll like 'em, Cole. JD is one fightin' hard-ridin' outfit."

"Sounds good," admitted Cole. He swung on his heel. "All right, Nat. If Dacey wants to talk to me I'll be around town some place."

He looked back as he turned into the street. Murran was again leveling the telescope at the Hachita road. The overdue stage was not yet visible to the naked eye, and all Cole could see was a distant haze of dust.

CHAPTER SIX

He came opposite the blacksmith shop. A girl was trying to quiet a black horse while the smith fitted a shoe. The horse reared, pulled his forefoot from the smith's clamped knees. The girl clung to the bridle, her voice scolding.

She glimpsed Cole in the doorway, spoke sharply. "Quick! Help me hold this darn fool colt!"

Cole's hand on the bridle, his quiet voice, steadied the nervous black, and after a moment the smith tried again. The horse trembled, but made no further attempt to pull back.

"You know how to handle colts," the girl said when the smith released the shod hoof from his knees.

"I've handled plenty," smiled Cole. "Nice colt," he admired.

"Diablo is just plain brute," she complained.

"He's still a colt," reminded Cole. "He'll settle down, make a good horse."

"I can handle him," the girl said with a toss of her head. "I'm not afraid of the brute." She was decidedly handsome, with a wealth of light brown hair under a white Stetson. She wore a white shirtwaist and faded blue levis over brown high-heeled boots, a long-legged, easy-striding girl with a hint of hardness in her.

"I'm obliged to you." There was frank appraisal in her blue eyes. It was plain that she liked what she saw. "I'll bet you're a cowman."

"You won't lose your bet," drawled Cole.

Her gaze followed him out to the street. "Who is he, Joe?" she asked the blacksmith.

"Search me." The smith, leaned on his bellows handle, pumped gently. "Never laid eyes on him before."

"JD could use a man like him," the girl said. "I think he stabled his horse in Nat's barn. I'll go ask Nat about him." She swung with easy grace into her saddle.

Cole caught a glimpse of her as she rode into the livery yard. His eyes narrowed thoughtfully. The black horse wore the JD brand. It was his guess the girl was probably Jasper Dacey's daughter. He surmised, too, with some amusement that it was her immediate purpose to question Nat Murran about him.

A light ranch wagon passed him and halted in front of the store. The driver climbed down, tied his team to the rail and went inside. A card in the window said "U.S. Post Office."

Cole looked up at the big sign on the store's false front. The postmaster was obviously the Silas Dunket announced as owner of the General Merchandise Emporium.

Cole hesitated, wondering if his expected letter had arrived. He decided to eat first before inquiring, and crossed over to Chang's restaurant, a flat-roofed building squeezed in between two saloons.

It was dark inside, after the glaring sunlight, and surprisingly cool. An elderly Chinese appeared from the kitchen, waited in silence while Cole pulled out a chair.

"Steak," Cole ordered laconically.

Chang was equally brief. "Me bling," he said, and shuffled back to his kitchen.

Cole tossed his hat on the opposite chair and gazed about the room. There was only one other customer, a big red-headed man who seemed to be dozing at his table on the far side. He wore a bandage on his head, and Cole suddenly realized that his lone fellow-diner was JD's foreman, Lute Soler.

Chang reappeared with cutlery which he placed in front of Cole, then after a hesitant glance across the room he shuffled over to Soler's table.

"Wantee more coffee?" he asked.

Soler lifted his head in a look at him. He was in an ugly mood after a night's hard drinking. His threatening expression frightened the Chinese who turned quickly away. Soler's chair crashed over as he lurched to his feet and grabbed hold of Chang's neatly-coiled queue.

"It's time you had a haircut, Chink," he said. "I'm startin' on your pigtail right now." He dragged the terrified old man back to the table, reached for the greasy steak knife on his plate.

Cole was on his feet. He called out harshly, "Turn him loose, mister!"

Soler's hand stopped in its reach for the knife. He turned, fingers still clutching Chang's long queue.

Drunken rage filled his inflamed eyes. "I'm cuttin' the Chink's hair, and you ain't got the guts to stop me!" he shouted.

"I'm not telling you again." Cole was suddenly moving fast. Soler seized a chair and hurled it at him. Cole dodged, landed a hard right on the JD man's chin. Soler staggered against the table which overturned with a crash, and free of the clutching fingers, Chang fled to his kitchen.

Soler disentangled himself from the table and sprang to his feet, hand reaching for his holstered gun. Cole whipped in a left and a right to his face and he went down again, the gun exploding as it fell from his hand.

Cole snatched up the revolver and tossed it beyond the drunken man's reach. He hoped Soler would decide to call it off. A brawl was the last thing he wanted in this town where he was a stranger.

Soler got to his feet, more slowly this time. Blood was streaming from a cut over his eye, and his nose was bleeding. He had the look of a man gone beserk.

"I'm killin' you with my bare hands," he said in a low, hoarse voice. "I'm tearin' you apart."

He was a good thirty pounds heavier, and as strong as a bull, and at this moment a completely mad bull. Cole tried to avoid his rush, but this time his battering fists failed to stop his opponent. He gave ground, anxious now to elude Soler's crushing arms and watching for the chance to land another devastating right.

Tables and chairs overturned as they battled across the room. Soler was pressing his advantage, his flailing arms reaching relentlessly for the bear's hug he wanted.

They crashed through the screen door to the sidewalk, where shouting men were spilling from saloon doors. Cole glimpsed the startled face of the girl he had met in the blacksmith shop, watching from the porch of the store.

They struggled through milling, excited bystanders into the street, and at last Cole got his chance. A terrific blow to the solar plexus made the JD man drop his arms, left him helpless to block Cole's savage left to the jaw. It was a wholehearted punch that rocked Soler back on his heels. He wavered, was suddenly down on his face.

A loud, raspy voice broke the momentary hush, and a long, lean man shouldered through the crowd. He wore a shiny star, and two guns in tied-down holsters.

"What's goin' on here?" he demanded. His eyes widened as he looked down at the senseless JD foreman. He scowled, stared hard at Cole. "Stranger here, ain't you?"

Cole guessed that the newcomer was Sil Turlo, the town marshal, the man Blackie Stenlo had said was a "good hombre." He was inclined to think that Blackie's enthusiasm was misplaced. The town marshal had a mean eye and a thin-lipped, cruel mouth. The man was a killer if he ever saw one, Cole thought, and his heart sank. Sil Turlo was going to be decidedly unpleasant.

The town marshal's voice was rasping at him. "We don't like strangers startin' brawls in this town." A gun slid with practiced ease into his hand.

"I didn't start it," Cole said. He gestured at the restaurant proprietor, peering anxiously from his wrecked screen door. "This man was abusing Chang, was going to cut off his queue."

"Your talk don't make hay with me," Turlo said belligerently. "Lute Soler's a peaceable man."

Somebody in the crowd guffawed. The town marshal's face reddened. His head swung in a slow, searching look for the offender. There were no more laughs, and his cold eyes fastened again on Cole. "I heard gunplay," he said ominously.

"It was his gun," Cole told him.

"I ain't believin' you!" Turlo rasped. "I'm takin' you to jail for an attempted killin'." He stepped quickly behind Cole, jabbed his gun hard into his back and deftly snatched the .44 from Cole's holster. "What do you say about it, Lute?" He looked at the JD man who was painfully getting to his feet.

Soler fixed bloodshot eyes on the prisoner. "He's a lot safer in your jail than runnin' loose in this town, Sil," he said with a malevolent grin. "I ain't finished with him — not yet."

"He says you were fixin' to cut off the Chinaman's pigtail," accused the town marshal, obviously making a pretence of fairness. "Is that right, Lute?"

"Chang knowed I was just foolin'," Soler answered. "Wouldn't have been no trouble a-tall if this feller hadn't jumped me — done his best to kill me."

"I reckon you've said enough, Lute," Turlo said loudly. "I'm chargin' him with attempted murder. I ain't lettin' no stranger mess things up in this town." His gun jabbed Cole's spine. "Get movin', feller. You're headed for jail right now."

A girl's voice, shrill, indignant, interrupted him. "You're not throwing that man in jail, Sil Turlo. I won't stand for it."

The blond girl was running across the street from the store. The crowd made way for her and she fixed a stormy look on Soler. "You tell the truth, Lute. You know darn well you started the fight. I know you, you big bully!"

"I'm gettin' me a drink," muttered JD's foreman. He started to push away from her. She clutched his arm. "I'll make Dad fire you!"

"I reckon he won't be doin' that," Soler told her with an ugly grin. He threw her hand off, lurched away and disappeared inside the adjoining saloon.

The girl faced the town marshal, her eyes bright with anger. "Give his gun back and turn him loose," she said, more quietly.

"Now, Belle," protested Turlo. "It ain't for you to tell me my duty."

"I'll tell Nat Murran," angrily retorted Belle Dacey. "He won't like it, Sil, if you put this man in jail." She flashed Cole an oddly concerned look. "Turn him loose or you'll be up to your neck in trouble."

The town marshal was breathing hard. "You shouldn't talk thataways to me, Belle," he said gruffly. "I'm the law in this town." He glowered at the grinning faces. "You don't want folks laughin' at the law, do you?"

Belle shrugged, turned away abruptly. "I'm telling Nat," she flung back at him.

Turlo's gaze followed her, and his expression told Cole that the man was worried. It was evident he had reason to fear Nat Murran. It was also plain that he was reluctant to turn his prisoner loose, make himself an object of ridicule.

"Get movin', feller," he said again.

He marched his prisoner up the middle of the dusty street, past the saloon which a big sign above the wide swing doors announced was Jake's Roundup. Several horses dozed at the long hitchrail. One of them was a black and white pinto. Cole's step faltered. The pinto was the same horse ridden by the man who had shot Jane Bowman's father from ambush.

He felt the jab of the town marshal's gun in his back, heard his raspy voice. "Move along, there, feller, or you'll be headin' for Boothill, 'stead of jail."

Cole reluctantly obeyed, heartsick at the scurvy trick fate had played on him. Somewhere near, perhaps in the saloon, or mingling with the crowd watching him being marched off to jail, was the pinto's owner, Lewis Bowman's would-be murderer. Discovery of his identity would have been an invaluable clue, helped bring to justice a thief and murderer whose trail had led down the long years from faraway Natchez.

The jail was a squat, adobe building that stood by itself between the town's main street and the few crumbling-walled adobes that comprised Old Town. A man appeared in the doorway of the office. The town marshal gave him a grin.

"Got a prisoner for you, Hoot," he said. "Done his best to kill Lute Soler." He prodded Cole through the door. "Shouldn't wonder but what the JD boys will be over and take him away from you and dangle him from the nearest tree. They won't like what he done to Lute."

Hoot scowled. He was a brutal-faced, stumpy man with the long arms of a gorilla. "I ain't buckin' the JD fellers," he said surlily. "If they want this jasper they get him."

Turlo holstered his gun. "He's *your* prisoner, now, Hoot. Won't hurt me none if that Dacey outfit comes and busts him out of jail."

"I sure won't buck 'em," repeated Hoot. He pushed Cole into a dark corridor. "All right, feller. I got a little room down this way, all fixed up with bars and nice clean straw."

The cell door slammed shut, bolt rasped into socket, and the jailer's footsteps faded down the corridor. Cole gazed gloomily at the small, iron-barred window. He had played the fool, putting off going to the post office. He might have found the letter promised by his old cattleman friend, gained possession of the proof that would have meant the end of the long trail that had led from the banks of the Mississippi.

CHAPTER SEVEN

Nat Murran removed his amber-tinted spectacles. It was like taking off a mask. The benevolent creases of his face were suddenly the hard lines of a scheming, ruthless man.

"It was a simple job," he said. "I don't like the way you handled it."

Jasper Dacey stirred uneasily in his chair. "You didn't give us much information," he said, defensively. "Ringo and Cherokee did the best they could, but the man was too smart."

"It's a mess," grumbled Murran. "You've got to pick up his trail."

"You can't even tell us what he looks like," complained Dacey. "All we've got is a dead horse. No brand and no mark on saddle gear." He gestured impatiently. "What makes you think some hombre from Santa Fé is on the prod for you?"

"What I know is *my* business," Murran said, a hint of sharpness in his voice.

"You're making this stranger that has you so scared *my* business," grumbled Dacey. "I don't like playing around in the dark, Nat."

Murran gave him a sour look. "It was something Pete Shedd let slip some time back."

Dacey nodded. He knew Pete Shedd. Pete's freight wagons came in from Santa Fé several times a year. "You mean it was Pete who tipped you off about this feller we're looking for?"

Murran hesitated. "Pete wasn't knowing I'd be much interested." He spoke slowly, almost reluctantly. "He said a Santa Fé feller was asking him if he knew a man in Boca Grande who might be wearing the name of Adna Fenn."

"I don't savvy why that should worry you," laughed Dacey. "Nobody here in Boca Grande using that name." He was suddenly silent, startled by the odd look in the other man's eyes.

"That's what I told Pete." Murran's tone was grim. "There are plenty hombres hiding out in this town, Jasper. We don't like it for folks to get nosy about names."

"We sure don't," muttered the big cattleman. He lowered his eyes as if afraid to meet the liveryman's unwinking gaze. "How do you know that the man Pete was talking to is the same feller who got away from Ringo and Cherokee?"

"No sense taking chances he ain't," Murran said. He paused, added softly, "Only one thing we can do. Savvy?"

Dacey nodded. "You mean we don't let strangers on foot reach this town alive. One of 'em would be the feller you want dead." His tone was matter of fact. He might have been discussing the cattle market.

"I don't care how many you fill with lead if one of 'em is this Santa Fé man." Murran's face wrinkled in a mirthless smile. "It's him dead awful soon, or the hangman's rope for you and me."

Dacey's face darkened. "For you, maybe," he said surlily. "It's not *me* this Santa Fé feller is looking for. I've built up a good name in this Boca Grande country. I'm not scared of every stranger's shadow, always watching the roads through a brass telescope." His clenched fist pounded the table between them. "I'm gettin' some tired of doing your dirty work, Nat. Wish to God I'd never got myself tangled up with you."

"You're forgetting that jail cell in Yuma," reminded Murran with another mirthless smile. "You'd be rotting behind those bars now, if I hadn't got you out." His mild voice was suddenly hard, venomous. "You wouldn't like to go back to Yuma. Don't be a fool, Jasper. You'd be dead before that gun was out of your holster."

The cattleman's head turned in a look at the beady-eyed face that peered at him from a curtained alcove. His hand slid from gun-butt. He gave the bald-headed liveryman a sickly grin.

"So you keep a killer handy, now," he sneered.

"His name happens to be Yuma," chuckled Murran. "That name is bad medicine for you, my fine friend, and don't forget it."

"I'll be on my way," muttered Dacey. He stood up, reached for his hat. "Promised to meet Belle over at the store."

"Sit down!" almost snarled the other man. "I'm not finished with you."

Dacey hesitated, glanced at the curtained alcove and slowly resumed his chair.

"Belle was in to see me," Murran continued. "She was some excited, wanted me to stop Sil Turlo from throwin' a young feller in jail." The liveryman paused, put on the amber spectacles and again his moon face beamed geniality. "Seems this young feller tangled with Lute Soler and beat him up. Sil figures to charge him with attempted murder."

"What has Belle got to do with it?" frowned Dacey.

"She liked the way he handled that black colt of hers over in the blacksmith shop." Murran's smile dripped benevolent amusement. "She's taken a fancy to the young feller, figures you can use him out at the ranch."

Dacey shook his head. "He wouldn't last long enough to hang up his hat, now that he's tangled with Lute. You know that redhead, Nat. He'd go for his gun."

"I reckon Lute will mind his manners if I speak the word," smiled Murran. He removed the amber spectacles, and his round face was suddenly like hard granite, his eyes sly, malicious. "I let you brag around that you're the owner of the JD ranch, but that don't make you the owner. You're just my hired man, Jasper, same as Lute Soler and the rest of the outfit. You make a good front for me, and that's all I want of you. I can send you and Lute and the rest of 'em to hell any day it suits me. Each one of you is on the dodge from the law, and you're safe only so long as you mind me. Savvy?"

Dacey nodded, his face averted, as if unable to bear the satanic glee in the other man's eyes.

"You're safe here because I'm the law in this town," continued Murran. His tone was suddenly boastful. "If I don't like a man, or if he's stopped bein' useful, he disappears."

"You promised to deed the ranch over to me," Jasper Dacey said. His voice was almost a groan. There was no arrogance in him now. "I've made that ranch."

"It makes us a good profit," smiled Murran. "I'm a smart man." A wicked laugh rose in his throat. "I reckon there ain't an honest-raised cow on the place. I've kept you some busy alterin' brands."

Dacey scowled. "We could stop rustlin', Nat, before it's too late. We've got plenty cows now and could run an honest business." His voice was oddly pleading. "I — I've got Belle to think of. I want her to be proud of JD."

Murran's murky eyes played over him. "We'll think about it," he finally said. "We've got to lay this Santa Fé man by the heels first, and I have ideas about the old Rivera range. Those Bowmans must be chased off that place, Jasper. You should never have let Bowman move in on you like you did."

"The girl heired it from her grandmother, she says," reminded Dacey. His eyes narrowed in a hard stare at the other man. "I reckon that shootin' out there was your work, huh, Nat?"

"Bowman is a dangerous man," Murran replied. "He's about as poisonous to me as the Santa Fé feller." His voice was thin, deadly. "Bowman and his girl must go, too, Jasper. They're in my way, and I don't like people when they're in my way. I get rid of 'em."

"You're a devil," muttered the cattleman. Beads of sweat broke out on his face. "That girl is a pretty little thing, and Bowman is a decent sort. Why don't you just scare 'em away?"

"Bowman won't scare," grinned Murran. "You see, I know something about him that you don't, and gettin' scared ain't one of his failings." He paused, drummed fat fingers on the brass telescope that lay on the table. "I want the Rivera place and I'm going to make sure I get it, and get it legal. There's silver in the canyon back of the springs. It's worth millions."

Dacey's eyes gleamed for a moment, then he shook his head. "All I want is my JD ranch," he said. "You count me out. I'm not lifting my hand against the Bowmans." He frowned, added in a puzzled tone, "Killin' the Bowman's won't give you legal title to the old rancho. You can't just move in and claim the place."

"I know a few things you don't," Murran said complacently. "After the Treaty of Guadalupe Hidalgo in 1848 the old Spanish land grants had to be confirmed by the United States Government, or their owners would forever lose title. Old Don Francisco died in Mexico, and his heirs never had their title confirmed by the new government. A lot of the old grandees lost their land grants that way." Murran's face wrinkled in a wicked smile. "The Rivera rancho is wide open to the first man who claims it under the law, and that's what I'm doing."

"They'll fight you in the law courts," argued Dacey.

"Won't do 'em any good to try," chuckled Murran. "A lot of 'em have tried and got nowhere." His face was suddenly an evil mask. "They won't have a chance to try. I'll make sure of that, and awful soon."

"You devil," repeated Dacey.

Murran seemed unmoved by the cattleman's horror. He said, slowly, significantly, "When the Bowmans ain't around to bother me no more, I'll maybe think about that deed to JD you're wanting from me."

"I — I don't know, Nat," mumbled Dacey. His face was ashen. "I — I've got to think it over."

"You'll come to it." Murran flapped a limp hand. "I warned you, Jasper. When folks stop bein' useful — they disappear."

Dacey's fingers spread open as if to claw at the butt of the gun in his holster. He glanced again at the curtained alcove, and the beady eyes he saw there made him draw his hand back.

Murran was speaking again, his voice placid. "There's a chance the Santa Fé feller got to the Bowman place. He'd likely show up at the Rivera rancho if he knew the Bowmans were there." His eyes stabbed at the sullen face opposite him. "You said you followed the trail up the arroyo where it makes the bend below the house. Did you see any sign of the feller when you talked to the girl and her dad?"

Dacey shook his head. "Bowman was lying there, near the corral, and the girl was fixing a bandage on him. I questioned both of 'em, but they said nobody had been to the house. I figured they told the truth."

"Lute Soler claims he run into the feller after he left you and headed for town." Murran smiled bleakly. "The feller sure outsmarted Lute, left him roped to his saddle and a gash in his head for Doc Johnson to fix up when he found him." He paused, added thoughtfully. "I questioned the doc hard, but he says he didn't see no sign of the feller at the Bowman place when he was there."

Dacey nodded. "I reckon he headed back for Hachita," he said sourly. "It's my notion he won't ever come back."

"I'm hoping he's some place close." Murran's voice showed alarm. "I want him bad, and I want him dead. You keep the boys on the lookout for him. He's got to show up, sooner or later."

"It's like looking for a woodtick in the dark," grumbled Dacey. "There's an awful lot of canyons to comb, and this feller is sure smart, or he wouldn't have got away the time Ringo and Cherokee laid for him up in the Big Hatchets."

"You've got to find him," reiterated Murran.

"Right now I'm getting over to the store and meet Belle." The cattleman pushed up impatiently from his chair. "You sure have me guessin', Nat, about this Santa Fé hombre that's got you so scared."

Murran stared up at him stonily. "I've got my reasons, and before you go I want to talk about this young jasper Sil Turlo has got in jail. I want you to put him on the JD payroll." He smirked. "Belle's taken a shine to him."

"He's in jail," reminded Dacey. His face reddened. "I ain't hirin' hands to please Belle."

"I'm taking him out of jail," continued Murran. "I'm Justice of the Peace, and I'm going to hand him a six months' sentence hard labor at the ranch, with pay." Murran smirked again. "Belle should make a good jailer."

Dacey shrugged. "You ain't foolin' me, Nat. You've got some idea back in your head."

"You've guessed it," Murran admitted, his expression suddenly hard. "He claims his name is Thomason, makes out he's on the dodge from the law. I want to know more about him. He hit town a couple of hours or so ago, and his bronc wears a Mex iron. He may be useful, or he may be plain skunk. If he's skunk you can turn him over to the boys to use their guns on."

"I savvy." Dacey turned to the office door, his expression gloomy. "Have him ready to leave for the ranch in the morning, Nat. Belle and I are staying over at the hotel, tonight."

The door closed behind him, and Murran was suddenly on his feet, gaze on the curtained alcove. "Yuma," he said softly.

The owner of the beady eyes stepped from behind the curtain. He was a scrawny little man with a thin slit of a mouth under a flat nose.

"I want Stinger to try it again," Murran said. "You know where to find him."

Yuma nodded, went on swift, soundless feet from the room.

The liveryman pondered for a moment, picked up the telescope and followed him into the yard. He went to the bench under the cottonwood tree, leveled the telescope at the horses at the rail in front of the Roundup Saloon, focussed the glass on the pinto Cole had noticed when on his way to the jail.

Murran smiled contentedly, lowered the glass, waited until Yuma turned in through the swing doors. He leveled the telescope again and in a few moments saw a man hurry from the saloon and swing into the pinto's saddle.

He continued to watch until horse and rider vanished behind the ridge south of the town. Again he lowered the telescope, leaned it against the bench and reached for his amber-tinted spectacles. He put them on, beamed benevolently at a freighter approaching the water-trough with a string of mules.

"Are you pullin' your wagons out today, Pete?" he asked.

The mule-skinner shrugged. "Figger to make Hachita come dawn if I don't have Injun trouble."

"Tough times," commiserated the fat little liveryman. He wagged his head sadly. "A man never knows what the dawn will bring."

The lanky freighter grinned. "I reckon so, Nat, but what the hell?" He gnawed at his plug of tobacco, stolidly watched his mules nose the cool water.

CHAPTER EIGHT

Cole stared gloomily at the small, barred window, yellow with the mid-afternoon sunlight. The situation promised grim possibilities. He was hopelessly trapped and could do nothing about it. There were no weak spots in the adobe walls, and the rusty bars were strong. Escape was impossible.

The jailer's callous hints of a lynching party worried him more than he cared to admit. It was easy to inflame a mob, especially if there were enough JD men in town to demand the border's rough and ready justice for the supposed attempt to murder their foreman.

His thoughts went to Jane Bowman, and dismay grew in him. He was convinced that Adna Fenn was responsible for the attempt to kill her father. The Bowmans were links to his past and it was his ruthless purpose to destroy them. Eventually he would have his way, despite Tranquilo Baca and his vaqueros.

For the first time in his life Cole found himself helpless to cope with the despair that gripped him. More than his own life was at stake. He had miserably failed Jane Bowman in her hour of peril.

He fought savagely for self-control. While life was in him he must hold on to his wits — his strength, keep alert and ready for any chance that offered. If no chance offered, he would have to make one, snatch victory from what now seemed sure defeat.

His panic subsided, and for long moments he sat motionless on his heels, coolly examined the various incidents that had culminated in his perilous predicament. The inquisitive hotel clerk, the livery barn and Nat Murran's offer to get him a job with Dacey, the brief interlude with Belle Dacey in the blacksmith shop, the restaurant — the brawl with Lute Soler. All commonplace happenings that quite failed to indicate the sinister hand of Adna Fenn. The only thing that tied up with Adna Fenn was the black and white pinto he had glimpsed at the rail in front of the Roundup Saloon.

Cole scowled at a skinned knuckle. He would have given a lot for a look at the pinto's rider. The man was a clue to the mystery of Adna Fenn, knew the name under which the murderer of Judge Spottisford masqueraded. It would have been trail's end, long deferred justice done, and something even more to be desired — safety at last assured for Jane Bowman and her father.

Careful scrutiny of his brief hours in Boca Grande satisfied Cole that Adna Fenn was not responsible for the town marshal's hostility. Sil Turlo was merely a sadistic bully who revelled in displaying his authority. The newly arrived stranger who had dared to use his fists on the foreman of the big JD outfit was a natural victim.

Cole felt he had found a satisfactory answer that explained why he had been thrown in jail. It was an answer that eliminated Adna Fenn and relieved much of his anxiety. There still remained the unpleasant possibility of a lynching party.

Cole got to his feet and went to the window. He had to get out of the place before it was too late. He wrenched savagely at the bars, realized the futility of his attempt to loosen them.

He turned away, desperate, his thoughts racing. Escape through window or walls was impossible, but a key could unlock the cell door. Perhaps Belle Dacey was the key to freedom. He recalled her indignant words: "*I'll tell Nat Murran . . . He won't like it if you put this man in jail . . . Turn him loose or you'll be up to your neck in trouble*."

Cole gazed thoughtfully at the door of his cell, a heavy, wooden affair with an iron grill used by the jailer as a peephole and through which he could pass a prisoner's scanty rations. It was an old door and showed signs of decay. Given a knife and plenty of time, he could cut the iron grill out, reach down to the outside bolt.

His lips twisted in a mirthless grin. The jailer had removed his knife, together with cigarette papers, tobacco and matches And even if he had his knife he certainly lacked the necessary time. The coming darkness might bring Lute Soler's friends.

His thoughts returned to Belle Dacey. Perhaps he was crazy, thinking she could effect his release. Her threat, though, to tell Nat Murran, had plainly disconcerted the town marshal. Apparently the genial-faced liveryman was a formidable power in the town.

The slam of a door sent an expectant thrill down Cole's spine. He listened, tense, a bit breathless, wondering if his crazy hopes were about to be fulfilled.

Heavy footsteps approached, and suddenly he saw the jailer's brutal face peering through the iron grill.

"You're wanted back in the office," Hoot said. He slid the bolt, swung the door, motioned at Cole with his gun. "Step lively, feller."

Cole preceded him down the corridor and into the dingy little office. He was not too surprised to see Nat Murran filling the chair behind the desk.

"Well, well, young man." The eyes behind the amber spectacles studied Cole attentively. "Didn't take you long to make plenty trouble for yourself in this town." The liveryman was not smiling now, and there was an ominous rasp to his voice. "You've been charged with attempted murder, Thomason."

Cole started to speak. Murran flapped a silencing hand at him. "Bring Lute and the Chinaman in, Sil," he called.

Shadows darkened the doorway and the burly town marshal stepped inside. Chang followed, long queue neatly dressed, hands folded over blue blouse. His downcast eyes lifted in a frightened look at the Buddha-like figure in the chair. Lute Soler pushed past him, hat on the back of his head, fingers hooked over gunbelt. Like the old Chinese there was apprehension in the quick look he gave Murran.

"I reckon the interested parties are all here," Murran said. He straightened in his chair, placed his hands on the desk, intoned solemnly, "Hear ye, hear ye! I declare this honorable court is ready to try this case." He gazed fixedly at Cole. "You look some surprised, young man, but I'm Justice of the Peace in this town, and that means I'm the law." He gave no time for Cole to speak. "Lute Soler, are you claimin' the prisoner tried to kill you?" He stared hard at the JD foreman.

Soler's swollen lips moved, but made no sound. It was the town marshal who answered.

"Your honor —" Turlo's manner was almost fawning. "Lute ain't pressin' no charge agin the prisoner."

Judge Murran frowned. "I've a notion to throw you in jail for contempt of this court." He glared at the uneasy JD man. "I'm finin' you ten dollars, Lute, for wasting my time, and you'd better have Doc Johnson fix up that black eye you're wearing. Fork up and get out of here." He transferred his judicial glare to the restaurant proprietor. "I'm fining you fifty dollars, Chang, for allowing your customers to disturb the peace of this town. Fork up and get out of here."

The two men silently produced the necessary gold pieces, laid them on the desk and left the office. Cole, gaze following the unfortunate Chang, was impelled to protest.

"It wasn't his fault," he said.

"Ten dollars for contempt of this court," snapped Judge Murran.

Cole shrugged, wordlessly laid a ten dollar gold piece on the desk. It was plain the town's Justice of the Peace was operating a profitable little gold mine. His law was also decidedly home-made to suit himself.

"Thomason —" The judge's voice was unexpectedly mild. "I should send you over to the county jail to stand trial for attempted murder. This court is disposed to be easy on you." The beam was back on his face. "Won't do to let you off too easy, so I'm fining you one hundred dollars and sentencing you to six months hard labor on Jasper Dacey's cow ranch."

Cole started to speak, remembered his ten dollar lesson, wordlessly counted out the required gold pieces and placed them with the growing stack on the desk.

Judge Murran beamed. "Six months hard labor," he repeated, "and I've fixed it up with Dacey for you to get top-hand pay."

Cole found his voice. "Thank you, Judge. I'm mighty obliged." He hesitated. "I understand Lute Soler is a JD man."

"Who told you?" rasped the liveryman.

Cole realized that as a stranger in town he was not supposed to know too much. "Why —" He nodded at the town marshal whose surly expression indicated disapproval of the sentence. "He was talking with the jailer, and something was said about the JD men getting up a necktie party because of the beating I gave their boss."

The explanation seemed to satisfy Murran. His genial smile returned. "I reckon sunup would have found you dangling from a tree, if I hadn't got you out," he said. He turned a complacent grin on the glowering town marshal. "All right, Sil. Give him his gun and things back and turn him loose." He got out of his chair, scooped the gold pieces into the pocket of his black alpaca coat. "Court is adjourned, and now, young man, you get over to the hotel and tell Dacey he's hired him a top hand."

Cole said, cautiously, "How about Lute Soler? He won't like having me in his outfit."

"Dacey will fix things up for you," reassured Murran. "Lute ain't one to hold a grudge." He beamed. "I reckon you'll get along fine with that outfit once they get to know you."

Hoot grudgingly handed over the confiscated gun. Cole examined it, saw the chambers were full. He slid the Colt into holster, gave the jailer a reproachful grin. "You're forgetting my knife — and the smokes," he reminded.

Hoot grunted, slapped tobacco sack and papers on the desk, reluctantly fished the knife from his vest pocket. "You're lucky to get 'em back," he growled.

"I'll say he's lucky," grumbled the town marshal. "All right feller. Get out of here, and watch your step in this town."

The last of the sunlight was fading when Cole turned into the main street. The wind was up, fresh and cool from the mountains. The clean air felt good after close confinement in Boca Grande's squalid jail. He owed a debt to Belle Dacey, a thought that vaguely worried him. He felt that the girl could be dangerous. She was high-strung and quick tempered and liked to have her own way. At least it was the impression she had made during those few minutes in the blacksmith shop.

Nevertheless, for some odd reason of her own she had persuaded Nat Murran to get him out of jail. He wondered with growing uneasiness if the sentence to "hard labor" on her father's ranch was the girl's idea. The challenge in her boldly appraising eyes had been too apparent to ignore. Belle Dacey liked him, wanted him around.

Cole leaned against a crumbling adobe wall and thoughtfully made a cigarette. Nat Murran was a puzzle he would like to solve. The town marshal's servility, Lute Soler's very evident awe of him, indicated there was more to the moon-faced liveryman than appeared on the surface. Hard-bitten men like Sil Turlo and JD's arrogant foreman were not the type to be easily cowed. It was plain that Nat Murran was a man to be feared.

Cole again recalled Belle Dacey's warning words to the town marshal. *"You'll be up to your neck in trouble."* His quick release from jail proved that her words were no idle threat, and also showed she had lost no time questioning the liveryman about the stranger who had helped her quiet the black colt. It was more than likely that Murran would have told her of his intention to ask her father to give the stranger a job with his JD outfit. The six month sentence *could* have been Belle's idea. At least Murran would let her think the plan was hers, and so conceal a personal and perhaps more sinister motive in wanting Cole on Jasper Dacey's payroll.

Twilight deepened in the street, and here and there lamplight began to gleam from windows. A pair of cowboys jogged past, off-saddled in front of the

Roundup Saloon. Cole was suddenly reminded of the black and white pinto.

The saloon's swing doors were still vibrating behind the cowboys when he reached the hitchrail. The line of horses was longer now, but the black and white pinto was not among them.

Cole turned, sauntered back along the rail for another look, wishing to make sure he had not missed the pinto in the growing darkness. As he came opposite the saloon the swing doors slammed and the two cowboys hurried out with Lute Soler. The JD foreman saw him, halted abruptly, and for a moment Cole thought he was in for more trouble. The red-headed man's friendly grin reassured him.

"Looks like they wasn't wantin' you in that jail," Soler said.

Cole grinned back at him. "Cost me a hundred dollars," he answered ruefully.

"I should split it with you." Soler thrust a hand into pocket. "I was sure actin' some mean with the Chinaman. Don't blame you none for gettin' on the prod."

"That's mighty white of you," thanked Cole. He smilingly shook his head. "You keep your money in your pocket. It was worth a hundred to find out you've got a tough marshal in this town. I'm sure going to watch my step from now on."

"Don't you get Sil Turlo wrong," protested Soler. "Sil's a good hombre and easy to get along with when he knows a feller." His hand came empty from his pocket and he glanced back hesitantly at the swing doors. "I should buy you a drink, only I got to fork saddle in a hurry and hightail in back to the ranch with Curly and Ben here." He nodded at his two companions whose poker faces relaxed in brief grins.

"We'll get plenty chances to buy drinks," Cole said. "I'm Cole Thomason, and if you don't already know it, Judge Murran has sentenced me to a six month's job with your outfit, Soler."

"Belle told me." There was no hint of animosity in Soler's grin. Only sly amusement. "If you can handle a rope as good as your fists, I'm bettin' you're a top hand."

"Thanks." Cole left them, crossed the street and climbed the hotel porch steps. It was very apparent from Soler's genial manner that he was obeying somebody's orders to be on friendly terms with the outfit's newest member. The foreman's admission that Belle had told him about the job worried him. The girl was already making it known that she regarded the new hand as her special property. She was going to be troublesome, one more problem to cope with.

Cole came to a standstill, one foot on the top step. Perhaps he was making a mistake. If he had any sense he would get his horse from the barn and put a lot of miles between himself and Boca Grande.

He thought of the black and white pinto, the clue that could lead him to Adna Fenn. The chances were good that he would see the pinto again, learn the rider's identity. The thought stiffened him. It was no time to let a girl frighten him from the purpose that had brought him to Boca Grande. There was more to the thing now than bringing to justice the man who had murdered old Judge Spottisford and stolen the gold so nobly offered on the altar of patriotism by a little group of Southern planters. Lives were at stake now, Jane Bowman's life, and her father's — his own life.

Cole's eyes hardened. There was no going back. He had to go forward, cling relentlessly to the trail he had followed from Santa Fé.

The screen flew open with a bang, and Belle Dacey smiled at him from the lobby entrance. "My goodness!" she exclaimed. "You look as savage as a mad grizzly bear!"

He forced a smile. "I've been through a lot of hell since I met you in the blacksmith shop," he said, truthfully.

Belle nodded, her expression sympathetic. "Sil Turlo is just too mean to live. I hate him!" Her fingers were on his arm, and there was a hint of possessiveness in the touch. "Dad is waiting for a look at his new top hand," she said.

CHAPTER NINE

Jane finished dressing, took a final brief look at herself in the mirror and went to the bedroom window. The distant mountain peaks were always at their best when touched with the early morning sun. She liked to think that her grandmother had probably enjoyed the same view from the same window in the long ago when she was Juanita Rivera. No doubt she would have shared the view with Carter Ruffin before he carried her off to her new home on the banks of the Mississippi. It was a pleasant thought, and always put a tender light in Jane's eyes. The few moments at the window where once her grandparents used to stand and watch the sunrise had become almost a morning ritual.

The sunlit peaks were still there, but for once they failed to hold her gaze. She found herself wondering about Cole Thomason instead, and to wonder about him put fear in her heart. He had been gone more than two days, and no word from him. The silence frightened her.

Sounds in the kitchen told her that Domingo was preparing breakfast. Domingo was one of the vaqueros and Tranquilo Baca had insisted that he take over the kitchen until the arrival of the women from Chihuahua.

It seemed that the soft-voiced, rather shy Domingo was a good cook.

She was still a bit dazed by it all, and grateful for the change and security wrought by the coming of Tranquilo Baca and his vaqueros. It was wonderful to know that these descendants of old Don Francisco's retainers had so miraculously rallied to the defence of the old rancho and its new mistress. For the moment her father was safe; and she was safe, but Cole Thomason was more than ever in peril of his life. The thought tortured her. She wished desperately that Cole Thomason would abandon the purpose that had brought him from Santa Fé. She feared for him, wanted him safely back from Boca Grande.

Jane was suddenly very still, her eyes fixed on the distant peaks but not seeing them. Instead she saw Cole Thomason, staggering toward her through the brush as she knelt by her father's side. She had snatched up her father's gun — almost shot him, but something in his white face had kept her from squeezing the trigger, something fine, honest — unafraid. To think of that moment filled her with horror.

Voices broke the stillness of the early morning, and several Mexicans appeared in the garden, began hacking at the brush with heavy-bladed *machetes*. Tranquilo Baca and two more of his vaqueros rode in from the back yard. The mounted vaqueros loosened their rawhide *reatas* and the men with the *machetes* made them fast to the growing piles of brush which the riders dragged away toward the arroyo.

Tranquilo saw Jane watching from her window. "We will make your garden beautiful again," he said in Spanish. The big Mexican's teeth flashed under his dark mustache. He looked very handsome in his silver-mounted saddle, hand lightly steadying the pawing horse under him.

"You are very good, Tranquilo," Jane said. "I think Heaven sent you."

He swept her a bow. "Nothing is too good for our señorita." He gestured. "Our fathers and our mothers were born on this old rancho. It is *our* home, too."

"We may have to fight to hold it," Jane said. "We have enemies, Tranquilo."

The chief of vaqueros gestured again. "We will fight them." His dark face was grim. "We will destroy the wolves who would do you harm." He looked at her searchingly. "You are worried about our young *Americano*, señorita."

"No word comes from him," Jane said. "He should not have gone to Boca Grande." Her voice was troubled. "Yes, I am worried."

"He is no fool," reassured Tranquilo. "Have no fears for him, señorita."

The two vaqueros returned at a gallop from the arroyo. They reined in close to Tranquilo and one of the men leaned to him from his saddle, showed something in the palm of his hand.

"We found it behind the big mesquite, where we dragged the brush over the bank," he said.

Tranquilo took the object between thumb and forefinger, examined it carefully, and Jane, watching from the window, saw that it was a brown cigarette stub.

"It is fresh," declared Tranquilo. He frowned. "A gringo cigarette."

"How do you know it is a gringo cigarette," Jane asked.

"We Mexicans do not smoke this *Americano* tobacco," explained Tranquilo. He shook his head. "The man who smoked this cigarette has not been gone long. What do you say, Julio?" He looked at the finder of the stub, a slim young vaquero with soulful brown eyes under long, almost girlish lashes.

"He came and went with the dawn," answered Julio. "His horse wore no shoes."

"Which way did he go?" questioned Tranquilo.

Julio pointed a thumb over his shoulder at the arroyo. "Straight down, but the ground is stony and there will be no trail."

"I do not like this," muttered Tranquilo. He spoke sharply to the brush cutters. "Leave your work and keep watch on the house. You will need your rifles." He swung his horse. "Come, Julio — Ramon. Show me this place where you found the cigarette."

Rifles appeared magically in the hands of the brush cutters. They scattered like quail, vanished in the chaparral.

Jane turned from the window, aware of a great thankfulness in her. The intruder, perhaps the same man who had shot her father from ambush, had been frightened away by the presence of the vaqueros. He had come with the dawn, a prowling, dangerous beast with the lust to kill. He must have been surprised to find that the Bowmans were no longer alone and helpless.

She found her father in the dining room. The vaqueros had cleaned out the cobwebs and dust and salvaged a table and chairs from the storeroom. The windows were still boarded up because of needed repairs, but the doors were open and let in bright sunshine from the little patio.

Lewis Bowman put down his coffee cup and looked at her questioningly as she pulled out a chair opposite him. He sensed from her expression that something was wrong.

"We've had an early morning prowler," Jane said. She told him about the cigarette stub. "Tranquilo is trying to pick up his trail."

Her father smiled. "The scoundrel must have had the surprise of his life." He fingered his beard thoughtfully. "Means that whoever sent him will soon learn we have plenty of help here."

"It terrifies me." Jane shivered. "He would have watched for us, waited for the chance to shoot us down."

"He won't come back for another try," Bowman said. "He knows we're not alone any more."

"Whoever wants to be rid of us will think up some other way," worried Jane.

Her father said slowly, not looking at her, "We can give the thing up, Jane . . . find us some other place a long way from here."

Her chin lifted. "We're Bowmans, and Bowmans don't run."

He was smiling at her. "No — Bowmans don't run, child." Domingo came in with bacon and *tortillas* and a fresh pot of hot coffee. "It is not a very good breakfast," he told her deprecatingly.

"It looks delicious," smiled Jane, knowing it was praise he wanted. "We do need such a lot of things, though; flour, bacon, eggs, milk — sugar and butter, and goodness knows what else."

"Tranquilo will get them." Domingo spoke confidently. "Tranquilo is very smart." He gave her a reassuring grin and went back to his kitchen.

"They regard Tranquilo as some sort of god," chuckled Bowman.

Jane sipped her coffee, put the cup down and gazed steadily at her father. "I'm thinking that God sent him," she said.

Bowman nodded, his face sober. "We were mighty close to the edge, Daughter, and that's a fact." He touched his bandaged arm, resting in a sling. "It's a miracle I'm sitting here with you this morning." His deep voice was very gentle. "I suppose you'll say God sent young Thomason along in time to save me from bleeding to death."

"Yes," Jane said. "God sent him, too." She faltered. "I'm frightened for him, Father."

"He's smart — like Tranquilo Baca," chuckled Bowman. "Cole's no tenderfoot."

His attempt to wave aside her fears failed to impress her. "You needn't pretend," she said. "You're quite as worried as I am."

Bowman was silent, and the anxiety he had been keeping from her was plain enough now in his eyes. Jane pushed her plate away. The thought of food at that moment revolted her.

"Cole shouldn't have gone to Boca Grande." A choke rose in her throat. "I — I can't bear it — thinking of him — alone in that town — and Adna Fenn perhaps knowing who he is." She got up from her chair. "I can't bear it!" she repeated. "We must do something — before it's too late."

Her father's shaggy brows lifted and he gave her an oddly speculative look. "You think a lot of young Thomason." His tone was dry.

"Why — of — of course. He — he's kin —"

Bowman continued to gaze at her, a mixture of concern and affection in his eyes. "Very remote kin," he reminded with a faint smile.

Spurs jingled and scraped in the kitchen and they heard Tranquilo Baca's sonorous voice. The door opened, framed the big Mexican, hat in his hand.

"A messenger," he announced.

Benito, and another man followed him into the room. Tranquilo motioned at the latter. "He is Mateo Cota who is a friend of our Benito. He brings a message from Señor Thomason." His hand gently pushed the man toward Jane. "Give our señorita the message, Mateo."

"Señor Thomason has taken a job at the Dacey ranch," the Mexican told her. "Señor Thomason says you will understand."

Jane's outstretched hand fell to her side. She asked disappointedly, "Is there no written message?"

Mateo shook his head. "It was not safe to write the words, señorita. He was afraid the letter would be dangerous for you if I were caught with it."

"Have you nothing more to tell me?"

Mateo hesitated, shook his head. "No, señorita."

Jane felt he was keeping something back, guessed that he was only obeying Cole's orders. "Are you returning to Boca Grande?" she asked.

"*Si.*" Mateo gave Benito a cryptic little smile. "Señor Thomason is my friend, and I am his ears — his eyes and can listen and watch for him in Boca Grande."

"Thank you for coming," Jane said. "I can see you are a brave and true man and a good friend."

The Mexican's eyes warmed. He fumbled his fragment of the little cross from inside his shirt, lifted it. "I have sworn on this to be his friend," he said simply.

The door closed behind the three Mexicans. Jane turned and looked at her father. "He was keeping something back," she said. "Something Cole didn't want us to know."

"I had the same impression," Bowman admitted. He frowned, shook his head. "I wouldn't worry too much. Cole has his reasons, I reckon."

"Why would he want to work for Jasper Dacey?" she worried. "He said we would understand, but I don't — unless —" She broke off, gazed uneasily at her father.

Bowman nodded, his face grim. "You mean he suspects that Dacey is Adna Fenn."

"What else could take him out to Dacey's ranch?" she asked unhappily.

Lewis Bowman got out of his chair. "Worry won't help anybody," he said. "Cole knows what he's doing." He paused, added with a cheerfulness he did not feel, "At least we know he's still alive." His good arm went around her waist. "Stop worrying, or I'll begin to think you're in love with the boy."

"Don't be foolish!"

Her father chuckled, rumpled her dark hair affectionately. "I'm going out to ask Tranquilo about that cigarette stub they found." He thought it best not to tell her that his real purpose was to ask Mateo Cota a few questions.

He was disappointed. Mateo Cota had already ridden away. He was in a hurry to get back to town and his job before his boss missed him, Tranquilo told Bowman. "Mateo does not want it known he has been here," Tranquilo said.

"I think he could have told us more than he did." Bowman looked hard at the big Mexican. "I think Thomason ran into some trouble he didn't want my daughter to hear about. Perhaps Mateo told you, Tranquilo."

"You have guessed it, señor." Tranquilo shrugged. "Señor Thomason had a fight with this Lute Soler hombre who is foreman of the Dacey cow ranch. He gave Soler a bad beating and was thrown in jail."

Bowman looked his bewilderment. "Mateo said Thomason has taken a job with Dacey's outfit. What do you mean — saying he's in jail."

"It is strange business, señor." Tranquilo shrugged again. "I know only what Mateo tells me. His boss, who runs the feed barn where he works is Justice of the Peace. He fined Señor Thomason one hundred dollars for disturbing the peace and sentenced him to six months hard labor on the Dacey ranch with pay." Tranquilo's tone was puzzled. "It does not make good sense."

"It's the craziest thing I ever heard of," puzzled Bowman. "I don't like it."

"We must not tell the señorita," warned Tranquilo. "It is Señor Thomason's command, Mateo says."

Bowman nodded, was silent, his expression thoughtful. It seemed that Cole had been *forced* to accept a job with the Dacey outfit. He was not at the ranch because he suspected Dacey was Adna Fenn. Which meant that Jane and he had jumped to a wrong conclusion.

He said worriedly, "My daughter must know the truth, Tranquilo. She is thinking the situation is worse than it really is."

"We must not make trouble for Mateo," objected Tranquilo.

"She must be told," insisted Bowman. "The news that Thomason is at the Dacey ranch has made her very anxious for him."

Tranquilo thought it over, his face troubled. "Our little señorita must not be unhappy," he finally decided.

"Tell her if you wish, señor. I will take the blame for Mateo Cota."

"Thank you, Tranquilo." Bowman gave him a relieved smile. "If Thomason doesn't like it, the blame will be all mine."

Tranquilo shrugged. He was watching two riders approaching from the arroyo. "Julio and Ramon return from the search," he observed. "Perhaps they bring news."

"It was lucky you were here," Bowman said, gratefully. "He must have been surprised, that prowler."

"It is a lesson for us." Tranquilo's eyes were hot with anger. "Day and night we will be on guard." He gestured at the garden. "You do not see them, but men lie concealed in the brush, their rifles ready for the next wolf who prowls near." His look went expectantly to the two vaqueros. "What is the news?"

"We followed the trail down the arroyo," Julio told him.

"You saw nothing?"

"We saw a horseman lined against the sky as he crossed a ridge," answered the young Mexican. "The sun was bright on him and on the horse he rode."

Tranquilo nodded. "You have the eyes of a hawk, Julio. You have more to tell me."

Julio looked pleased. "The horse was a black and white pinto," he said.

Bowman met Tranquilo's inquiring look. He nodded, his face grave. "Cole Thomason said the man who took that shot at me was riding a black and white pinto."

Anger rasped in his voice. “He was back for another try, Tranquilo.”

The big Mexican scowled. “When we catch this wolf I will cut off his ears,” he promised. “He will be very dead.”

“It’s the man who hires him we want dead,” Bowman said grimly. He went gloomily back to the house.

CHAPTER TEN

The somber look on Jasper Dacey's face warned his daughter of an impending storm. She halted her impetuous rush into the office, gazed at him uneasily.

"What's wrong, Pops?"

"You," Dacey said.

Belle's chin lifted. "What do you mean?"

"I'm sending you to Santa Fé," her father told her gruffly. "There's a school there that learns a girl how to be a lady."

"I'm lady enough to suit me," laughed the girl. "Don't be an idiot, Pops."

"I mean it." Dacey glowered at her. "This ranch isn't a good place for a young girl, not when she doesn't know how to behave. First thing I know you'll be acting the fool with some no-count cowhand."

"There isn't a man in the outfit I'd look at a second time," angrily retorted the girl. She was suddenly silent, confused by the disbelief she saw in his eyes.

Dacey smiled grimly. "You could have said that yesterday," he told her. "Saying it today makes you a liar."

Belle stamped a foot. "You mean the new man!" she flared.

Her father nodded. "You're all set to play the fool with him, and that's why I'm sending you off to Santa Fé."

"Cole Thomason is the first decent man ever on JD's payroll," Belle said stormily. "I like him, Pops. I like him a lot and I'm old enough to know what I want."

"A girl doesn't have much sense at seventeen," grumbled Dacey. He shook his head. "No use to argue. I can't send Thomason off. I've got to keep him here for six months, so that means you go to Santa Fé."

"You can't make me go," she defied. Her eyes narrowed in a slyly speculative look at him. "Nat Murran won't let you, if I ask him."

Dacey's face reddened, went suddenly white. "Don't talk to me like that," he said thickly.

"Nat likes me," continued Belle. "He wants to marry me." She lifted a disdainful shoulder. "I don't like the smell of a livery stable."

Dacey leaned back in his chair, shocked gaze on her. He was seeing his daughter with new eyes. At seventeen she was no longer a long-legged tomboy. She had miraculously grown up, was a remarkably handsome woman.

His dismay pleased her. She felt she had the whip hand. "Lute Soler wants me, too. He's always trying to get me off alone some place." She giggled, patted the little revolver in the Mexican hand-carved leather holster belted to her waist. "The last time he got fresh with me I told him I'd shoot him — the whiskey-smelling wolf."

The significance of her talk about Soler drew an explosive ejaculation from her father. He said savagely,

"You should have told me Lute was bothering you. I'd have used my own gun on him."

"I can take care of myself," Belle reassured him with a malicious smile. "Lute's not the only JD man who's found *that* out." She went back to the Santa Fé matter, her voice hard, determined. "You forget this idea you've got about sending me away, Pops. I'm staying here on the ranch, or I'll make trouble for you with Nat Murran."

Dacey gazed at her dully, wondered how much she knew. "I'm not wanting trouble with Nat," he finally acknowledged.

"You're afraid of Nat," Belle said frowningly. "A lot of people are afraid of him." She paused, added in a puzzled voice, "Just a little bald-headed, potbellied livery man and he has you all minding him like he was God. What's the secret, Pops?"

Dacey said hoarsely, "You wouldn't understand. Get out of here and forget it."

"Nat hires all your men for you," charged the girl. "You have the toughest bunch of renegades on the border and I'm old enough to do some wondering."

"Get out of here," he repeated. His clenched fist thumped the desk. "Wondering will do you no good."

Belle fired a parting shot. "I told Nat to make you hire Cole," she said, and added complacently, "Nat will do anything I ask."

Dacey gave her a strange look. "Don't fool yourself, girl. Nat Murran didn't sentence Thomason to work six months on this ranch just to please you."

"He certainly did," declared Belle. She smiled back at him from the door. "At least Cole Thomason is one decent man here a girl can talk to and have some fun with. I like him, and if you have any sense you'll kick Lute off the ranch and give his foreman job to Cole Thomason."

"Nat Murran thinks Thomason is maybe on the dodge from the law," Dacey said.

"You could say the same of the whole JD outfit," retorted Belle. She gave her father a sharp look. "I hope that doesn't explain why Nat has so much to say about this ranch." The dark scowl on her father's face suddenly frightened her. She pulled the door shut.

Dacey remained rigid in his chair for long moments. He wondered again how much Belle knew of his unfortunate experience in Yuma. It was not possible for her to know anything, unless Murran had talked, and Nat was not one to talk. She was smart — had realized that some dark and sinister cloud shadowed his life.

He reflected gloomily on those days in Yuma. It had not really been murder. He would have been killed if he had not shot first. Unfortunately, the dead gambler had influential friends.

To think of it still filled Dacey with horror. Nat Murran had managed his escape from the grim prison, provided the boat to cross the river, kept him safely hidden until search had been abandoned. Gratitude had made him willing to listen to the schemes of the man who had saved him from hanging.

The following years had seen the schemes prosper. He had balked at times, but Murran had always overcome his scruples. Murran could send him back to Yuma if he disobeyed. Obedience meant prosperity. Disobedience meant death. It was easier after the first year. Lust for wealth and power hardened him. The lawless border country was accustomed to violence. It was the day of bitter war between nester and cattleman, and Dacey's ruthlessness had made JD the biggest cattle ranch in the Boca Grande, and himself both respected and feared.

Belle thought she was his own daughter. She had never learned about the nester and his wife, found murdered and their cabin in ashes. An Apache raid was the story Dacey had spread. He knew the story to be a lie. It was the nester's own fault. He had been warned to leave or expect trouble. He had chosen to put up a stubborn fight. The memory of the ruthless affair sometimes worried Dacey. His men had obeyed orders a little too thoroughly, but there was nothing he could do about it, only care for the year-old baby girl, lone survivor of the massacre. As his supposed daughter, Belle had become the one clean, bright spot in his life, the only thing he loved.

Ugly fears mounted in him. Nat Murran had no intention of keeping his promise to deed the ranch to him. The man was evidently scheming to take Belle from him. He could easily rob him of Belle's affection by telling her the truth about the murdered nesters.

The big cattleman's face hardened. Not since that fatal day in Yuma had he actually killed a man. He felt now that he could kill Nat Murran. He was certain that Nat would not hesitate to have him killed when he had ceased to be useful. Nat had bluntly said as much. "*If I don't like a man, or if he stops bein useful, he disappears*." The warning was unmistakable.

Thinking of Nat Murran sent a chill through Dacey. He had always been a mystery. Never once had he spoken of his past life or the source of the money found for his many enterprises. Where he was from was a secret he kept to himself. Dacey had soon learned that personal questions were best left unasked. The little liveryman was as deadly as a rattlesnake.

Who Nat Murran really was, or the reason that had brought him to the Boca Grande, did not particularly interest Dacey. He had sometimes wondered why Nat chose to make his livery barn his headquarters. The man was rich, probably had money in a dozen banks under as many different names. He could have lived anywhere. Santa Fé, Albuquerque, New York, but he preferred his livery barn, spent hours on his bench in the yard, always scrutinizing the roads with his long brass telescope. It was obvious that the man was obsessed with some deadly fear. His frantic efforts to find and destroy the stranger from Santa Fé seemed to prove such a belief.

Dacey clenched a big fist. Nat Murran was watching the roads for some danger known only to himself. He would be surprised to know that he was in a more immediate danger. His broken promises about deeding the ranch meant a showdown. The ranch was all Dacey wanted from him as his share of their long years of lawless partnership. He wanted to break with the man for all time, to live the life of an honest and respected cattleman. An impossible dream while Nat Murran continued to live and hold the threat of Yuma over him. Also there was the deed to be considered. He could think of no way to force Nat to give him the deed, unless at gun's point. The fact that Nat now kept a hired killer at his elbow made the problem no easier. He was determined to kill Nat, but he must get the deed first or he would lose the ranch which in truth was really Belle's ranch. The murdered nester, her own father, had located the half section on which the house now stood. Belle was the rightful owner of JD, a startling fact that Dacey had not thought of until this moment. His determination hardened. He would have to get the deed from Murran — and then kill him. There was no other solution. In the meantime he must be careful to avoid a premature break with the man. There was still a chance that Murran would keep his promise and deed over the ranch. He recalled the liveryman's words: "*When the Bowmans ain't around to bother me no more, I'll maybe think about that deed to JD you're wanting from me*."

Dacey's fingers drummed thoughtfully on the desk. Murran's meaning was clear enough. He wanted the Bowmans dead as the price for the coveted deed to JD. It was a grim price, and yet — and yet — Again he was hearing the smooth voice of the tempter: "*You'll come to it . . . Bowman and his girl are in my way . . . There's silver in the canyon*." Sweat suddenly beaded Dacey's face. He shook his head, sprang from his chair. The price was too big. He could not do this thing to the Bowmans. They were nice, the kind of people he wanted for neighbors. The Bowman girl was a lady, would make a good friend for Belle — could do a lot for Belle.

Again Dacey shook his head, angry now for allowing pity to soften him. No matter how nice they were, the Bowmans must go. Getting rid of them was the price he must pay for the ranch. If he did not do it, Murran would make other arrangements. They were doomed even though he withheld his own hand against them.

He paced the floor, a haggard-faced man shaken with the turmoil of his thoughts, striving desperately for some solution that would satisfy Murran. He could warn the Bowmans as a friend that only immediate flight could save them from certain death. If they refused he would send masked men to ride them across the border. The experience would weaken their resistance and they would never return to the rancho. No need to tell Murran they were not dead and buried. But first he would do the friendly act, warn the Bowmans to go before it was too late.

His hard decision made, Dacey jerked the ranch bellrope, three sharp peals that would tell Lute Soler he was wanted at the office. He returned to his chair, found a sheet of paper and began a hasty scrawl.

Dear Bowman:

I have learned that you and your daughter are in terrible danger if you do not immediately leave the Boca Grande country. I cannot help you, or I would. For God's sake get out before it's too late.

He scrawled his signature, folded and thrust the note in an envelope, wondered grimly what Lewis Bowman would do about it. "*Bowman won't scare*." That was what Nat Murran had said. Perhaps Nat was right. Dacey stared morosely at the envelope. He had done all he could. It was going to be up to Bowman now. Get out or likely find himself feeding the buzzards.

Lute Soler stamped into the office. He gave Dacey a lop-sided grin from swollen lips. "That new feller sure can ride 'em. He forked the worst broncs the boys had in the remuda." Soler's grin faded. "What's on your mind, boss? You look some worried."

"Nat Murran wants the Bowmans run off the Rivera place," Dacey told him.

"You want the boys to do the job?" Soler's tone was callous. "Won't be the first time they've fixed a nester."

"Bowman is not a nester," reminded Dacey. "His girl inherited the rancho." He shook his head. "No rough stuff right now, Lute. I'm giving them a chance to get out."

"Bowman ain't the kind that scares easy," grumbled the foreman. "I'm thinkin' Nat figgers there's only one way to get rid of Bowman for keeps. Hand him a dose of lead poison — him and the girl both."

Dacey gazed at him suspiciously. "Do you know anything about the attempt to ambush him the other night?"

"I can make a guess," chortled Soler. "I reckon Nat Murran ain't leavin' it *all* to us."

"It's bad business," worried Dacey. "I don't like it."

"Nat won't like it, nuther, if we don't do something about it like he wants," Soler said with a shrug.

"I'm giving them a chance first," repeated Dacey. He tapped the envelope. "I want you to get this note over to Bowman on the jump."

Soler hesitated, thoughtfully fingered the bandage under his hat. He had strong misgivings that he would not be welcome at the Bowmans. The errand was sure to end most unpleasantly — for himself. "I've got other things to do," he reminded. "There's a chance the Santa Fé feller is holed up over in Lost Horse Canyon. I figgered to head over that way with some of the boys."

"We've got to find that man," Dacey said. "Nat wants him bad — alive or dead." He stared pointedly at the foreman's bandaged head. "After what he did to you I reckon you won't be taking him alive."

Soler's answer was a sour smile. It was his own story and he was not going to change it, give Dacey his *real* reason for not wanting to carry the note to Lewis Bowman.

"It's up to you to find him," warned Dacey. He stared reflectively at his foreman, Belle's story about him suddenly in his mind. He would like an excuse to get rid of the man. "*Kick Soler off the ranch and give his job to Thomason*." Belle's idea was good, but firing Soler was easier said than done. He was beginning to suspect that Soler had a secret understanding with Nat Murran. It would account for his arrogance, his mounting insolence. And it was obvious that the JD outfit regarded him as the real boss. Something would have to be done about Lute Soler, something more drastic than merely kicking him off the ranch. Perhaps Thomason was the answer, a carefully planned feud between the two men — gunplay, with Soler on the receiving end of a fatal bullet.

Soler waited, puzzled by the long silence. “I’ll be goin’,” he finally said. “The boys are waitin’ for me.” He lit the cigarette he had been shaping, added casually, “You could send Cherokee.”

Bowman nodded. “Send Thomason, too,” he said. “I wouldn’t trust Cherokee to get my note to Bowman. He’d likely head for town instead and get drunk.”

“I was figgerin’ to take Thomason along with us,” demurred Soler. “That feller can handle a gun. He’s been showin’ us some fancy shootin’.” He grinned. “He’d sure be bad medicine for that Santa Fé jasper we’ve been huntin’ for.”

“I reckon Nat had him sized up for a man we could use,” smiled Dacey. “Good with his fists, too, huh, Lute?” he added maliciously.

The big foreman’s face darkened. “I’ll work him over worse than he done me next time we mix.”

“Nat thinks he’s on the run from the law, or wanting us to think he is.” Dacey chuckled. “We’ll have to keep an eye on him, Lute. He’s maybe a range detective.”

“You ain’t telling me nothin’,” growled Soler. “Be too bad for him if he’s a law man on the prowl.”

Another chuckle came from Dacey. He said, with feigned amusement, “Belle likes him a lot. She’ll likely get him to talk about himself, kind of lead him on.”

Soler’s eyes took on an ugly glint. “Leadin’ a feller on is somethin’ Belle’s good at —” He broke off, forced a grin. "I'll tell Cherokee and Thomason you're wantin' 'em," he finished.

Dacey's gaze followed him to the door, his expression bland. He felt that he had planted his seed for discord between the two men rather well. Suspicion — jealousy. He hoped that Lute Soler was right about Thomason's fast trigger-finger. It was a good way to get rid of his dangerous foreman. What happened to Thomason would be up to Thomason. The outfit might decide he was a good man to let alone, accept him as their new foreman.

The harassed rancher's big frame sagged deeper in the chair. He was crazy, trying to find a shred of hope in the new man who for all he knew might be one more spy that Nat Murran had foisted on the payroll. The thing smelled like one of Nat's sly tricks.

Dacey's eyes narrowed thoughtfully. Belle was smart, and the fact that she liked Thomason was a good sign. Belle was frank in her appraisal of the men on JD's payroll. She had no use for any of them, from Lute Soler down. "*Cole Thomason is one decent man here a girl can talk to and have some fun with*." Belle would not have said that without good reason. Her finer perceptions had sensed that Thomason was a man to be trusted, which meant he was no spy. He might be hiding out from the law because of some shooting scrape, but he would not be the *first* good man in that kind of trouble. The thought drew a wry grimace from Belle's foster father. He had reason to know.

The cattleman shook his head impatiently, surprised by his fleeting sympathy for young Thomason.

Excepting where Belle was concerned he was stony ground for kindly emotions. His suddenly awakened interest in Thomason was merely a matter of self-preservation, a desperate gamble he had to take if he hoped to save himself from Nat Murran's fast-spreading web of treachery and death. More than his own life was at stake. Belle — the ranch.

Dacey's decision hardened. Thomason was an unknown quantity, but he would have to use him. From Lute Soler down, there was not a man in the outfit he could trust. He had no alternative. He must take a chance on Thomason, hope that Belle's influence would make him a useful and dangerous weapon against the man who was scheming to destroy him.

Cherokee pushed the screen door open, poked his head inside. "Lute says you want me, boss."

"I'm sending you and the new man over to the Bowman place with a letter," Dacey told him.

"Don't need *two* of us for that job," Cherokee objected. "I was figgerin' to hit the trail for town. Ain't been in town for a coon's age."

"Thomason doesn't know the way to the Bowman ranch," Dacey said. "No more back talk, Cherokee. You can go to town some day when I don't need you."

"I'll go throw on a saddle," Cherokee said sulkily. He glanced over his shoulder. "Here's Thomason comin'. I'll be waitin' in the yard."

"Tell Cookie to fix some sandwiches for you," Dacey called after him. He greeted Cole with a genial smile. "Well, young man, how are you making out?"

"No complaints," grinned Cole.

"Lute Soler says you can ride the worst we've got," smiled Dacey.

Cole shrugged, waited for the cattleman to continue. Soler had merely told him that he was wanted at the office and he was wondering what was in Dacey's mind. He was not deceived by the show of geniality. The smile was too fixed. It was obvious that something seriously worried the man.

Dacey picked up the envelope. "I want to get this over to the Bowman ranch."

Cole managed to keep a blank face. "You'll have to tell me how to get there," he said.

"I'm sending Cherokee with you. He knows all the short cuts." Dacey smiled. "I could send Cherokee alone, but I thought you'd like a chance to see the country — learn the trails. You'll be riding on JD range most of the way."

Cole nodded, took the envelope. "A right smart idea," he agreed.

Dacey regarded him thoughtfully. "There's more to it than that," he finally said. "Lute and the boys are heading over to Lost Horse Canyon to look for a man we think has got himself lost in the hills. Leaves only Cherokee I can send to the Bowman place, or you, and you don't know how to get there."

"I've been riding the chaparral a lot of years," Cole drawled.

"Sure you have," interrupted Dacey. "But this letter is important and I want it there in a hurry. By yourself you'd lose time hunting trail, and if I send Cherokee alone he'd likely head for town first. He's got a thirst on and when he's that way you can't trust him."

Cole shrugged. "I savvy —"

"Pick yourself any bronc you fancy," Dacey said.

"I'll take my own Buck," Cole decided. He was gazing at a saddle that hung by its stirrup from a wall-peg. He knew that saddle. It was the one left on his dead horse at the scene of the ambush in the Big Hatchets. "Nice-looking rig." His pulse was jumping a bit but he managed to hang on to his lazy drawl.

"Well —" Dacey's tone was grim. "That saddle is one reason I'm thinking Lute and the boys won't find the man we're looking for. Not over in Lost Horse Canyon, or any place. It's my idea he's dead."

"Why do you think he's dead?" Cole asked.

"Take a close look at the saddle," Dacey said.

Cole already knew what he was expected to see. "I reckon a bullet made that gash," he commented. "Tore a hunk clean out of the horn."

"Glanced off and caught the rider in the belly," Dacey guessed. "That's why Lute won't find him in Lost Horse Canyon. He's up in the Big Hatchets some place and by now the buzzards won't have left more than his bones."

"How do you know it was up in the Big Hatchets?" Cole was careful to keep his voice casual, his face averted from the man in the chair. He was afraid his expression might betray him.

"Some of the boys were looking for strays up there," replied Dacey. "They found his horse, dead in the brush. Said there was no trace of the rider but they brought the saddle in with 'em."

"A nice rig," repeated Cole. He was wanting that saddle. "I like a 'center fire'."

"Most all the outfit use the Texas rig." Dacey's tone indicated he was no longer interested in the saddle. "Cherokee is waiting for you," he added pointedly.

Cole was racking his brains for some way to regain possession of the saddle. He had good reason for wanting it. "If the man who owned it is dead maybe we can make a swap," he suggested. "My Texas rig for this California rig." He grinned. "I'd throw in a couple of dollars."

Dacey chuckled. "Take it along with you, Cole." His voice hardened. "I'm gambling the feller won't show up here looking for it. If he does it'll be up to you to make the swap stick."

Cole slung the saddle over a shoulder, turned to the door. "It's going to take some talking to talk me out of my swap."

Dacey's rumbling laugh came again. "Cherokee's going to wonder how come you got that saddle away from me. It was Cherokee who took it off the dead bronc."

If Dacey could have looked into Cole's eyes at that moment, he might have done some wondering himself. Fortunately for Cole he was already pushing through the screen door.

CHAPTER ELEVEN

Cherokee's furtive glances at the buckskin's saddle grimly amused Cole. The cowboy was puzzled, uneasy. It was plain he recognized the saddle as the one he had stripped from a dead horse in the Big Hatchets. He had last seen it hanging from a wall-peg in the ranch office.

Cole made no attempt to relieve the man's curiosity. He was content to let Cherokee worry. The cowboy did not seem overbright, might betray himself. His sly interest in the saddle indicated a guilty knowledge of the ambush that could solve the mystery of Adna Fenn's identity.

Adna Fenn was undoubtedly responsible for the near-fatal ambush of his camp, but Cole was convinced now that Jasper Dacey was not Adna Fenn. The fact that Cherokee was a JD man did not prove that Dacey had planned the attempted murder, although his anxiety to track down and capture the intended victim indicated a sinister link between him and Fenn.

Cole recalled the brief scene in the ranch office. Dacey's blustering geniality had failed to conceal the fact that he was a very worried man. A great fear rode him, something to do with his ranch, or Belle — with life itself. *The fear of death*.

Cherokee's voice interrupted his puzzled speculations. "Squaw Crik, yonder." The cowboy halted his horse. "Reckon I'll make me a smoke."

Cole felt for his own tobacco sack, his mind again searching for an answer that would explain Dacey. The cause of his fear could not be the stranger from Santa Fé for whom Lute Soler and his riders were now combing Lost Horse Canyon. Cole was himself the man they sought. And the purpose that had brought him to the Boca Grande country was the capture of Adna Fenn, thief and killer. Not Jasper Dacey.

Cole thoughtfully put a match to his cigarette. It must be that Adna Fenn was the source of Dacey's fear. Fenn had some hold on him, was tightening the screws.

Cherokee was eying him curiously. "How come you got that there saddle from the boss?" he asked.

"You know this saddle?" Cole fingered the bullet-scarred horn, gave the cowboy a faint smile.

"Sure do," Cherokee said. "I fetched that saddle down from the Big Hatchets couple days ago." He paused, added cautiously. "Was the boss tellin' you it was me fetched it down?"

"That's right." Cole's smile widened. "He said Lute and the boys are headed for Lost Horse Canyon looking for the man who used to own it."

"He's one slippery hombre," grumbled Cherokee.

"He was too smart for you," grinned Cole. "You got his horse, though." He was watching the man carefully, saw quick suspicion flare in the beady eyes.

"How come you think it was me killed the bronc?"

"That's what you told the boss." Cole snubbed his cigarette on the saddle horn, flipped the butt aside. "He says we've got to get that Santa Fé hombre alive — or dead."

Cherokee's lean, dark face showed an odd relief. He had mixed blood in him, Cole decided, and none of it good. The man had the low cunning of a brute killer. Cole knew now that he was looking at the desperado who had tried to murder him from ambush. Almost unconsciously his hand lowered to the gun in his holster. He restrained the movement. It was not Cherokee he wanted. Cherokee must wait until he had learned more, found the trail that would lead to Adna Fenn.

"I reckon the boss told you plenty," Cherokee was saying. He gave Cole a rueful grin. "Don't savvy yet how come I didn't get the feller. I sure had a bead on him, only he jumped his bronc so quick I got the saddle 'stead of him. He lit out of that saddle fast as greased lightnin' and it was the bronc got my second bullet." The cowboy swore softly. "Won't miss him next time I meet up with him."

"You'll have to be awful fast," smiled Cole. "Like you said, I reckon he's some slippery."

They rode on, crossed the sandy shallows of Squaw Creek. Cherokee was more friendly now, disposed to talk.

"You ain't said yet how come you got that saddle away from the boss," he reminded.

"Talked him into a swap," chuckled Cole. "I like these California center-fire rigs."

"She's a right smart saddle," admitted the cowboy. His head turned in a critical look at the damaged horn. "Braid some rawhide over that gash and she'll be fine as new."

"That's what I figured," agreed Cole, and carelessly added, "Sure feels good under me again."

"Huh?" Cherokee's eyes swiveled in a sharp look at him. "No savvy."

Cole could feel suspicion oozing from the man and cursed himself for the unfortunate comment. "I mean it's good to have a California rig under me again." He grinned. "I thought my three of a kind would win the pot, but the other fellow held four aces. So that's where my old saddle went." As an explanation it was not very plausible, Cole realized when he saw the doubt plain in Cherokee's eyes. A cowboy would gamble his last dollar on the turn of a card, but rarely risk his saddle. Without his saddle a cowboy was on foot, a fate to be abhorred.

"Sure was tough luck," was Cherokee's laconic comment. His glances became furtive again. It was obvious that he was doing some hard thinking. Cole's hand lowered to gun-butt, ready for the trouble he sensed was brewing.

They reached a fork in the canyon, and Cherokee broke his silence. "South Fork heads for the Rivera ranch. Wish we was headin' up North Fork. That way goes to town. I sure crave a drink."

Cole wondered if the man was contriving some plan to leave him and go to town, carry his newly aroused suspicions to his real boss who no doubt was Adna Fenn. Cherokee's next words left no room for doubt.

"I reckon you can find your way from here. Just follow South Fork till you hit the pass. There's a dead pine marks where the trail drops to the big arroyo. The Rivera place is a couple of miles down the arroyo. You cain't miss it."

"I think we'll stick together until we get there," Cole said.

"Who says so?" Cherokee's tone was ugly.

"Dacey said so," drawled Cole. "What's eating you, Cherokee?"

"Do you know what I think," demanded the cowboy. "I think Dacey was loco, puttin' you on the payroll."

"Dacey didn't," Cole told him. "Judge Nat Murran put me on the JD payroll."

"Huh?" Cherokee's tone was disbelieving. It was evident that he had not heard the story. "Murran hired you?"

"That's what I said."

Neither noticed Belle Dacey round the bend behind them. She halted her black horse, watched the two men absorbedly.

"Do you know what I think?" repeated Cherokee. His eyes were suddenly bits of obsidian, without expression.

"I don't care what you think," Cole replied. He was watching the man intently. "Dacey hired me because Murran told him to." As he repeated the fat little liveryman's name he was conscious of a galvanic shock. Murran — Murran — *Adna Fenn*. He also became aware of the gun in Cherokee's hand.

"I'm tellin' you what I think." A grin twisted the cowboy's thin-lipped mouth. It was not a pleasant grin. "I'm thinkin' you're that Santa Fé feller Murran wants us to catch for him."

"You're crazy!" Cole kept his voice steady. He had underestimated Cherokee. The man was not as stupid as he looked. That little slip of the tongue about the saddle had not escaped him.

"You went and made a swap with Dacey for the saddle that's under you." Cherokee's voice was a low, deadly whisper. "Then just a while back you said you was glad it was under you ag'in. You sayin' that got me to thinkin'."

"You think fool things," Cole said. He sat easily in the saddle, relaxed, careful not to move his gun-hand, but ready to seize the chance when it came. "You're just red-eyed because you don't want to go to Bowman's. You want to take the North Fork trail to town — and the Roundup Bar."

"I like to think," Cherokee boasted. "Nat Murran could tell you I'm a right smart thinkin' gent."

"I thought Dacey was your boss," Cole said, pretending bewilderment. "Nobody ever told me Murran is boss of JD."

Cherokee shook his head impatiently. His wrinkled brow indicated he was doing some more heavy thinking. His gun though, was ominously steady. "I ain't figgered what to do with you," he finally said. "I reckon Murran would like to hold palaver with you."

Any straw to grasp seemed good at that moment. "It's all right with me if you want to take me to

Murran," Cole said. A lot could happen before they reached Boca Grande, he told himself. All he needed was a chance, and right now he had no chance. Not with the cowboy's gun threatening instant death.

The same thought of a possible escape was in Cherokee's mind. He shook his head again. "Cain't risk takin' you to town," he decided aloud. "Nothin' I can do but make cold meat of you right now."

Cole was conscious of rage at himself for letting the cowboy gain his terrible advantage. He began protest, heard another voice, a girl's voice, sharp, furious.

"Don't do it, Cherokee! I'll kill you first!"

The cowboy spat out a startled oath, and in the brief instant it took to turn his head, Cole's gun was out and spurting flame. Cherokee's gun dropped from his smashed hand, he reeled in his saddle, lost his balance as his frightened horse jumped from under him.

Cole slid from his own saddle and ran to the prostrate man. Cherokee wore two guns and was still more dangerous than a rattlesnake. He was already trying to get the second gun from his holster when Cole snatched it. He heard Belle Dacey's voice behind him.

"Quick work, mister!"

Cole moved to the other side of Cherokee where he could look at her and at the same time keep the cowboy under his eyes. "I don't understand why you are here," he said. "I only know I'm mighty glad you got here. Cherokee was all set to squeeze trigger."

Belle holstered her gun. Her hand was shaky and her eyes very big in her white face. Her voice though, was composed, almost gay, a hint of challenge in it. "I'm beginning to think I'm your guardian angel. I get you out of jail, then stop Cherokee from killing you." Her voice changed, became wondering, deeply curious. "Why did he try to kill you?"

"He thinks I'm the man your father is looking for, some man from Santa Fé whom Nat Murran wants alive — or dead." Cole's attention was mostly on Cherokee, but her complete bewilderment was too pronounced for him to miss. "Lute Soler and the rest of the boys are combing Lost Horse Canyon for the mysterious stranger now," he added dryly.

Belle's puzzled look went to Cherokee. "You must be crazy," she scolded. "Cole Thomason isn't *that* man!" She broke off, worry suddenly deep in her eyes. "You're lying, too," she went on, her voice shrill. "The man you're all looking for is a friend Nat Murran has been expecting from Santa Fé. You found his dead horse, Cherokee, up in the Big Hatchets, and Nat and Father are terribly worried because he's lost somewhere in the hills. That's why we're all looking for him."

Cherokee made no answer, sat on his heels, stared glumly down at his bleeding fingers.

"It's his story," Cole said. He was grateful for the miraculous intervention, but resentful that it had to be Belle Dacey who had supplied the chance he needed. He could not help liking her, despite her only too evident feeling of ownership in him. She was as wild as any untamed mustang off the range, entirely without inhibitions. She wanted what she wanted and she was making it plain she wanted Cole Thomason. He was at a loss to know what to do about it.

His smile though, was genuine, when he spoke. "I owe you a lot, Miss Dacey. It was lucky for me you happened along, but I'm puzzled *why* you happened to be Johnny-on-the-spot."

"*Belle*," she said, with a toss of her head. "It's Belle, when you speak to me, Cole. And I didn't just *happen* along." Her laugh rippled. "I was in the kitchen when Cherokee came and told Cookie to put up sandwiches for you two, heard him say you were going to the Bowmans with a note from Pops."

"Do you mean you decided to go to Bowman's ranch with us?"

"What do you think I'm here for?" Belle laughed again, an odd little laugh that made Cole look at her suspiciously. "I happen to know there's a girl lives on that place. I met her once at a dance in town. She's awfully pretty and I'm not letting you be alone with her — not for one minute."

Her frankness increased the dismay in him. He managed to say, a bit stiffly, "I'm not interested in girls. I've a job to do, deliver your father's letter to Mr. Bowman."

"I'm not taking chances," Belle declared. "I'm going with you, Cole." Her attention went to Cherokee, morosely nursing his bullet-gashed hand. "You catch your horse and trail back to the ranch," she told him. "Pops will fix up your hand for you. He's fixed plenty gun wounds and is as good as a doctor."

"He'll kill me," muttered the cowboy. "He'll kill me when I tell him this feller got away from me, and you ridin' off alone with him."

"I don't care much if he does kill you," Belle said with an indifferent shrug. "I hate you, Cherokee, for lying about Cole — and trying to kill him."

Cole was doing some fast thinking. He would never dare go back to the JD ranch if Cherokee got to Dacey or Nat Murran with his story. In fact he had planned not to return to the ranch. There was nothing more there of use to him. He had already learned enough to satisfy himself that Dacey was not Adna Fenn. Cherokee had said enough to convince him that the genial little liveryman was the murderer and thief whose trail had led down the long years from the banks of the Mississippi. The thought stirred him, stiffened his resolve. Cherokee must not be allowed to warn Murran or Dacey that Cole Thomason was the man from Santa Fé.

His grim face seemed to fascinate Belle. She stared at him wonderingly, almost fearfully. "You look so savage!" she exclaimed. "I've never seen so terrible a look on a man's face! You frighten me!"

Cole gazed at her with hard eyes. "Cherokee is not going back to the ranch," he said. "I'm taking him to the Bowmans, and *you* are going home."

"Who'll make me?" she flared. Her eyes sparkled. "Not *you?*"

"It will be dark hours before we could get back to the ranch," Cole argued. "Your father will be crazy with worry, not knowing what has become of you." He smiled placatingly. "He'd likely shoot me on sight."

Belle's mouth took on a stubborn look. "I'm going with you. I'm not going to let that Jane Bowman get her hands on you. I have some rights, haven't I, after just saving your life?"

Cole held his temper down, his voice quiet. "Your father will do what Cherokee tried to do," he pointed out. "You wouldn't like that, Belle? You wouldn't like to see your father shoot me down because of your foolishness."

She was momentarily impressed, then her full, red lips parted in a dazzling smile. "I told Pops I liked you a lot," she said. "He'll let me have anything I want." Belle caressed the gun in her belt. "Why — he'd have to shoot me first, and he darn well knows it."

Cole gazed at her, anger struggling with an odd admiration. She had him baffled and he did not know what to do. One thing was firm in his mind. He was going to hang on to Cherokee. He could learn a lot from Cherokee, get the proof he would need.

Belle sensed a temporary advantage. "We'll send Cherokee back to the ranch," she said. "He can tell Pops where I am, if *that's* all that's worrying you." Her smile was confident. "Pops likes you, Cole. Why — you mind yourself with him and you'll be foreman of the ranch any time you want." She fastened a contemptuous look on Cherokee. "You can kick *him* off the place, along with the rest of the renegades on JD's payroll, including that Lute Soler wolf."

Cherokee's eyes lifted in a venomous glance at her. "You sure have growed up with no sense, sister," he said in his thin voice. "You ain't nothin' but a silly, bawlin' calf."

Belle's fingers clenched over the braided rawhide quirt that dangled from her wrist. "I'll slash your ugly face!" she stormed. "Shut your nasty mouth!"

Cole interrupted her. "Listen, Belle! I've got to get your father's letter over to Mr. Bowman. It's important, he said. You shouldn't be holding me back. Go on home and let me do my job. I'm taking Cherokee with me because I'm afraid to trust him alone with you, not after the way you spoiled his chance to shoot me."

Cherokee spoke, bitterly. "You won't never see him at the ranch ag'in, sister. Ain't you got eyes for that saddle on his bronc?"

Belle's head turned in a look at the saddle. "It's the one you brought in the other day." Her tone was thoughtful. "The one you found on the man's dead horse."

"Sure is," Cherokee said with a rasping laugh. "This here feller made a swap with the boss for it, let on to me he was glad to have it back ag'in." The cowboy's beady eyes flashed a triumphant look at Cole. "That's how come I savvied he's the Santa Fé feller what was on the bronc I took the saddle from."

"I — I don't believe you," Belle said, weakly. She turned, gave Cole a searching look.

"You hightail it for the ranch and tell the boss," Cherokee advised. "He'll have Lute and the boys headin' this way on the jump."

Belle paid no attention to him. "Is it true, Cole?" she asked, her voice dull, all life gone from it. "Is it true — what he says about you?"

"Yes," Cole answered, his voice harsh. "I'm the man Nat Murran and your father want to find — and kill."

She gazed at him with stricken eyes. "Not — not my Pops! He — he doesn't kill people — murder people."

He made an attempt to soften his words. "I don't understand what your father has to do with it," he said, more gently. "Perhaps he really believes I'm just a lost friend Murran wants him to find." He shook his head, finished worriedly, "I don't know, Belle."

She studied him, anxiety, fear, in her eyes. "Do you mean my father harm, Cole?" she asked, her voice low, troubled.

Cole hesitated, shook his head. "I'm not interested in Mr. Dacey." He hesitated again, watched the relief flooding across her mobile face. "I'm interested in only one man. No, Belle, I don't mean harm to your father."

She continued to regard him, thoughtful, now, and a hint of understanding in her grave eyes. "You mean — Nat Murran?"

"I'm beginning to think so," Cole replied.

"I'm frightened," Belle said. "I've never felt so frightened." Her breath quickened. "For all of us — for you." She paused, added in a half whisper. "For you — most of all."

"There is nothing you can do about it," Cole told her. He smiled as if to reassure her. "Go back home, Belle. Tell your father if you must, but telling won't help and could only make things worse for him. I don't want him to get mixed up in this business."

"He's already done mixed hisself up in it," muttered Cherokee.

"Shut your mouth!" Belle lifted her quirt, gave the cowboy a furious glance. Her look questioned Cole. "What will you do with him?"

"Take him along to Bowmans." Cole shrugged. "I'm not turning him loose."

Her fingers were toying with the butt of the gun in her holster.

Cole said sharply, "Don't try something foolish."

"It's not *you* I'm wanting to kill," Belle said. Her gaze went to Cherokee, fierce, menacing. "Why take him along with you?"

"He's more useful to me alive." Cole looked at her curiously. The girl was half woman, half child, and had the primitive directness of a savage. "You go back to the ranch," he advised. "I'll handle Cherokee."

She gave him a piteous look. "I — I don't want to go back." Her voice faltered. "I — I want to stay with you, Cole. I want to go where you go."

"It is best for you to go back," he insisted. "I'm telling you the truth, Belle. If you don't go back, it will mean my finish. You'll be missed and they won't be long picking up your trail. Lute Soler and his bunch will be after us like a pack of wolves."

"I don't want to make things harder for you, Cole." She turned away, slowly, was suddenly running to her black colt. She snatched at his tie rope, flung herself into the saddle. "All right —" Her chin was up, but there were tears in her eyes. "I'm going back — and Cole —" Her voice softened, and she looked at him steadily. "I'm not telling Pops, even if you don't come back." She whirled the black horse, spurs raking him.

Diablo squealed, went into a wild frenzy of bucking. Her quirt swung from side to side, left welts on his satiny skin. Cole knew she was loosing her emotions on the unfortunate horse. She had to expend her rage on something and the horse was the only thing handy. She wanted him to buck, wanted to fight him.

"The little hellcat can sure ride," muttered Cherokee. He stifled an oath, glowered at his bullet-gashed hand. "Turn me loose, mister," he pleaded. "Turn me loose and I'll make tracks a long ways from here. I savvy when I'm licked. You turn me loose and my shadder won't never cross your trail no more."

Diablo was "licked," too, and so were Belle's pent-up emotions. She rode the subdued horse close to Cole, leaned down to him, her face serene, eyes extraordinarily gentle.

"I mean what I said, Cole. Your secret is mine, too." Her mouth pressed down on his, warm, soft, clinging, and then she was gone, the big black colt on the dead run.

Cole watched until the bending trail took her from view. The manner of her going left him conscious of disturbing emotions, uneasily aware of an odd stirring in him. He scowled, shook his head. He was a fool to let a young girl's kiss explode the blood in his veins.

Cherokee, still sitting on his heels, nursing his wounded hand, grinned up at him. "A lot of 'em have tried to git what she gave you," he said. The frosty eyes Cole turned on him wiped the grin from his face.

"Climb your saddle," Cole said, curtly.

The cowboy sullenly obeyed. His injured hand made it awkward for him. Cole did not offer to help, watched in grim silence.

"Where are we headin'?" Cherokee asked. His face was gray from pain. "I gotta git my hand fixed . . . she sure hurts bad."

Cole went to him, tied the uninjured hand to saddlehorn. "Nothing we can do for your hand until we get to the Bowman ranch," he said.

He put the cowboy's horse on a lead-rope, examined the confiscated guns, threw out the shells and thrust them back in Cherokee's holsters. "I know a man who can use these guns," he said. "You can give 'em to him for tying up your hand."

Cherokee cursed him. "I'll git you good, some day," he promised.

"You've had your last chance to get me," Cole told him with a grim smile. He climbed into his own saddle. "Let's go," he said. "We've got a letter to deliver for your boss."

CHAPTER TWELVE

The trail crossed a boulder-strewn dry wash that sprawled at the mouth of South Fork Canyon. It twisted up through a spindly growth of junipers and finally straightened out across a narrow strip of mesa and then plunged again into the depths of the gorge. There was water here, a shallow stream that trickled down the rocks. Cole halted, let the horse drink at one of the little pools, and after an appraising look at his prisoner he slid from his saddle.

"I'll fix a bandage for you," he said.

He took the cowboy's bandanna, washed it in the pool and in a few moments had the wound cleaned and bandaged. "You're lucky, Cherokee," he commented. "That bullet only raked your knuckles. No bones broken."

"Hurts like hell," muttered the cowboy.

Cole made a cigarette, stuck it in the man's mouth, put a match to it. Cherokee relaxed in his saddle, sucked smoke into his lungs. He made no comment, but there was a glint of surprise in his hard eyes, a grudging thanks.

Cole made a cigarette for himself. He was wondering if Mateo Cota had managed to get his message to the

Bowmans. The few fast-moving hours in Boca Grande had made it impossible to keep the rendezvous with Mateo Cota in Old Town. He suspected his movements would be watched and he did not like the thought of making trouble for the Mexican. He used the only means left that would give him a few moments with Mateo. His talk with Jasper Dacey at the hotel had been brief.

"Nat Murran tells me you're wanting a job," the cattleman had said. "I can use a good hand." Dacey had smiled at his daughter. "Belle says you're good, from the way you handled that black son of Satan she rides."

The business finished. Dacey had invited him to share the evening meal with them at Chang's restaurant. It was easy enough when they left Chang's to say he wanted to go to the livery barn for a look at his horse. Mateo was still there, was obviously amazed to see him, also vastly relieved. He had heard of the trouble with Lute Soler.

Cole snubbed his cigarette under bootheel. He hoped that Mateo had got word to the Bowmans. To hear that he had taken a job with Dacey would surprise them, but he thought they would understand, realize he was following the long trail of Adna Fenn. He had warned Mateo to say nothing of the jail episode that had led to his impressment on JD's payroll. They were due for another surprise, when he appeared with his wounded prisoner.

He took Dacey's letter from his pocket, eyed it curiously. Something to do with the trouble that was worrying the cattleman. A warning, perhaps. A warning for the Bowmans to leave the country. Dacey would resent their presence on the ranch he had long considered JD range. If it had not been for the Adna Fenn angle there would have been every reason to believe that Dacey was responsible for the attempt on Lewis Bowman's life.

Cole slowly returned the letter to his pocket. The appearance of Dacey and his riders so soon after the shooting was decidedly suspicious. The cattleman's surprise though, was genuine. He had been really concerned about the affair, had insisted upon sending for Dr. Johnson. His anxiety to learn from Jane if she had seen the ambusher indicated a certain guilty knowledge, was proof that he suspected the would-be-killer had been sent by Nat Murran. The Bowmans were a dangerous link to the past. Murran would want them removed, knew the killing would be laid at Dacey's door.

Cherokee was watching him curiously. He spat the cigarette from his mouth. "You ain't told me yet what for you swapped that saddle with the boss."

Cole gave him a mirthless smile. "You can keep on wondering, Cherokee," he said. "I had my reasons for wanting the saddle. That's all I'm telling you, right now."

"You're sure one smart hombre," muttered the cowboy. "I ain't buckin' you no more, mister. Turn me loose, like I said, and I'll make dust so far from the Boca Grande it'll cost a million *pesos* for a postcard to catch up with me."

"Save your breath," Cole advised with another mirthless smile. "I'm thinking you're going to be mighty useful, Cherokee." He paused, eyed his prisoner thoughtfully. "Maybe you can tell me about a man who rides a black and white pinto. He sometimes ties up in front of the Roundup Saloon in town."

"We can maybe make a trade." Cherokee's eyes narrowed in a crafty look at him. "Turn me loose, and I'll palaver with you."

Cole shook his head. "I reckon not, Cherokee."

"You figger to know somethin' I can tell you," argued the cowboy. "I'm smart, too, mister. I've gotta price, like I said. Turn me loose and I'll tell you about that black and white pinto and the feller that rides him."

Cole gazed at him, his eyes bleak. "Have you ever heard the story about a maverick on the end of a rope?"

"Huh?" Cherokee's sulky rejoinder showed that he understood.

"You're on *my* rope," chuckled Cole. "I'm not trading you for a dozen mavericks running loose in the brush. Savvy?" He climbed into the buckskin's saddle.

The trail went up steeply from the stream, circled great boulders, hung precariously to sheer cliffs, finally straightened across the mesa.

Cherokee spoke from his horse on the lead-rope. "We turn left where that dead pine is I told you about."

Cole had already seen the lightning-blasted pine. It was not the first time he had seen the tree. It came to him with something of a shock that hardly more than forty-eight hours had elapsed since his stumbling feet had passed it, carried him into the arroyo in time to see

Lewis Bowman shot down in his own ranch yard. So much had happened during those hours. He had met Jane Bowman! There was no doubt in him now. Jane was the most important thing that had happened since that first passing of the giant pine. It was for Jane he was fighting Adna Fenn. Bringing him to justice meant more than avenging Judge Spottisford, the little group of betrayed Southern planters. Jane's life was at stake — her father's life — his own. There could be no compromise.

Cherokee's thin, nasal voice interrupted his troubled reflections. "Been called the hangin' tree, that old pine. A lot of fellers has dangled from that tree."

Cole fastened hard eyes on him. "You'll dangle there, too, maybe —"

"I'm thinkin' about it," Cherokee said.

"Do some thinking about that pinto," Cole suggested. "You told me you're a right smart thinkin' gent."

Cherokee gazed thoughtfully at the gaunt-limbed pine. "I sure don't crave to dangle from that tree," he said. "I reckon I've gotta think awful fast."

"Make it smart thinking, and no lies," Cole warned.

The trail dropped them steeply into the wide wash of the arroyo, now sweltering under the blistering midday sun. No life stirred in that inferno of heat. Cole found himself wondering how he had managed to survive the torturing hours of flight from the men who had sought to kill him. The man on the horse behind him was one of those would-be-killers. The thought brought a blood-mist over his eyes and he found his hand closing hard on holstered gun.

The cold fury in his backward look must have shocked Cherokee. He lifted his bandaged hand, whispered hoarsely, "Don't use your gun on me, mister!"

The man's horror brought Cole to his senses. His fingers loosened from gun butt. It was the heat, getting him, he told himself. He must watch his step, hold fast to the purpose that had brought him from Santa Fé. He wanted no blood on his hands. He must leave Cherokee and his fellow renegades to the law.

A voice crackled from the high slope above, a harsh blast of sound in the stillness of the wash. Cole halted the buckskin.

The voice came again, curt, challenging, and Cole now saw the glint of sunlight on metal. A rifle, and the man holding it was crouched behind a clump of buck brush.

Cole grinned up at the sentry. "Tell Tranquilo Baca it is Cole Thomason who comes," he called in Spanish.

"*Si, señor.*" The sentry revealed himself, and Cole recognized the slim youth whose name was Julio. "It is all right, señor, for you to come." Julio was smiling. "The señorita will be very happy for you to come."

"You keep good watch," Cole called back.

"*Si, señor.*" Julio's voice was like steel. "We watch for wolves."

He waited by the trail while Cole and his prisoner made the steep climb, horses' shod hoofs digging into slippery shale. His eyes hardened questioningly on Cherokee.

"*Quién es?*"

"One of the wolves," smiled Cole.

The young vaquero's soulful brown eyes were suddenly like rapier points, deadly, menacing. "We should make him a very dead wolf," he said. "A good wolf is a dead wolf, no, señor?"

"I need him alive." Cole spoke firmly. "It will be your job to keep him safe, and alive, Julio."

"Only Tranquilo Baca gives me orders," Julio said discontentedly.

"I will tell Tranquilo to so order," Cole told him. He sent the buckskin up the trail, Cherokee's horse following on the lead-rope. The cowboy's hoarse whisper reached him.

"What in hell's goin' on here? That Mex feller on lookout and his talk of wolves." The worried cowboy swore softly. "My gawd, he was all fixed to stick a knife in me."

Cole glanced back at him. "You're in for a big surprise, Cherokee. You'll understand why I'm not letting you get back to Dacey with the news." His voice took on an edge. "Or should I say, back to your *real* boss. You know the name."

"I ain't talkin' yet," muttered the cowboy. "Not till you say you'll trade."

"Remember this," warned Cole. "You can die very soon unless I want to keep you alive. I'm your only protection from sudden death here."

"I'll maybe do some talkin' right soon." Cherokee sagged dejectedly in his saddle, worried gaze on his stained bandage.

Two more alert Mexicans challenged them as they rode out of the arroyo. Cole recognized Ramon and

Manuelo. They greeted him with equally recognizing smiles, waved him on down to the ranch yard, a very different yard now, the brush chopped out and dragged into piles for burning.

Jane heard Tranquilo Baca's welcoming shout. She ran to the window in time to catch a glimpse of them disappearing past the house. Delight, enormous relief widened her eyes — and amazement. The man trailing Cole on the led horse was one of the JD cowboys who had helped carry her wounded father to his bed. She had reason to remember him. His name was Cherokee and Jasper Dacey had sent him to get the doctor from Boca Grande. She was not sure, but she had the impression that the man was a prisoner.

Cole was down from his saddle by the time she hurried through the kitchen door. She wanted to run, restrained the impulse, but her quick step turned Cole's head in a look at her. His face lighted and he was suddenly moving toward her.

"Jane!" he said.

She saw the amusement in her father's eyes, Tranquilo's indulgent, knowing smile, wondered if her joy was too transparent. She was not caring much, but managed to keep her voice steady, almost casual.

"Why, Cole! This *is* a surprise."

He stopped abruptly, something like disappointment shadowing his face, and then he saw the look in her eyes that she could not hide. His smile warmed again.

"I'm surprised, too," he said. "It's the way things have worked out. I didn't know a few hours ago that I'd be here this afternoon."

"I've been afraid, terribly afraid." Jane broke off, dismayed by the unmistakable emotion in her voice. Her look went to Cherokee, slumped dejectedly in his saddle. Her impression had been correct. One of his hands was tied to the saddle horn. Cole *had* brought a prisoner to the ranch. The cowboy's bandaged hand indicated there had been serious trouble.

Her father, his arm still in a sling, was frowning at a letter in his hand. He met her inquiring look. "It's from Jasper Dacey," he told her. "Cole brought it."

"I don't know what it's about," Cole said. "I can make a good guess, though." He smiled at Tranquilo Baca. "I'm thinking you got here just in time," he added.

"We keep a good watch," Tranquilo said with a grand gesture. "Julio has the eyes of a hawk, the ears of a wildcat. It will be too bad for one who is not a friend."

Jane was studying her father's worried face. "What does the letter say?" she asked.

"I'll read it aloud," Lewis Bowman said. His wrathful voice rumbled out the brief lines.

Dear Bowman:

I have learned that you and your daughter are in terrible danger if you do not immediately leave the Boca Grande country. I cannot help you, or I would. For God's sake get out before it's too late.

Tranquilo Baca's deep laugh broke the momentary silence. "We have the big surprise for him if *he* is this terrible danger." The big Mexican gestured his scorn.

"We do not fear his wolves. We will make them very dead."

Bowman crumpled the piece of paper, his expression thoughtful. "This thing proves my suspicions. It was Dacey who sent that skulking killer to get me the other evening." He looked at Jane. "I didn't want to tell you that night, Daughter, but I found a warning pinned with a knife on the barn door. It said. '*Get out or you get this*.' You got mighty upset when I hinted that Dacey would make trouble for us, would try to run us off this ranch he's ranged his cattle on so long." Bowman's frown deepened. "Dacey sent his killer to get me, sure as the sun rises, and now he's promising worse things, even threatening to harm you."

"I can't believe he'd be so vile." Jane looked at her father with shocked eyes.

"You don't need to believe it," Cole said. "I have reason to think Dacey was not responsible for the shooting of your father."

Bowman scowled at the crumpled note. "He sent this, didn't he? You said he did."

"That's right," admitted Cole. "Dacey sent you that warning, but I've an idea he's only the tool of a far more dangerous man." He paused, added thoughtfully. "I think Dacey means what he says in that note. He'd help you if he could. He's doing the best he can, warning you to leave the Boca Grande country before it's too late." Cole smiled grimly at Tranquilo Baca. "He doesn't know you have good friends here."

Tranquilo slapped the long-barreled .45 in its holster. "We will fight him, or anybody who comes," he rumbled.

Bowman was gazing at Cole doubtfully. "What do you mean, saying that Dacey is only the tool of a far more dangerous man?" he asked perplexedly.

"It shouldn't be hard for you to guess," Cole answered.

"Adna Fenn?" Bowman's eyes took fire. "Do you mean you have located the scoundrel?"

Cole gestured at Cherokee. "He let something slip that got me to thinking. Dacey sent him along to show me the trail to the ranch. Something *I* said made him suspect I was the lost Santa Fé friend Dacey told you he was searching the hills for the evening he was here. He tried to kill me, but wasn't fast enough with his gun."

Cherokee glared at him from his saddle. "I'd have killed you all right if the gal hadn't horned in on the play." He spat the words viciously.

"I'll explain about her, later," continued Cole, uncomfortably aware of Jane's quick look of surprise. "I couldn't let Cherokee get back to the ranch, spread the news, especially when he let slip it was really Nat Murran who wanted me, either alive or dead."

"Murran!" exclaimed Bowman. "You mean the little fat man who runs the livery barn in Boca Grande?"

"I've been awfully dumb," Cole grumbled. "I should have guessed the truth about Murran a lot sooner. He's the big boss in that town, and the *real* boss of Dacey's bunch of renegades. Dacey's boss, too, for that matter."

"Adna Fenn," muttered Lewis Bowman.

"I'm thinking he is." Cole's face was a hard mask. "I've yet to get the proof, but Cherokee is a good start.

He's valuable, Tranquilo. He can tell us a lot we want to know."

"We will keep him safe," promised the Mexican. The smile he turned on the prisoner was not pleasant. "We have ways to make a man loosen his tongue."

"I told Julio to guard him." Cole said.

Tranquilo shook his head. "Julio's hawk's eyes are needed to watch for wolves," he demurred. His voice lifted. "Pedro — come!"

"*Si!*" answered a voice from the barn. The owner of the voice hurriedly appeared, pitchfork in hand.

"A job for you," Tranquilo said.

Pedro, a short, stocky man, leaned the pitchfork against the barn, sped across the corral.

"Watch this gringo day and night," Tranquilo ordered with a gesture at the cowboy. "The old *cárcel* we used in Don Francisco's time is still strong," he added.

"*Si.*" Pedro nodded. "I will use the chain that once held *El Gato*, the *bandido*. He will not get away from me, señor."

The chief of vaqueros waved him off. "Take him, and if he escapes I will have your ears."

"I wish to keep my ears where they are," grinned the stocky Mexican. He seized the bridle, led horse and prisoner into the corral. Cherokee wore the haggard look of a very worried man.

Bowman's gaze followed him, came back slowly to Cole. "So he tried to kill you?"

Cole said, not looking at Jane. "He told the truth. He was about to squeeze trigger when Belle Dacey gave me the chance to shoot first."

Jane made no comment. Her eyes were wide with curiosity. It was her father who asked the question in her mind.

"What was the Dacey girl doing there?" he asked.

"She was out with a black colt she's breaking." Cole was suddenly angry at his embarrassment, his attempt to withhold the facts. "I might as well tell you she got the idea she wanted to come with us. I sent her home." He forced a smile. "It's not really important, except that her being there saved me from Cherokee's bullet."

Jane said, quietly, "I think it's very important that she saved your life."

Cole's eyes thanked her. "I'll tell you more about it, some day, perhaps."

"She's as wild a filly as I ever saw," chuckled Bowman. "You remember her, don't you, Jane? We met her at the dance."

"She's very beautiful," Jane said, not looking at Cole now. Her voice lacked enthusiasm.

"Well —" Her father turned away. "Let's get into the house and have a powwow. I want to hear about what happened in Boca Grande." Grim amusement touched his voice. "Mateo Cota got here with your message telling us you'd taken a job with Dacey's outfit."

"I was hoping he'd make it to the ranch," Cole said. His look went to the old Mexican approaching down the slope from the spring. "Benito!" he called. "Come here. I've got something for you."

"*Si, señor.*" Benito hurried his step, a wide grin on his wrinkled brown face. "It is good to see you, señor," he greeted. "There has been fear in our hearts when we heard the news."

Cole took the little piece of silver cross from his shirt pocket. "I bring it back to you, Benito. It brought me good luck — and a good friend, as you promised it would."

The old Mexican took it from him, kissed it reverently and fastened it to the chain inside his shirt. "Mateo Cota says you are a man, señor," he said simply.

"We learned more than your message told us," chuckled Bowman.

Cole frowned inquiringly at Benito. The Mexican gave Tranquilo a worried look.

"I will take the blame," the chief of vaqueros reassured him with one of his grand gestures.

"No," interrupted Jane's father. "The blame, if any, is mine."

"As you will, Señor Bowman." Tranquilo shrugged, relief in his smile.

"I made Tranquilo tell me what he learned from Mateo Cota," Bowman explained to Cole. "I refer to the jail episode."

"I didn't want you to worry," Cole said with a wry grin. "You see, Nat Murran happens to be Justice of the Peace. He sentenced me to serve six months on the Dacey ranch, and that's how I got on the JD payroll. I think he suspected I was a range detective, wanted Dacey to watch me."

"I had to tell Jane," confessed Bowman. "She was worried, and so was I, when we got your message about taking a job there. We thought it was because you suspected Dacey was Adna Fenn. We didn't know what might happen."

"It all turned out for the best." Cole spoke soberly. "I learned enough to know that Dacey is not Adna Fenn, and I managed to get the saddle Cherokee admitted he took from my dead horse in the Big Hatchets. I was wanting that saddle." He went to the buckskin, drew a claspknife from a pocket and slit the leather stitching under the cantle. His fingers searched inside the opening, drew out a piece of metal. "I wanted this," he finished.

They stared at the thing lying in his open palm. Bowman muttered an exclamation. "A United States Deputy Marshal badge!" he marveled.

"*Por Dios!*" ejaculated Tranquilo Baca. Respect deepened his voice.

Jane said nothing, gazed with fascinated eyes at the silver emblem that armed Cole Thomason with the might and majesty of the Law, a token of power in this lawless border land of the Boca Grande.

Cole slid the badge into a pocket, glanced at the buckskin. Tranquilo understood. "Stable the horse, Benito," he ordered "Feed him well."

"He's a good horse, Tranquilo," thanked Cole. He gave the chief of vaqueros a rueful grin. "I owe you for the saddle I swapped for the one he's wearing."

"It is nothing." Tranquilo began another of his lordly gestures, stopped the sweep of his hand in midair. "Listen!" he said, excitement in his voice.

They heard now what his keen ears had caught, the low monotonous murmur in the distance. Cole recognized the sound for the bawling of cattle — an approaching trail herd.

Their gaze followed the direction of Tranquilo's pointing forefinger, fastened on the trailing banner of dust, still a pale haze in the distance.

"The herd comes," Tranquilo said, his voice vibrant, exulting. "The Rivera herd comes back to the old rancho, my señorita!"

CHAPTER THIRTEEN

The midmorning sun was bright on the trail that dropped to the valley from Apache Pass. Something moved there, took shape under Nat Murran's long, brass telescope. Quick flurries of dust said the lone rider was in a hurry.

The liveryman continued to watch, and there was a tenseness in him that betrayed an extraordinary anxiety. A bend in the trail hid the rider for a few minutes, and when he reappeared, lower down and a good quarter of a mile closer, the telescope clearly showed that the horse under him was a black and white pinto.

Murran leaned the telescope against the bench and felt in a pocket for his amber-tinted spectacles. He put them on and after a moment's frowning thought, glanced at a clump of bushes that grew between the water-trough and the yard fence. His hand lifted in a furtive beckoning gesture, and almost instantly Yuma appeared from behind the screening branches and strolled toward him.

"What's the trouble, boss?" asked the gunman. He perched on the edge of the long trough, the eyes in his sinister, flat face roving, watchful.

"He's coming." Murran spoke fretfully.

"Stinger figgered he'd mebbe show up before noon," Yuma said. "He was all set to do the job quick."

"He's coming too fast," worried Murran. "Something has gone wrong. He's coming down that trail like the devil was on his tail."

"I reckon he figgers you'll be wantin' to know he's done the job," grinned Yuma.

Murran removed his amber spectacles, and the look in his uncovered eyes made the renegade visibly flinch. "Something has gone wrong," he repeated impatiently. "You get over to the Roundup. He'll be there in a few minutes."

Yuma said nothing, slid from his perch on the trough and started for the dusty street. His scrawny frame was deceptive. He was as tough as weathered rawhide and the guns in tied-down holsters could leap into his hands with the speed of a striking snake.

Murran lifted the telescope again. The dust-drift was rapidly approaching and before Yuma was half way to the saloon, the pinto horse came into view, on the dead run down the street, rider bent low in the saddle.

The telescope almost dropped from the liveryman's hands. He sprang from the bench with a startled grunt. Stinger was not pulling in at the Roundup, and in his haste failed to see Yuma or heed his yell to stop. He swung into the livery yard, jerked the pinto to a sliding standstill.

Murran's face emerged from the cloud of dust that followed the quick halt. "You fool!" he said in a low, furious voice. "I told you never to bring that horse into this yard, or show yourself here."

Stinger slid from the trembling horse, a lean dark man with cold slate eyes. "Looks like hell's bust loose at the Rivera place. Figgered you'd want to know in a hurry. Just about killed the bronc gettin' here."

A rancher in a light farm wagon, a sun-bonneted woman by his side, drove into the yard. Murran hastily put on his amber spectacles, greeted them with his benevolent smile as they passed. "Get that horse out of sight," he muttered to Stinger. "I'll be in the office." He tucked the telescope under an arm. Yuma, hurrying in from the street, followed him into the office. At a nod from Murran he went to his curtained alcove.

Mateo Cota had witnessed the brief scene from the darkness of the barn. His curiosity jumped to fever heat. Señor Thomason had questioned him about a mysterious man who rode a pinto horse. *Verdad!* This was the man who had tried to kill the father of the little señorita.

He was careful to conceal his suspicions when Stinger led the tired pinto inside the long runway behind the stalls. The man gave a surly refusal to his offer of help.

"I ain't wantin' the saddle off the bronc," he said. "Leave him be, Mex. All I want is for him to cool off some before I hightail it away from here." His cold, slate eyes fastened a threatening look on Mateo. "Savvy?"

"*Si*." Mateo gestured indifferently, turned his attention to the rancher who was leading in his team of horses. He shook down some hay, listened to the rancher's instructions about a feed of grain when the horses had cooled off; and when the man had rejoined his waiting wife outside, took a look at the pinto horse concealed in the box stall. The man's demand for a box stall strengthened Mateo's suspicions about him. It was plain he wanted the pinto kept from sight.

The Mexican, an eye on the door against a surprise return of the owner, gazed at the horse thoughtfully. The pinto's heaving sides showed he had traveled far and fast. There was a rifle in scabbard, no doubt the same that had spat attempted death at the señorita's father.

Excitement mounted in Mateo, and a growing anxiety. It was possible the man had just come from the old Rivera rancho, perhaps with news that a second attempt at murder had been successful. Or perhaps it was to tell Señor Murran that the señorita and her father were now surrounded by brave men who would fight to the death for them.

The suspense was too great for Mateo. He felt he must know what was happening in the office of Señor Murran. A crisis was imminent and it would be necessary for Tranquilo Baca to be on his guard.

The Mexican hurried through the rear door that opened into a corral. He climbed over the fence and went stealthily to a little alley between the office and the barn. There was a small window, usually kept open an inch or two for ventilation. The window was covered with gray paint, which lessened the risk of being seen by anybody inside, but a man outside could peer through the narrow opening, see and hear.

Murran was sitting at his desk, gazing incredulously at the man opposite him. "Say that again." He breathed noisily. "You're lying!"

Stinger said, softly, "I ain't takin' that kind of talk from no man, Murran." His slate-colored eyes remained steady under the liveryman's venomous look. "It's like I told you. There's a bunch of Mex fellers holed up at the Bowman place, armed to the teeth and lookouts posted all over."

"Who are they?" Murran toyed with the amber spectacles on the desk. His tone was less belligerent, perhaps because of the other man's refusal to be cowed.

"Ask me somethin' easy," growled Stinger. He lit a cigarette. "I crave a drink," he added.

Murran took a bottle from a drawer, pushed it across the desk. Stinger said "*Gracias*," tilted it to lips, drank, gasped, replaced the bottle on the desk and wiped his unkempt mustache with the back of his hand.

"A rattler could use that stuff for poison," he complained.

"You don't have to drink it," Murran said. He leaned back in his chair, round eyes hard, unwinking. "Anybody see you?" he asked.

Stinger nodded. "Sure did. If they'd got any closer I wouldn't be here now. I'd be layin' some place in that arroyo." He reached for the whiskey bottle.

"I suppose they got a look at the horse," grumbled the liveryman.

Stinger shrugged. "I reckon so." Whiskey gurgled down his throat.

"I don't like bunglers," Murran said.

"Huh?" The renegade put the bottle down, stared intently at his employer. "What do you mean?"

"I hired you for a job," Murran said. "You've bungled it, laid a trail to me."

"You're talkin' loco talk," protested the man. "I ain't left no trail."

"You let them see you and that pinto horse of yours." Murran was breathing hard again. "I'm an important man in this Boca Grande country, respected, trusted. Hundreds of people for miles around know me, use my livery barn, borrow from me, bank their money in my safe. They know that Nat Murran is a good friend." His voice was suddenly a husky whisper, deadly, menacing. "And you lay an attempted murder trail straight to my door."

"Loco talk," repeated the desperado contemptuously. It was plain he was not impressed by the anger of the little fat man in the desk chair. His hand though, slid unobtrusively to gun butt, an instinctive response to the malignant threat he read in Murran's unwinking gaze. "I'm headin' back for the Panhandle," he continued. "Just as soon as you hand over the five hundred you promised I'm sayin' *adios* and hightailin' away from your damn Boca Grande country."

There was a brief silence, and when the liveryman spoke, his voice was quiet, almost bland. "You're not quitting, Stinger. You're fired. You're no use to me any more. When a man is no use to me I get rid of him."

"Fork over the *dinero* and I'll be a long ways from here come sundown," Stinger assured him with a thin smile.

"You bungled the job," reminded Murran, his voice still a soft purr. "You get no money from me, you poor fool." His look slid past the man to the curtained alcove.

The renegade growled an oath, half rose from his chair, fingers wrapped over the butt of the gun in his holster. He went suddenly rigid. Something hard was pressing against his spine. No need for him to look over his shoulder. He knew that death was whispering in his ear, warning him to be very good, or else he would be very dead.

"Search him," Murran ordered.

Yuma reached for Stinger's gun, laid it on the desk. "Turn round, feller," he said. "Keep your hands up high, agin' the wall."

Stinger obeyed, and the deadly little gunman made a quick search. "Ain't no more guns on him," he said to Murran. "No knife, nor nothin'."

The liveryman got out of his chair, reached for the confiscated gun, leveled it at the prisoner's back. "Get a rope," he told Yuma.

Yuma took a coil of rawhide rope from a peg, cut off a length with his knife. "Get your hands down." He worked swiftly, jerked Stinger's arms back and tied his hands. "He can't bust *them* knots," he told Murran. "What do you figger to do with him?"

"For the present I'm leaving him here with you," answered the liveryman. His smile was vicious. "I don't want this office messed up or I'd end the business now."

"Turn him over to Sil Turlo," suggested Yuma. "Sil can keep him safe in jail for you."

Murran frowned, shook his head. "I want this man in a safer place than Sil's jail." He continued to gaze at Stinger's back. "Get a rope around his legs. He's too tough for us to take chances with."

Obeying Yuma's gruff command, the prisoner lay face down on the floor. Yuma cut off another piece of the rope and tied his ankles. "All right, boss," he said. "He's hawg-tied for sure, now."

Murran laid the gun on the desk, put on his amber spectacles and reached for his hat. "I'm going up the street." He hurried outside. Yuma listened until his footsteps faded into the distance, then sat down in the chair recently occupied by Stinger. He holstered his gun, took a long drink from the whiskey bottle and began making a cigarette.

Stinger twisted his head in a look at him. "Turn me loose," he said in a hoarse whisper. "That devil figgers to kill me."

Yuma grinned at him. "Sure does, feller."

"I figgered him wrong," groaned the renegade. "He's a devil — that little fat-bellied pizen toad."

"Sure is," agreed Yuma with another mirthless grin. He was suddenly on his feet, moving with the swiftness of a cat to the little gray-painted window. He jerked it wide open. A quick look reassured him. The little alley was empty of life. Only some bits of discarded wagon gear, a piece of paper fluttering in the wind.

Yuma closed the window, returned to his chair. "Thought I heard somethin' out there," he said to

Stinger. "Piece of paper blowin' in the wind." His hand went to the whiskey bottle.

Mateo, crouched close to the side of the barn around the corner of the alley, reached inside his shirt for his piece of the little silver cross. He kissed it with a prayer of thanks to his favorite saint for the narrow escape. An instant's delay would have betrayed his presence in the alley. Yuma would not have hesitated, would have shot him down.

Shaken by the close call, the Mexican hastily made his way back to the stable. He was at a loss to know what to do. It was very evident that Murran wanted Señor Bowman dead. It was Murran who had sent the rider of the pinto horse to kill the señorita's father. The liveryman now knew that many armed men were protecting Señor Bowman and it was plain he was very puzzled. It was equally plain that he did not want it known he planned murder, which was why he was so angry with the pinto's owner. *Verdad!* It looked like a quick finish for Stinger.

The worried Mateo listlessly fed the rancher's team of horses their grain, his mind a conflicting whirl of emotions — fear, horror, despair. Señor Murran was a terrible man — a devil. He would find some way to accomplish his purpose. He wanted the old Rivera ranch. He would use all his powers, and they were great. Tranquilo Baca would not be able to keep up the fight long. There would be much bloodshed and Tranquilo Baca and his vaqueros would soon all be dead — the little señorita and her father dead.

He thought unhappily of Cole Thomason, but the young gringo was now at the Dacey ranch, unable to help the señorita in this time of dreadful peril. Señor Thomason would be surprised to learn that it was Murran who had sent the owner of the pinto horse to kill Señor Bowman. Señor Thomason had been most anxious to learn the identity of the pinto's rider whose trail could lead him to Señor Bowman's unknown enemy. *Por Dios!* It was a problem to know what to do!

Decision came to the Mexican while he slowly cleaned the stalls. He could not get word to the young gringo, risk going to the Dacey ranch, but he could carry his tale to Tranquilo Baca, warn him of the señorita's growing peril. He must be careful not to betray his purpose to Señor Murran who would most certainly kill him. He must make an opportunity to get away, plead bad pains in the head and say he must go home and lie in the bed until the pains went away. In the meantime he must keep eyes and ears open, try and learn what was in Señor Murran's mind.

CHAPTER FOURTEEN

There was much in Murran's mind as he hurried up the street. Stinger's news about the Mexicans guarding the Bowman ranch shocked and frightened him. He could not imagine who the Mexicans were or where they came from. It was possible that Bowman had discovered the rich silver deposits in the canyon above the big springs, was preparing to open the mine.

The liveryman's short steps quickened, his black alpaca coat billowed behind him. Alive or dead, Bowman was destined to lose. Legal title to the Rivera rancho was no longer vested in Jane Bowman. The heirs of Don Francisco Rivera had failed to have the old Spanish grant confirmed by the United States Government. Any day now, the papers would come from Washington, acknowledging his own claim as legal owner of the land. Perhaps the papers had already come on the morning stage, were now at the post office. He would soon know.

The thought somewhat reassured him, but in no way allayed his awareness of a danger that might be closer than he suspected. There would soon be prison bars, a rope around his neck, if Bowman learned that Nat Murran was Adna Fenn. He had immediately recognized Bowman when the former Confederate cavalry officer arrived in Boca Grande with his daughter less than a month ago. They had stayed the night at the hotel. He should have got rid of them at the time. The shock had numbed his wits. One thing was certain, he was not safe while the Bowmans lived. Stinger had failed him and now it was up to Dacey to act — and quickly. Dacey was getting chicken-hearted, puffed up with pride of his position in the Boca Grande as a big cattleman. Fortunately, he had the power to bend Dacey to his will. A raid would do the job. He could enlarge the JD outfit, hire a hundred men, tough border renegades. No matter how many died if he was forever rid of the Bowmans. The man from Santa Fé must be found, too, and removed from life.

None in the street could have guessed the fat little liveryman's murderous thoughts as he hastened to the post office. His bespectacled, chubby face beamed benevolence, his voice, smooth, bland, made genial response to greetings from his fellow townsmen. He climbed the hotel porch steps and pushed into the lobby.

"Is Sil Turlo up in his room?" he asked Blackie. He knew the town marshal rarely went to bed before dawn.

"He ain't up yet," Blackie answered. Perhaps the clerk was one man who was not deceived by the liveryman's beaming face. He leaned hairy forearms on the untidy desk, lowered his voice confidentially. "Somethin' up, boss?"

Murran was silent, his expression thoughtful. Blackie Stenlo was too good a man to be wasted behind a hotel desk when emergency called for grim action. Among all the border desperados on his secret payroll, Blackie was the most ruthless. His stupid, beefy face masked the cunning and ferocity of a wolf. Only Yuma could match him for sheer viciousness.

The big man seemed to sense his thoughts. "I'm cravin' excitement," he said. "Gettin' some sick of ridin' herd on this damn desk."

Murran made up his mind. "Tell Turlo I want him down at the office." He paused. "You, too, Blackie. I've a job for you."

Blackie nodded. "I'll fix it with Reno to take the desk." His bulging eyes took on a wicked glint. "I'll be right down, quick as I can drag Sil out of bed."

Murran turned to the lobby door. "If you and Sil get there before I do, tell Yuma I sent you." The screen door slammed behind him.

Blackie stood for a moment, gaze on the fly-specked screen. He jerked at a drawer, took out a half-filled whiskey bottle, eyed it with a grin and started for the stairs, big fingers wrapped around the neck of the bottle. It would be empty by the time he had the town marshal headed for the livery barn office. Sil hated to be dragged out of bed so early in the day, would likely act as ugly as an old range bull on the prod. Whiskey would fix him up, though, get him on his feet and started for the office.

The storekeeper was behind his post office grill, sorting out the mail, popping envelopes into pigeonholes. He returned Murran's cheery greeting with a stiff nod. He disliked the liveryman who he suspected was the secret backer of the new store soon to be opened across the street. There were rumors the new store would also be the town's new post office, which meant that Silas Dunket would no longer be postmaster. The loss of the post office would result in a loss of trade, and Dunket was worried about it. He would be forced out of business and out of Boca Grande much to Nat Murran's secret gratification.

"Anything for me, Silas?" asked the liveryman, face at the little opening in the grill. "I'm expectin' important mail from Washington."

The craggy-faced storekeeper slid a handful of letters through the grill. "Nothing from Washington, Nat," he said with a wintry smile. "I guess the Postmaster General ain't got around to you — *yet*."

Murran let the gibe pass. "Nothing but feed bills." He stuffed the envelopes in a pocket. "I'm going out to Dacey's ranch this afternoon," he went on. "I'll take the ranch mail along, Si."

Dunket offered no objection. He was aware that Murran was supposed to have an interest in the big cattle ranch, held a mortgage, or something. He often took out the ranch mail.

The liveryman sorted the bundle pushed through the grill. A few letters, a Montgomery Ward catalogue. No letter bearing a certain name he had hoped to find.

"Is this all of it?" he asked.

Mr. Dunket's chin whiskers bristled. "I don't overlook anybody's mail," he retorted. "You can't send *that* kind of lie to the Postmaster General."

Again Murran ignored the thrust. Dunket would soon be hauling his big sign down and looking for a new town. He pawed through the letters, shook his head. "Should be one here for young Thomason." The postmaster's quick look at a pigeonhole was not lost on him. "Thomason is out at the ranch, now," he added. "If you've got anything for him I'll take it along with me, Si."

Dunket hesitated. "I'm not supposed to hand over a man's letters to anybody who asks," he said. His look went to the pigeonhole again. "A letter came on this morning's stage for Cole Thomason, but he'll have to come and get it in person, not having left word for me to hand it over to you or anybody else."

Murran beamed at him. "I don't blame you for being particular, Si," he chuckled.

"A postmaster has to be particular," Dunket said stiffly. "I run this office according to regulations."

"You don't understand the joke about this Cole Thomason," smiled Murran. "He's the young stranger who got into that fight with Lute Soler. I liked him, and instead of sending him to jail I got him a job with Dacey. I knew Jasper was looking for a top hand."

"I see." Dunket looked interested. "He's *that* feller." He smiled. "I saw the scrap. He sure was treating Lute Soler mighty rough. I was all for him, and so was the Dacey girl. She was here in the store when those two came tumbling out of the restaurant."

"He's the man," chuckled Murran. "Well, he's on the JD payroll now, and I'm thinking he'd like any mail you've got for him, Si."

“I suppose it’s all right,” reluctantly assented the storekeeper.

“Of course it’s all right,” Murran assured him. “He went off to the ranch so early yesterday morning he must have forgotten to tell you he’d be out at Dacey’s.”

Dunket turned to the pigeonholes, silently fished out a letter and pushed it through the grill.

“Thanks.” Murran stuffed it with the others in his pocket, seized the bulky mail-order catalogue and hurried away, followed by the postmaster’s uneasy gaze. Mr. Dunket was wondering if he had made a mistake.

Murran went directly to the livery barn office, the letter burning a hole in his pocket. He would soon know something about the young stranger he had made Dacey put on the JD payroll. A growing uneasiness gnawed him. Mexicans! That is what Stinger had said. A lot of Mexicans camped out at the Bowman place. Thomason had appeared in town riding a horse wearing a Chihuahua brand. Hardly a coincidence. The thing smelled of danger.

Mexicans at the Bowman place. The young stranger — his Mexican buckskin horse.

The liveryman’s agitated thoughts set his heart to pumping. Coincidence was out. Cole Thomason was the man from Santa Fé. Lewis Bowman had recognized him, knew he, Murran, was Adna Fenn — had sent word to Santa Fé.

He heard again Pete Shedd’s gravelly voice. “*Met a feller in Santa Fé. Said he’d heard I was haulin’ to Boca Grande . . . asked me if I knowed a feller name of Adna Fenn.*” The mule-skinner had chuckled. “All I could tell him was to look you up. Told him you knowed just about all the folks within a hundred miles of Boca Grande."

The distraught liveryman pushed at his office door. It was locked on the inside. A key scraped and the door swung open, revealed Yuma's flat face.

"Heard you coming, boss. Sounded like you was on the lope."

Murran swore at him, sank breathless in his desk chair. He was glad that Blackie Stenlo and the town marshal had not arrived. He wanted time to recover his composure, time to think — make plans. He heard Stinger's satanically amused voice. "You look like the devil was grabbin' at your heels."

Murran gazed at him with grudging admiration. Stinger was under no illusions. He was well aware his end was close. The desperado's iron nerve was food for thought. Perhaps there was still room for Stinger in the plans he must make to survive.

He said, musingly, a hint of promise in his voice, "I'll maybe change my mind about you."

"I sure crave you'll change your mind awful fast," muttered Stinger. "Ain't likin' layin' here all fixed for them buzzards."

Murran was tearing at the envelope addressed to Cole Thomason. His hands were clammy, dampened the letter he extracted. He removed his spectacles. They were only colored glass and he could read better without them. The pencilled scrawl carried no heading or signature.

. . . and the letter written some twenty years ago by your grandfather has only just been found in an old trunk. It confirms the rumor you picked up. Fenn was actually seen in Boca Grande by the man who carried the news to your grandfather, whose death soon afterward put an end to the search. I believe that the man who recognized Fenn is also dead. His story indicates that Fenn was using the name of Nat Murran . . .

Murran stared at the letter like a man who sees a ghost. *Your grandfather. Cole Sims. Cole Thomason was his grandson*. No further room for doubt, now. Thomason was the man from Santa Fé, for whom Dacey's outfit was still searching the hills. Only they would never find him in the hills. He was one of them, looking for himself, laughing at them all for fools.

The liveryman started to tear the letter to shreds, changed his mind and thrust it in a pocket. Cole Thomason was in his hands now, doomed to die. Before he died he could have the pleasure of reading the letter that came too late for him to learn that Nat Murran was Adna Fenn.

The thought amused Murran. He was suddenly in high humor. Cole Thomason — the Bowmans. A simple matter now to deal with them. They were finished. The fears of the past month would soon be done with. No more need to watch the roads, the trails, through his telescope. He could give his time to more pleasant things — the fine, brick building that was to be his bank, the Boca Grande Bank, the new General

Merchandise Store, the new Boca Grande Hotel, the great house on the mesa, overlooking the river — Belle Dacey.

Murran put on his amber spectacles, beamed at Blackie and the town marshal as they pushed through the screen door. A gun belt was strapped around Blackie's bulging waist and his beefy face wore a wide smile in sharp contrast to Turlo's scowl. The town marshal looked the worse for wear, his eyes bloodshot, his expression morose.

"Hell of a note," he grumbled, "draggin' me out of bed, and me up all night keepin' law and order in this damn town." He saw the whiskey bottle on the desk, started for it. Murran's sharp voice halted him.

"Leave it alone, Sil, and listen to me."

Turlo's reaching hand dropped to his side. "All right." His tone was sullen. "I'm listenin'." His eyes widened on the bound prisoner. "What for you got Stinger hawg-tied? Want me to throw him in jail?"

"Listen to me," repeated the liveryman. "I'm leaving for the Dacey ranch in a few minutes." He paused, looked at Yuma. "Tell Mateo to harness the Morgans and have the buckboard ready right away."

Yuma nodded, made his soundless exit. Murran's look returned to the glowering town marshal. "Young Thomason fooled us plenty," he said.

"I figgered you was wrong, turnin' him loose," Turlo growled.

Murran's smile was wicked. "I'm smarter than you think," he said. "I didn't turn him loose. I only turned him over to Dacey to keep safe for me."

"What for you want him now?" Turlo asked.

"He's that Santa Fé man I told you to keep on the watch for. I've just learned the truth about him."

"From him?" The town marshal gestured at the bound man on the floor.

"Not from Stinger." Murran chuckled. "I have my ways of learning things."

"You want me to go out to JD and haul the feller back to jail?" Turlo looked puzzled. "Why don't you just pass the word along to Lute Soler. Won't be no chore for Lute to fill him with hot lead."

"I'm taking care of Thomason," purred the little fat man. "I've another job for you, Sil. Just a little job." He flapped a limp hand at the prisoner. "Stinger bungled things at the Bowman place, let them see him and that pinto he rides and left a trail straight to this office."

There was a brief silence. Turlo and Blackie exchanged understanding looks. "I reckon I savvy," Turlo said. "You want me and Blackie to leave 'em lay out in the brush some place. Him and the bronc, huh?"

Murran shook his head. "Only the bronc, and that's *your* job, Sil. Blackie is going to Dacey's with me, and so is Stinger."

Stinger asked, in a hoarse whisper, "Why ain't you killin' me now and be done with it?"

"I've changed my mind about you," Murran told him placidly. "You're a fast man with your gun. You can be more useful to me alive." He glanced at the town marshal. "Cut the ropes off him."

Turlo opened a claspknife, cut the rawhide thongs, gave Stinger a hand and helped him to his feet. The desperado rubbed chafed wrists, stamped numbed feet, a dazed look on his hard face.

"Help yourself to the whiskey," smiled Murran.

Perhaps Stinger remembered his comment about the contents of the bottle. He had told Murran a rattlesnake could use it for poison. Or perhaps he wanted to keep his mind clear, make the best of this surprising chance to stay alive. He shook his head. "*Gracias*." His grin was apologetic. "Ain't cravin' likker right now."

"*I'm* sure cravin' likker," Turlo said with a defiant look at the liveryman. He seized the bottle, gulped thirstily, set the bottle down with a bang, exclaimed in a shocked voice, "Sure is pizen, that likker." He shuddered, gave the grinning Murran an indignant look.

"I don't drink myself," the liveryman said placidly. "I wouldn't know good whiskey from bad. All of the stuff is poison for all I know about it." His voice was suddenly brisk. "I'm fixing for a showdown with that Bowman outfit. Stinger tells me Bowman has a bunch of Mexicans there and it looks like we've got a fight on our hands. Just as quick as Mateo has the team ready we're leaving for the Dacey ranch." He smiled at Stinger. "That's why I've changed my mind about you. I need your guns."

The renegade's pale slate eyes showed no expression. He nodded, reached the confiscated .45 from the desk and slid it in holster.

"I want you to round up a bunch of good men," Murran continued, his gaze on the town marshal.

"Top-hand pay on JD's payroll — and a bonus when the job's done." He paused, his expression murderous. "All the men you can get, Sil, and the quicker you can start them for the ranch the better. We've got to clean up this job fast."

The town marshal nodded. "I'll get movin'," he said. "I reckon I can round up fifteen or twenty fellers."

"Don't forget Stinger's pinto," reminded Murran. "Wait until after dark, then take the bronc off in the chaparral some place."

"I savvy —" Turlo turned to the door.

Stinger's voice held his step. "I sure hate to see old Paint made into buzzard's meat."

"Your own fault," snapped Murran. "Count yourself lucky you're not sharing the pinto's fate."

Stinger said no more. He stood there, rubbing the numbness from his wrists, his strange eyes devoid of expression. Wheels rattled up the yard from the barn. Murran got out of his chair. He crammed hat on head, took a key from his pocket.

"Let's go —" He waved the other men through the door, followed them, paused a moment and turned the key in the lock. "You in the front seat with Yuma," he said to Stinger. He climbed into the buckboard's back seat with Blackie, beckoned to Mateo to come closer.

"I'll be in sometime tomorrow," he told the Mexican. "You can handle things here while I'm away."

"*Si señor*." Mateo's eyes were busy, for all their sleepy look. His ears were busy, too, overheard Murran's low-spoken words to the town marshal. "Don't forget that pinto."

"I'll come and get the bronc after dark," Turlo promised. "Don't you worry about that paint horse, boss. Come dawn and he'll be layin' some place in the brush."

Yuma lifted the reins, the black Morgans sped away, the buckboard swaying, wheels rattling. Dust lifted, drifted. Mateo stood there, watching, wondering about Murran's reference to the pinto horse. There could be only one answer. When night came, the horse was to be taken to some lonely canyon and shot to death. It was evident, too, that the pinto's owner was not to die. He had gone with the others, unbound, his gun again in holster.

Mateo shook his head. It was all very puzzling. Señor Murran was a devil. It was hard to know what was in his mind. Only one thing was certain. Whatever came from his mind was evil. *Verdad!* Señor Murran was indeed the Evil One.

The Mexican's keen eyes never left the fading haze of dust. He knew the fork in the road. The dust drift had shifted to the left fork, the road to the Dacey ranch. Only matters of great importance would be hurrying Señor Murran to the Dacey ranch with those three bad men in his buckboard. They were killers, men who lived on blood.

Mateo pushed at his sombrero, worriedly fingered his graying thatch of hair. He knew so little. Yuma had told him nothing, only that the señor desired the black Morgans immediately hitched to the buckboard. One fact alone seemed clear. Señor Murran's hurried trip to the Dacey ranch meant trouble for the little señorita and her father.

The dust haze was gone. Mateo scowled, pulled the sombrero low over his eyes. *Por Dios!* He was wasting time! Only one thing he could do. Get out to the old ranch as fast as a horse could travel.

He wanted to run, made himself walk leisurely back to the barn. Nobody must suspect the excitement seething in him. His departure from Señor Murran's livery barn must not attract unwelcome attention.

The darkness of the stable closed over him. He halted, aware of a pounding heart under the faded blue shirt. He was getting old, too old.

He waited for a few moments. No! He was not too old. He thought of days long gone, himself — Benito shoulder to shoulder, guns blazing — Comanches tumbling from fast-moving ponies. The odds against them were big, but they had won through.

Other thoughts were also in Mateo Cota's mind. He was moving again, fast now, and he went to the box stall that concealed the pinto horse Señor Murran had doomed to die.

He released the tie-rope, led the horse through the rear door of the barn, and across the maze of corrals to a gate opening into the green meadow. He swung into the saddle. He knew where he was going. The trail in the canyon below the mesa was a short cut to the old ranch. No gringo knew of the great caves that shortened the distance by several miles.

Mateo muttered a pious ejaculation. Thanks to his knowledge of the secret trail through the great caves he had managed to get back to the livery barn before Stinger's arrival with the news so disturbing to Señor Murran. The fleeing renegade was already gone by the time he himself arrived at the rancho with Señor Thomason's message for the little señorita. *Verdad!* The old Apache trail had saved him from running into Stinger, enabled him to return in time to avoid awkward questions about his prolonged absence from the barn.

The old Mexican flung a fierce look back at the huddle of buildings, sent the pinto horse down the steep trail. He was finished with their evil owner, was on his way to the little señorita — to Tranquilo Baca.

CHAPTER FIFTEEN

Curly and Ringo halted their horses on the rimrock, narrowed their eyes at the dust drifting up from the south. They exchanged speculative looks, and Ringo said, in a surprised voice, “Sure is cows, makin’ that dust.”

Curly pushed up his hat, rubbed unruly blond hair. He was hardly out of his ’teens, but in his face there was a maturity, a hardness, that made him seem years older.

“Headin’ this way,” he said.

The two JD riders watched for several moments. It was Curly who broke the silence. “Looks like that herd is makin’ for the old Rivera place.” He paused, added in a puzzled voice, “There’s wagons trailin’ the *remuda* comin’ ’round the bend yonder.”

“Sure has me guessin’.” Ringo wrinkled his brow at the younger man. “Where’n hell is that outfit comin’ from, you reckon?”

“Only one place them cows can be trailin’ from,” Curly answered.

Ringo nodded. “The border, huh?”

“Cain’t be no place else,” drawled Curly. He gazed intently at the distant herd, mystification deepening in his eyes. "All them chuck wagons don't make sense. There ain't more'n five or six hundred cows in that bunch."

"Looks like there's wimmen in them chuck wagons," observed Ringo. He turned a baffled look on Curly. "What do you make of it — all them wimmen?"

"Mexicans," Curly answered. "It's a Mex outfit, but what for they're headin' thisaways has me buffaloed." He wheeled his horse back to the trail that had brought them up from the vast gorge of Lost Horse Canyon. "Let's go tell Lute," he said.

Julio's hawk eyes had spotted the two JD riders. He made haste to warn Tranquilo Baca. The chief of vaqueros was already on his horse, his intention being to meet the approaching herd below the mouth of the little ravine behind the corral. Julio's startling news of spies on the rimrock changed his plan. He had learned from Cole that Dacey's men were combing Lost Horse Canyon for the elusive stranger from Santa Fé. Apparently the search had brought them dangerously close. Anything might happen. Less than half a dozen vaqueros accompanied the herd. A surprise attack could easily stampede the cattle, scatter the *remuda*, do irreparable damage. The gringos would be ruthless, perhaps burn the wagons.

Jane heard the commotion in the yard, excited shouts, the quick thud of shod hoofs. She ran from the house in time to glimpse Tranquilo and his vaqueros riding at a gallop into the ravine. Old Benito stood by the corral gate, a rifle in his hands. His worried eyes met her startled look, went to Cole and her father coming on the run from the *cárcel*.

"What's wrong?" Bowman asked.

"I don't know." Jane gestured at Benito. "Ask *him*."

"Bad men have seen the cattle," Benito told them. "Señor Baca has gone to fight them off."

Cole swung toward the stable. The old Mexican's voice halted him. "No, señor. Tranquilo asks that you and Señor Bowman stay with the señorita."

Gunfire crackled in the distance. Cole began to run. Jane and her father followed him to the arroyo bank. Beyond the sharp bend of the big wash they could see the approaching herd, the strung-out *remuda* with some half dozen wagons in the rear. Horsemen were pouring from the mouth of Lost Horse Canyon. Their purpose was clear even to Jane. The attackers planned to cut off the wagons and stampede the herd into the canyon. It looked to the observers on the arroyo as if the raiders would accomplish their purpose.

Jane clutched Cole's arm. "Tranquilo!" she exclaimed. "Oh — they'll shoot him!"

The chief of vaqueros tore out of the little ravine, his big golden horse on the dead run, the vaqueros a hundred yards behind. Guns crackled again from the opposite slope. Answering shots came from the wagons. The vaqueros with the herd were too busy to use their guns. They were urging the cattle into a run toward the ravine.

Cole's eyes glinted approval. Let them stampede as long as they ran in the right direction. Tranquilo and his riders also understood. They began a circle that would place them between the cattle and the would-be rustlers. Julio was suddenly off his horse, taking deliberate aim. They heard the sharp report of his rifle, saw one of the raiders tumble from his saddle. Again the young Mexican's rifle spat smoke. Another rider pitched from his horse. And now the wagons were at a standstill, the drivers prone on the ground, their rifles spouting flame and smoke.

The unexpected resistance was more than Lute Soler had bargained for. He was the first to swerve aside. In another minute the raiders were in desperate flight back to Lost Horse Canyon. Not all of them. Two lay where they had fallen. A third man struggled free from his dead horse, started to scramble up the rocky slope. Tranquilo's lariat snaked out, looped tight over the rustler's arms.

The few hectic minutes had averted the stampede. The cattle stretched out in a long line, moving fast but pointed for the ravine that would take them to the new corrals the Mexicans had made ready. Manuelo and Ramon were in the lead, slowing them down and other vaqueros fanned out after the stragglers. The raid was over.

Jane heard her voice, shaky, breathless. "It doesn't seem real," she said. "It was like something out of a — a book." She repressed a shiver, added in a low voice, "It's terrible!"

"It's life on the border," her father said grimly.

Cole said nothing. He was wondering about the rustler stumbling along at the end of Tranquilo Baca's rope. If they had guessed right, the prisoner was a JD man. He had been having a talk with Cherokee when the alarm had hurried him from the *cárcel*. Cherokee was a stubborn nut to crack, wanted his freedom, a chance to put a lot of distance between himself and the Boca Grande. Tranquilo's captive might prove useful, more easily persuaded to talk than Cherokee.

Tranquilo had turned his prisoner over to Julio and was taking a short cut across the arroyo. He drew up, swept off his hat to Jane, gestured at the wagons now again in motion. "The wives and the children come, my señorita," he said. "Soon they will serve you as their mothers served the Señorita Juanita who was your grandmother and the daughter of Don Francisco Rivera."

Jane had no words. She could only look at him, her eyes very bright, her breath quickening.

It was Lewis Bowman who spoke, his voice thoughtful, touched with worry. "Can they stay here in New Mexico, Tranquilo? They come from Mexico and it is possible the United States Government will say they must return to Mexico."

Tranquilo Baca shook his head. "Not so, señor. All of them, like myself, were born on this rancho. We are citizens, señor. This is our country, and to be back makes us happy."

"I'm only too glad not to argue the point," Bowman moved close to the big Mexican's sweat-lathered horse, held out his hand. "I'm mighty glad to have your kind of American on our side, these days, Tranquilo."

They gripped hands, and Tranquilo said, his sonorous voice deep with emotion, "*Si señor. Americano.*" He drew himself up proudly in his resplendent saddle, smiled at Jane. "We will build a school for the little ones, my señorita. We will teach them to be good *Americanos*."

"Yes," Jane said. "Good Americans like you, Tranquilo, and your vaqueros." Her look went briefly to the distant slopes of Lost Horse Canyon. A pair of buzzards were already hovering there. She closed her eyes, added faintly, "You were all so brave."

The chief of vaqueros made one of his grand gestures. "We are Americans," he said simply. He wheeled his horse. "I must see to the herd."

"Was that Dacey's outfit you chased away?" Cole asked.

"*Si, señor*." Tranquilo glanced at the circling buzzards, added grimly, "Two of them will not return. They are very dead."

"You took one man alive," reminded Cole.

"He will make three who will not return," Tranquilo said with a shrug. "He will look well, hanging from a tree."

"No!" exclaimed Jane. Her eyes reproached him. "We will leave him to the Law."

"We have no law," Tranquilo grumbled.

"The Law will come," Jane said positively. "You must help us bring the Law, Tranquilo. Good Americans live by the Law."

The big Mexican looked at her soberly. "*Si*, my señorita. You say true words. We will have the Law on this rancho — in all this country of the Boca Grande."

Jane's father chuckled. "That's the talk, Tranquilo. We'll maybe make you sheriff, some day."

Tranquilo's head lifted in his deep-throated laugh. "*Por Dios!* I will soon fill all the jails in the Boca Grande." He rode off to the corrals.

Cole left Jane and her father watching the approaching wagon-train. Luke Soler's attempt to stampede the cattle gave him food for troubled speculation. Dacey would soon learn of the strange happenings at the old Rivera rancho. He would realize that his plan to frighten the Bowmans had failed. They were no longer helpless nesters, to be chased away. A miracle had occurred under his very nose. Overnight the old rancho had taken on a new lease of life, with cattle on the range — a tough, hard-fighting outfit on guard.

Jasper Dacey was due to be a very puzzled and outraged man, and whether or not he wanted to, he would be forced to act quickly. Fear of Nat Murran would drive him to ruthless extremes.

Cherokee eyed him curiously as he pushed through the *cárcel* door. The cowboy sat on his heels, his back against the adobe wall, a chain clamped around an ankle.

"Seems like I heard shootin'," he said. "Can hear cows bawlin', too," he added.

Cole studied him, wondering how to make the man talk. Tranquilo Baca had offered certain suggestions he guaranteed would make the most stubborn man speak the truth, suggestions Cole rejected as too primitive.

His silence was getting Cherokee uneasy. "Sure sounds like cows bawlin'," he repeated.

Cole kept his silence, tossed him tobacco sack and papers. Cherokee's eyes lifted in a curious look at him, fingers expertly shaping a cigarette.

"You sure have me guessin', Thomason." There was mild wonder in his voice. "If you was me and me *you*, you'd be danglin' from a tree, or layin' out in the brush."

The sincere admiration in the desperado's voice was not lost on Cole. He caught the tobacco sack, the papers Cherokee tossed back at him, reflectively made a cigarette. He stripped a match from the block of sulphur matches in his pocket, lit Cherokee's cigarette — his own.

The cowboy relaxed against the adobe wall, drew smoke into his lungs, meditatively watched the blue haze curl from nostrils. He lifted his chained ankle, shook the heavy, rusted links. A worried scowl darkened his face.

"That Pedro feller says you figger to slice my ears off," he muttered. "Ain't likin' the way that Mex comes in and looks me over and then goes to fingerin' that damn *machete* he wears." Cherokee's voice lifted plaintively. "Why ain't you sayin' something, mister?"

"The Panhandle is a long way from here." Cole spoke musingly. "Too bad you ever left the Panhandle, Cherokee."

"I crave to git back there," Cherokee said violently. "Once I git back to Texas I ain't never leavin' it no more." He stared gloomily at his fettered ankle. "Don't seem like I'll see the Panhandle ag'in."

"Your time is running out," Cole said. "Talk fast, if you hope to get back to Texas."

Cherokee thought it over, smoke curling from nostrils, his expression irresolute. "You ain't said you'd turn me loose," he complained.

"Your time is running out," Cole repeated. "Things have been happening. Lute Soler tried to pull off a raid. He left two of his men lying out there — dead. We have another prisoner, Cherokee. It's your last chance to talk before he does."

"Who's the feller you got your rope on?"

"I'm not telling you," answered Cole. He could have added that as yet he was himself unaware of the captured JD man's identity. He had left orders for the prisoner to be held in the barn when Julio brought him in.

"Listen —" Cherokee spoke earnestly, almost pleadingly. "I ain't done no killin' my own self since I been with JD —"

"You did your best to kill me — twice," reminded Cole.

The cowboy shrugged, gave him an embarrassed grin. "Cain't claim you're a liar. I'm just tellin' you I ain't done no killin' since Nat Murran hired me, put me on JD's payroll."

"Keep on talking," encouraged Cole.

"You're a white man." Cherokee's cold eyes took on an odd warmth. "If I'd knowed you a few years back I wouldn't have got to rustlin' cows. That's how come I landed in Boca Grande a couple of jumps ahead of the sheriff." He scowled. "Nat Murran is sure the big boss in that town. Once a feller gets tied up with him it's do what he says and no back talk. When a feller stops bein' useful he disappears awful sudden."

"Keep on talking," Cole repeated.

"Like I told you, I'm smart," continued Cherokee. "Seemed kind of queer the way Murran done all the hiring for Dacey. Ain't a man on JD's payroll he ain't hired, all of 'em on the dodge from the law. Murran's the real boss of JD and I reckon he's got Dacey in the same fix as the rest of us. Dacey's got to do what he says or he's sure headed for plenty trouble."

"Was Dacey responsible for the ambush in the Big Hatchets?" Cole asked.

Cherokee shook his head. "It was Nat Murran fixed it for me and Ringo to lay for you. I fetched your saddle in like Dacey told you. He didn't know then it was me shot your bronc. He knows now, 'cause Murran told him he had to get you alive or dead."

"Do you mean Dacey really thought I was a friend Murran was expecting?" Cole asked.

"He sure did, until Murran told him different." Cherokee paused. "You want to know about the feller that rides the pinto horse. It was Murran sent him here to kill Bowman."

"Do you know the man's name?"

Cherokee hesitated. "Wears the name of Stinger," he finally answered. "He's a tough hombre. I figger Murran got him here special for the job." He leaned forward, snubbed his cigarette on the rusted chain, tossed the stub aside. "You ain't said nothin' yet about turnin' me loose."

Cole looked at him thoughtfully. "How do I know you won't make tracks back to the Dacey ranch, or Boca Grande?"

"Mister —" Cherokee was breathing hard. "Once I get goin', the Boca Grande will never see me no more. I'm headin' for the Panhandle, and when I get there I'm keepin' inside the law. I'm done with rustlin'."

Cole turned to the door, beckoned to Pedro, dozing in the sun, back against the stump of a tree. "Unlock the chain," he ordered.

The old Mexican rubbed his grizzled thatch of hair, his expression dubious. "Señor Baca," he began. Cole's gesture silenced him. He produced a huge key, reluctantly unlocked the fetter and went back to his stump.

Cherokee got to his feet, stood for a moment, a curious incredulity in his eyes. "I reckon you mean it," he said finally, his voice husky. "I reckon you're turnin' me loose."

"That's right," Cole said. "Maybe I'm a fool, but I've an idea you'll go straight, once you're back in Texas."

"I reckon it ain't too late," muttered the man. He continued to gaze at Cole. "Ain't forgettin', Thomason. You're sure one white man." He hesitated. "There's more I'm wantin' to tell you. Dacey ain't Belle's own father. She don't know it, but her dad and ma was killed in a raid Murran had Dacey pull off. They was homesteaders and Murran wasn't wanting 'em around. The ranch-house stands where the shack they lived in was burned down. Belle was only a baby then.

Dacey took her and raised her up for his own daughter. I reckon she's the real owner of that ranch."

Cole asked, quietly, "How did you learn this story?"

Cherokee shrugged. "I kind of listened one night when Murran and Dacey was talkin' in the office. They wasn't knowin' about me layin' under the window." His lips twisted in a mirthless grin. "Like I told you, I'm smart, kind of like to know what's goin' on."

Cole felt a bit sick. "It's bad business," he said gloomily. "I'm glad you told me." The cowboy floundered, lowered his eyes. "I — I figgered you'd want to know, her likin' you the way she does."

Cole said nothing, waited for him to continue.

"Murran takes what he wants," Cherokee said. "He'll get her. Dacey won't dare stop him."

"How do you know all this?" Cole asked.

"Lute passed us the word to lay off of her," Cherokee said. "Wasn't hard for us to savvy why." His eyes took on a malicious glint. "Lute was after her his own self. He sure quit foolin' 'round her awful sudden."

"It might have been Dacey himself who didn't like you boys fooling around with her," argued Cole.

"It wasn't Dacey," insisted the cowboy. "He'd have bawled us out plenty his own self if he'd knowed we was chasin' that gal. He thinks the world an' all of her."

"Well —" Cole frowned, shook his head. "If Dacey thinks so much of her he'll tell Murran to leave her alone."

"I'm tellin' you Dacey won't dare stop him," reiterated Cherokee. He shrugged. "It's up to you, if you're likin' the gal your own self."

Cole was more worried than he let the cowboy know. He turned abruptly to the *cárcel* door. Cherokee followed him to the corrals. From down the little ravine came the low bawls of the approaching herd. Tranquilo was nowhere in sight. Cole guessed he had gone to meet the herd. Domingo and Benito, lounging by the water-trough, stared with hostile eyes at the JD man. It was plain they were puzzled, uneasy.

"Your horse is in the barn," Cole said. "Throw on your saddle and get away fast. Head for the border and swing north for El Paso."

Cherokee nodded that he understood, disappeared inside the barn. Cole's look went to the pair of glowering Mexicans. "I'm turning him loose," he told them. "He's given me valuable information."

"He will go back to the wolf-pack," Domingo grumbled.

"He won't stop until he gets to Texas," reassured Cole. "He is not to be harmed. Understand?"

"*Si señor*." Ramon lifted an expressive shoulder. "It will be too bad for him if he ever comes back."

"He won't," smiled Cole. He went inside the barn, took a gun belt from a peg and carried it to the stall where Cherokee was hastily saddling his horse. "Here's your gun," he said.

Cherokee gave him a wondering look, silently buckled the belt around lean hips, and at a gesture from Cole, followed him out with the horse. He swung into the saddle, looked at Cole soberly with eyes that had curiously lost their hard, vicious glint. They were warm, sincere, almost shy. He said softly, "*Adios*. I won't be forgettin'."

Cole watched until he disappeared in the arroyo. He was confident Cherokee would not return to Boca Grande, less sure of the man's regeneration. It was not going to be easy for Cherokee to shed his villainy. There were hundreds like him, products of a lawless environment that gave them small chance. One push in the wrong direction and they were riding with the "wild bunch."

Jane and her father had seen Cherokee vanish down the arroyo trail. They hurried into the yard, dismayed, bewildered. Cole forestalled their questions. "I turned him loose," he told them. "He did some talking and that's all I wanted from him."

"The scoundrel wasn't deserving mercy from you," grumbled Lewis Bowman.

"I got what I wanted from him," Cole said in a hard voice. "He was *my* prisoner and I was finished with him. You'll never see him in the Boca Grande country again. He's on his way to the Panhandle."

Jane's eyes were on his face, intent, probing. She sensed some desperate purpose hardening in him, said in a troubled voice, "You look so worried, Cole."

"It's Belle Dacey —" Cole broke off, arrested by Jane's almost indignant expression.

"What do you mean?" The warmth was gone from her voice. "Why should you worry about Belle Dacey?"

"She is in great danger," Cole said.

His grave tone impressed her. She asked more quietly, "In danger from what?"

"Cherokee told me that Dacey is not the girl's father. She doesn't know it, yet, nor the very dreadful truth that he seems to be responsible for the murder of her parents when she was a baby."

Jane gazed at him speechless, horror in her eyes. It was Bowman who broke the brief silence. "Can you believe Cherokee?" he asked, doubt in his voice.

Cole nodded. "They were nesters and Nat Murran wanted the land. Cherokee says Murran is the real owner of JD, and that every man on the payroll is a fugitive from the law, including Dacey himself."

"It's hard to believe," Jane said unhappily. "I rather liked Mr. Dacey."

"The ranch-house now stands on the land stolen from Belle's murdered parents." Cole's tone was grim. "Perhaps Dacey only intended to frighten them away. Something went wrong and there was shooting."

Lewis Bowman drew the crumpled letter from his pocket, eyed it with a scowl. "He sent me two of these warnings." He looked at Cole. "I reckon there'll be shooting here, too."

Jane spoke again. "What has Belle Dacey got to do with it?" she asked. "Why should she be in danger?"

"Murran wants her," Cole said. "Dacey will be unable to protect her."

Lewis Bowman glowered at him. "There is *one* way you can stop Murran cold. Use your authority as United States deputy marshal and throw the scoundrel in jail."

Cole grimaced. "Easier said than done." He shook his head. "As a matter of fact, I have no actual proof that he *is* Adna Fenn."

"What can you do about it even if you get proof?" Jane asked worriedly. "You can't go to that dreadful town alone — arrest him."

Cole shrugged. "I'll have to manage it in some way." He gave her a faint smile. "I could take him by surprise — get him out of town before his friends knew what was going on."

"You could swear in Tranquilo's vaqueros as deputies," suggested Bowman.

"It's an idea." Cole was silent for a moment, gaze on the first of the wagons to appear around the bend in the arroyo. His expression hardened. "I've no time to waste," he said. "I must get Belle Dacey away from that ranch immediately."

"No!" exclaimed Jane. "You are not going back to Dacey's. You won't have a chance." Her voice faltered. "You — you'll be killed."

"Dacey doesn't know who I *really* am," argued Cole. "He'll be expecting me to return."

"He'll want to know what has become of Cherokee," reminded Bowman.

"I can tell him the truth," smiled Cole. "I'll tell him Cherokee decided to hit the trail for the Panhandle."

"I don't see why it is up to you to risk your life for that girl." Jane spoke half angrily. "Why *should* you, Cole?"

Cole looked at her steadily. "I'm remembering that Belle saved my life this morning."

Jane gazed back at him with stricken eyes. "Yes," she said, faintly. "I'm afraid I was *not* remembering." There was self-reproach in her voice. "I take it all back, Cole. Of course you must go and help that poor girl."

His eyes thanked her, and he was suddenly hurrying to the barn. Jane watched until the darkness of the stable hid him. A second wagon was following the first one down to the yard. Two Mexican vaqueros were behind it. She wondered vaguely why they looked so solemn, held their flat-crowned hats in their hands. Tranquilo Baca rode out of the little ravine beyond the corrals. Julio appeared, and behind him, stumbling at the end of a rope, was a young gringo cowboy. He had curly, straw-colored hair and he looked very frightened.

Jane felt suddenly ill. She could find no joy now in those wagons, the bellowing herd coming up the ravine. She flung her father a piteous look, fled into the house.

She went to her bedroom window, the one that every morning showed her the sun lifting above the distant hills. It also overlooked the road from the yard.

She stood there, watching, and soon she saw Cole. He was riding the Chihuahua buckskin horse, and his face made a hard profile against the late afternoon sun. There was resolute purpose and courage there, and in the lean, hard-muscled body so lightly erect in the saddle.

Jane's heart went out to him. She longed to be riding by his side, share the dangers of the trail ahead. There was nothing she could do. She could only pray.

CHAPTER SIXTEEN

The drumming hoofs of a fast-running horse sent old Sam on the run to the yard gate. He swung it wide, stood ready to give the black colt's rider his customary grin. Belle tore past without even a glance, and by the time the choreman closed the gate she was in the barn and feverishly stripping off saddle and bridle.

Sam watched in silence from the stable entrance. He made no attempt to help. He knew she would refuse. She allowed no man in the outfit to touch the black colt. She had gentled him, broken him to the saddle. Diablo was a one-man horse, ready to let fly with his heels at anybody except Belle. It had been Cole Thomason's easy mastery of him in the blacksmith shop that had so amazed her. The incident was in her mind as she drew off the saddle. She had never known the black colt to show such confidence in a man, and a stranger at that. Diablo had the same feeling about Cole that was hers. Cole was a man to trust — to *love*.

Belle was suddenly running from the big stall that was her black colt's special domain. She never even saw the choreman as she brushed past him. His wondering look followed her across the yard. He shook his head, combed fingers through drooping grizzled mustache.

He had never seen such sheer misery on her face. Something was wrong. She had not even stopped to attend to the vicious offspring of the devil she quite properly called by the name of Diablo.

The old choreman shrugged, climbed into the hayloft and grudgingly forked some hay into the black colt's manger. He liked Belle. She was always nice to him, gave him warm smiles, something she held back from the others of the outfit. Perhaps it was because he was old, and lame, and had been with Jasper Dacey since she was a baby.

Sam shook his head, jabbed his fork back into the hay and climbed out of the hayloft. There were things he could tell Belle. He knew he never would. It could do her no good now to hear the story of a nester's cabin burned to the ground — the man and woman found dead in the ashes.

The old choreman limped outside and perched himself on the corral fence. The afternoon wind was astir, rustled the cottonwood trees that shaded the water-trough. He fingered a piece of plug tobacco from a pocket, reflectively studied the clouds piling over the distant mountain peaks. Rain coming, or it might be wind — a sandstorm.

Sam gnawed frowningly at his plug tobacco. Sandstorms were bad, made life hell while they lasted. Cows turned their backs to a sandstorm, drifted miles. It always meant hard work rounding them up. He hoped he was wrong, but those clouds looked like wind to him.

Habit drew his gaze to the road that crawled over low desert hills to Boca Grande. The faint haze of dust was a familiar sign. The Dacey ranch was at road's end. Dust lifting beyond the buttes meant visitors within the hour.

Belle was too busy with her unhappy thoughts to notice the approaching telltale dust. She slammed through the garden gate and hurried into the house. The sharp rap of her bootheels sounded loud to her ears, increased the feeling of loneliness in her. The big, sprawling house was always so silent. She was weary to death of its silence. No friends to fill it with the sound of living. Her father always glooming in his ranch office, especially the last few weeks. Only her own voice, her own footsteps. She wanted more from life. She had dreaded coming back to the ranch, spent hours down in the creek willows, thinking about Cole Thomason, wondering what to do.

She flung into her bedroom. It was a large room. Her father had spent a lot of money on its furnishings; the great Spanish bed from Santa Fé, the huge mirror in its gold frame, the dressing table, the paintings, the frescoed ceiling. She instinctively knew that something was wrong. The huge bed did not belong in a young girl's room, nor did the massive chairs, taken from the ruins of an abandoned old mission church. Bitter thoughts churned in her. She hated it all. Life on the ranch was woefully lacking in the finer things good for a girl to know. Excepting an occasional visit to Hachita she had never been beyond the borders of the Boca Grande.

Belle frowned at the face frowning back at her from the mirror. She lifted the quirt dangling from wrist, slashed viciously at the glass. It shivered into countless tiny cracks, and now the face she saw was a distorted, grimacing mask from which she fled with a stifled sob back into the hall and out to the long *galería*.

Dacey sprang from his desk chair, alarm in his eyes as she jerked the screen open and paused in the doorway. "Belle!" Fear constricted his throat. "Belle!" he repeated.

"I'm doing what you want, Pops." Her chin was up, her smile hard. "I'm going to that school in Santa Fé — learn to be a lady."

Dacey lowered slowly into his chair, his gaze not leaving her. "I — I thought you were ill, or something —" His look left her, went to the paper spread out on his desk. "I'm very busy —"

"I'm worse than ill," she flared. "I've just decided I'm sick of living here with nobody to talk to who's decent. I want to get away from this ranch."

Dacey's frown deepened. "You've changed your tune from this morning."

She lifted a shoulder, closed the door and took the chair opposite him. "I'm growing up, Pops."

"It's about time you did," Dacey said, his look returning to the paper on his desk. "I'm arranging to have this ranch put in your name, Belle. This Santa Fé school is a good idea, and I'm glad you're willing. You'll be a rich young woman, owner of one of the best cattle ranches in New Mexico."

"Pops —" Belle toyed with her quirt, eyes downcast. "Let's both of us go to Santa Fé — any place to get away from here."

"Don't be silly." He spoke gruffly.

"Before it's too late," she urged. "Before something terrible happens."

He gazed at her, eyes suddenly wary. "Something has frightened you," he said. "You looked scared to death when you came in just now."

She wanted to tell him about Cole and Cherokee. She had promised Cole to keep his secret. "*Tell your father if you must, but telling will only make it worse for him.*" Worse for Cole, too, if her father knew what she knew about Cole.

Dacey was saying impatiently, "What's the matter with you? What's got you so scared?"

She remembered what Cole had said about Nat Murran. "*There is only one man I'm interested in . . . I'm beginning to think he's the man.*"

"It's Nat Murran," she answered. "I'm frightened of him, Pops, and so are you."

Dacey was silent, his attention seemingly on the paper spread before him.

"You don't deny it," Belle said, violently. She was suddenly by his chair, looking over his shoulder at the document on the desk. Her eyes widened. "Why Pops, that's not a deed of the ranch to me! It's a deed from Nat Murran to you — and he hasn't signed it."

Dacey said sharply, "Mind your own business."

She went back to her chair, but did not sit down, looked at him with sick eyes. "You mean JD is not our ranch." She spoke in a low, appalled voice. "I — I *am* frightened, now, Pops. What does it mean?"

Dacey's big frame slumped in his chair. He seemed unable to meet her accusing gaze. He mumbled words that made no sense.

His obvious panic had a surprising effect on Belle. Her near hysteria subsided. She said quietly, "I understand now, why Nat Murran hires the men on JD's payroll. He's the *real* owner — their boss — *your* boss." Her smile was hard, edged with contempt. "I don't see why *you* should be afraid of that fat little man. You could twist his neck with one hand."

"He's a devil," muttered Dacey.

Scorn fired her eyes. "Devil or plain skunk, I'll bet Cole Thomason could handle him."

Dacey's eyes lifted in an odd look at her. "I've been thinking of Thomason. Lute Soler says he's lightning fast with a gun." His voice grew heavy with decision. "I'll have a talk with him the moment he gets back from Bowman's."

Belle was horrified to hear her voice say, "Cole won't be coming back."

Dacey's hands gripped the arms of his chair. "What do you mean, girl?" He flung the question savagely.

"Why —" She floundered, came to a decision. After all it was Nat Murran her father feared for reasons unknown to her, and it was also Nat Murran who for equally unknown reasons was the objective that had brought Cole Thomason from Santa Fé. Perhaps Cole was the answer to the sinister problem that threatened her father with ruin, or worse. Nat Murran apparently had some dreadful hold on her father. It was a chilling thought, stiffened her resolution to tell him about Cole and Cherokee.

He listened with frowning attention, and, she realized with some dismay, a certain grim despair.

"I wish I'd known," he muttered. "I could have used him — made a trade with Nat for the signature I want on this deed." He slammed a fist on the document. "It's not too late. I can send Lute and the boys after him."

Belle was more than dismayed now. She was horrified, doubted her ears. She had betrayed Cole's secret, thinking to give her father a weapon against the man he so dreadfully feared. Instead of taking fresh courage her father was callously eager to throw Cole like a bone to a hungry dog; use him to pacify Murran and get his signature on a deed. For the first time in her young life she was aware of frightening thoughts about her father.

She said huskily, "No, Pops. I — I'd hate you."

He seemed not to hear her. Her news about Cole's identity had surprisingly restored his self-confidence. "I'll tell Lute to fix the Bowmans, too," he said, unconsciously thinking aloud. "No sense wasting time."

"Pops!" exclaimed Belle.

"It's for *your* sake," Dacey said harshly. "Thomason, the Bowmans, don't mean a thing to me. They do to Nat Murran. I don't know why. I only know he doesn't want them around and his price to get rid of 'em is his signature on this deed."

Belle could only look at him, wonder if this father she had so adored could have suddenly gone mad. Misery welled in her heart as she stood there, stricken eyes on him. He was like the others, hard, ruthless. *Not my pops. He doesn't kill people*. That is what she had told Cole. The blood in her turned to ice. She was wrong. Her father was worse. He hired others to do murder for him. She was suddenly afraid of this man. He was like a stranger, sitting there in the desk chair.

She found her voice. "I don't want the ranch, if murder is the price." He was looking at her strangely. "I won't let you do it," she defied. "I'll tell Cole. I'll go to the Bowman ranch and warn Cole — warn the Bowmans."

Dacey was out of the chair before she could reach the door. He stood in front of her, his face dark with anger. "You little fool!" He reached for the key, turned it in the lock, slid the key in a pocket. "Sit down and behave yourself."

Belle was glad to sink back into the chair. Her knees felt queer, like the time when Diablo had bucked her from the saddle. She had climbed right back in the saddle, ridden the young horse to a standstill. Only this time it was not a horse that was making her knees trembly. It was her own father.

"Listen —" Dacey kept his voice low. "More than the ranch is at stake. Your own happiness, perhaps even my own life is at stake if I don't obey Nat Murran."

Belle shook her head. "You can leave my happiness out of it." The words came in a painful whisper. "I don't care about *me* — now."

"You've done some guessing about Murran," continued Dacey. "He can make a lot of trouble for me, ruin me and worse. Thomason, the Bowmans, can do the same to him, ruin him, put a rope around his neck. He told me as much, and that is why he wants to be rid of them. It's their lives, or Murran's and mine. Once they are out of the way our troubles will be over, the ranch mine — yours."

"There must be other ways." Belle was struggling to clear away the blackness that numbed her mind. "Nat Murran will do anything I ask. He — he wants to marry me."

Dacey said nothing, went back to his chair. He had the look of a man suddenly stricken with a mortal illness.

"I could bargain with him, tell him I'll marry him if he will promise not to harm Cole — or the Bowmans." She spoke quietly, almost confidently. "He's crazy about me."

"I'll kill him, first," Dacey said hoarsely.

"I'd rather die than marry him," Belle shuddered.

"It's a crazy idea," Dacey said in a louder voice. "Nat would never keep a promise. Forget it." He paused. "You go and pack up. I'm sending you to Santa Fé on the morning stage." He got out of his chair, unlocked the door, forced a smile. "Our troubles will all be done with when you come home for a holiday from school."

Belle brushed past him, her face averted. She did not want to look at him, this stranger who was her father. There was no love in her for him, only horror. She felt lost in a black forest of fear and despair.

Back in her room she flung herself on the bed. She had never felt so helpess, unable to think. She wanted to cry, but crying could do no good. One thought alone burned like a tiny spark in her. She must manage to warn Cole Thomason.

Sounds reached her from the yard. The rattle of wheels, voices. One voice stood above the others, shrill impatient, demanding. Her heart shriveled. Nat Murran's voice. She sprang from the bed, ran into the hall, huddled close to the door where she could watch the *galería*.

The garden gate creaked and Nat Murran appeared, almost on the run, black alpaca coat billowing. Three other men followed. She recognized Yuma and Blackie Stenlo. The third man was a stranger. They hurried past the hall door, unaware of her peering eyes. She heard her father's voice, surprised, apprehensive, as the visitors crowded into his office.

Belle stood in the darkened hall, irresolute, wondering what to do. She wanted to know the reason for Murran's very evident agitation. No doubt something to do with Cole Thomason — the Bowmans. The three men with him were heavily armed. It was peculiar that the hotel clerk was one of them. The lazy, good-natured grin was gone from Blackie Stenlo's moon face. He looked decidedly formidable with the two guns in his low-slung holsters. Obviously he was another of Nat Murran's hired killers. His presence indicated a fast-approaching crisis.

She went on quick, light feet to the rear door, slipped into the garden. The trees and bushes were thick here and it was easy to reach the back window of the office unseen. She worked her way stealthily under a low-growing shrub, close to the window. The sky was darkening, and a hot wind was blowing in from the desert. If the men inside heard any sound they would think it was the wind making noises in the trees.

She flattened down, lay very still, heard Nat Murran's querulous voice. "We'd have got here a couple hours sooner if we hadn't busted a wheel crossin' Squaw Creek."

"Hit a rock and sure smashed that wheel," broke in Yuma's thin voice. "I had to ride the Morgans clean back to town and fetch out another rig. Lost some time, Mateo not bein' there to help me hook up."

"I'll give that Mex hell when we get back," Murran said viciously. "Sneaking off the moment my back's turned."

"Well?" Her father's voice had a hollow sound to Belle. "What's the trouble, anyway, Nat? You look loaded for bear, bringing Yuma and Blackie and Stinger along with you."

"I've come to get Thomason," replied Murran. "Sam says he doesn't know where he is unless he's with Lute and the boys over to Lost Horse Canyon."

"I sent Thomason and Cherokee over to the Rivera place with a note warning Bowman to get out of the country," Belle heard her father say. "They should be back any moment now. Lute and the boys, too. Lute had a notion that maybe the Santa Fé fellow was hidin' out over there." It was plain that Dacey was unwilling to let Murran know he was aware of Cole's identity.

"You blundering fool!" snarled Murran. "Thomason's the man we've been hunting for these past three days." He tossed the letter intended for Cole on the desk, the one the postmaster had so reluctantly given him.

“Why didn’t you say so when you turned him over to me yesterday?” Dacey’s voice showed proper indignation. He glanced over the letter quickly. “Didn’t know your real name is Fenn.”

“You know it now,” grumbled the liveryman. His fist slammed the desk. “What’s the idea, anyway, sending a note to Bowman, warning him off? I told you that he and his girl don’t leave there alive. I’m sick of your bungling.” He pushed the letter back in the envelope.

“No harm done,” argued Dacey. “Bowman won’t scare. He and the girl will still be there when we pull off the raid.”

“I ain’t so sure, now that Thomason has got to him,” Murran said fretfully. “He’ll likely have the Bowmans leave there in a hurry — go off with them. He’s smart.”

“Thomason doesn’t know you want to get rid of the Bowmans.” There was real bewilderment in Dacey’s voice. “All he cares about is picking up *your* trail. He never heard of the Bowmans until I sent him over there with Cherokee. He’ll head back here with Cherokee all right.” The cattleman’s laugh came hard, almost gloating. “Thomason doesn’t know we savvy who he is. He’ll walk right into our hands, Nat.”

“You still don’t understand.” Murran spoke viciously. “Thomason and Bowman are wrapped up in the same package that’s dynamite for me. We’ve got to work fast, fix things before it’s too late.” He was suddenly silent, and when he again spoke, there was worry, almost fear in his voice. “I’m forgetting about those Mexicans,” he said.

"Mexicans?" Belle knew her father's surprise was genuine. "What are you talking about, Nat?"

"Stinger says there's a bunch of Mexicans camped out at the Rivera ranch. They chased him off, almost nabbed him."

There was a silence, broken by Dacey's voice. "First I've heard of it," he said. "I didn't see any Mexicans when I was over there couple of days ago — the evening Bowman was shot."

"The yard was full of 'em," broke in another voice. Stinger's, Belle guessed.

"I'm thinking it won't be so easy to fix the Bowmans, now." Dacey's tone was worried. "It will mean a shooting raid, Nat."

"Sil Turlo is rounding up a bunch of fellers," Murran said. "He'll have 'em out here by morning."

"We'll have to wait for them," Dacey decided. "No sense taking chances. If it comes to a fight we've got to make sure we can finish the job." He paused. "Sounds like Lute and the boys out in the yard."

Belle heard the familiar commotion that told her the outfit had returned from what she now knew was a futile search. The gate slammed. She recognized Lute Soler's step. He was running, in a hurry to get to the ranch office. She lay very still, her heart beating fast. Something had happened.

The screen door slammed; she heard Lute's excited voice. "Boss, hell's bust loose —" There was a brief silence and Belle guessed the JD foreman was suddenly aware of Dacey's visitors.

Murran's acid voice broke the silence. "You ain't telling us news, Lute, unless you mean you brought Thomason back with you."

"Hell, no," rasped Soler. "Him and Cherokee went over to the Rivera place. Ain't seen 'em since they rode off." His voice lifted angrily. "Listen — I'm tellin' you we ran into plenty trouble over at Bowman's. Curly and Ringo spotted a trail-herd comin' up from the border, a big remuda and a lot of wagons with women and kids in 'em. Me and the boys got down there fast, figgerin' to pull off a stampede, head the cows into the canyon. First thing we knowed a bunch of Mex riders come on the jump from Bowman's place, guns pourin' lead at us." JD's foreman swore luridly. "They was too many for us. We had to leave there mighty fast." His voice hushed. "Left Ben and Ringo layin' in the brush, both of 'em dead. Ain't knowin' for sure about Curly. I reckon they got Curly, took him back to the ranch." He paused, added thoughtfully. "Looks like Thomason and Cherokee are in the same fix as Curly, ridin' over to Bowman's like they done."

"Don't you worry about Thomason," grumbled Murran. "He's the Santa Fé feller we've been looking for, and he's laughing at us for a pack of dumb fools."

The ranch bell clanged out the supper call, and Belle heard her father's voice. "You and the boys go eat, Lute. Come back to the office soon as you can."

"Sure will, boss," Lute said. He paused, added savagely, "I crave to get my gun on Thomason, foolin' us the way he done." The screen door slammed.

"You go and eat, too, Blackie," Dacey said. "You and Stinger and Yuma. I've some private business with Nat."

"They stay here," Murran said curtly. "They'll eat when we do, Jasper."

Belle heard the rustle of papers, her father's voice, stiff with poorly repressed anger. "Look this over, Nat, and get your signature on it."

"I don't need to look it over," Murran answered. "I'm not signing that deed, Jasper. You haven't earned it, and now it's too late."

"What do you mean?" The anguish in Dacey's hoarse whisper sent a shiver through the girl crouched under the office window.

"You are finished here," purred Murran. "You bungled things with Bowman and Thomason. You're not useful to me any more, and when a man stops being useful I get rid of him."

There was a silence, and when her father spoke again, his quiet voice surprised Belle. "I'm not thinking of myself, Nat," he said. "I'm thinking of Belle. This ranch really belongs to her. Her parents settled on this land before we took it from them. I'm only asking you to do the right thing."

Belle was conscious of a paralyzing horror as she listened. Her father was calmly saying that he was not her father. She must be going crazy, imagining things. Nat Murran was talking now, saying shocking words that appalled her ears.

"Do you want Belle to know the truth about those nesters who were her parents?" Murran's laugh made the girl shudder. "It was *you* who warned them to get out — or else."

"I didn't tell the boys to shoot them down!" almost shouted Dacey. "*You* told them to use their guns, Nat. It was *you* who really murdered Belle's father and mother, stole the land this house stands on."

"You poor fool," snarled Murran. "You won't even have the chance to go back to Yuma and hang for that other killing."

"So that's why you brought your killers? You plan to close my mouth for keeps? Is that it, Nat?" Dacey's voice was quiet again. "All right, only sign that deed. Put Belle's name in, instead of mine. I love her, Nat. She's the only thing that's been worthwhile in my rotten life."

"I'm taking care of Belle." There was an ugly smirk in Murran's voice that drew another shiver from the girl listening outside the window.

She wanted to run away from there. Horror held her rigid, unable to move. The evening sky had a murky look, and fitful gusts of wind roared through the trees. The stillness inside the office terrified her. She wanted to look, scream defiance at Nat Murran. The wind subsided, came again, a shrieking blast through the open office door. A paper came whirling from the unscreened window. Instinctively her fingers closed over it, and above the uproar she heard Dacey's voice, hoarse, defiant.

"Not Belle, Nat! I'm killing you first!"

She heard the rattle of an opening drawer, a shot, followed almost instantly by two more shots. She screamed, found herself on her feet, face pressed to the open window. Dacey lay slumped across his desk, hand still on the gun in his drawer. Lying on the floor, near the opposite wall, was Yuma, dead, and near the door, the long, lean man they called Stinger. He was on the floor, too, blood rapidly staining the front of his shirt, and behind Murran's chair she saw Blackie Stenlo, a smoking gun in his hand. "I'd like to have got you, too, Murran," she heard Stinger say. He was clawing for his fallen gun. Blackie shot him again.

It was a horror picture and her dazed eyes could make no sense of it. She had no more time to do any thinking. Arms were suddenly around her, drawing her quickly from the window. She heard Cole Thomason's whispered voice.

"Let's get away from here."

Feet were pounding along the *galería* as he half carried her into the growing darkness of the trees.

CHAPTER SEVENTEEN

The feel of Cole's arms, the sound of his voice, startled Belle out of her near-hysteria. She said, breathless, "I'm all right," ran by his side into the deepening darkness under the trees.

Clawing underbrush slowed them down. Cole halted. "There's an opening somewhere close," he said. "We'll have to crawl."

Belle leaned against him, small hand clutching his. "I know." She spoke in a whisper. "I used to play Indian here when I was small. I cut a tunnel through the cat's-claw and made a trail down to the creek."

"I found it," Cole said. "I began to think I'd never get through that cat's-claw."

"It's awfully thick all along this side of the creek — keeps the cattle out." She choked off an hysterical giggle. "I never thought that hole might *really* save my life some day."

"Listen," he said.

Voices came faintly above the tumult of the wind in the trees.

"I don't think they heard us," Cole hoped. "Not with all the noise the wind is making."

Belle was suddenly trembling again. "I think I'd have died, if you hadn't come. I could hardly believe my senses when I heard your voice, felt your hands dragging me away from that window."

His fingers tightened reassuringly over hers. "I didn't know you were there until you screamed."

Belle shuddered. "It was horrible. Those men, dead — my pops —" She broke off, added in a low whisper. "Cole he's not my — my father."

"Cherokee told me," Cole said. "That's why I'm here, Belle."

She repressed another shiver. "I never dreamed you were so close."

"I had to get you away," Cole told her. "I was down in the willow brakes below the gate when I saw Murran drive into the yard."

"Cole —" She pressed against him. "Murran knows who you are. They'll kill you on sight."

"I heard him," Cole said. "I saw it all."

"I'm still in a daze about it," Belle said. "I couldn't see — only hear. What happened, Cole?"

"Dacey wasn't liking what Murran said about you. He tried to get his gun from the drawer. Yuma shot him, and then for some reason I don't understand, Stinger shot Yuma."

"I never saw Stinger before," Belle said.

"Queer, his killing Yuma," puzzled Cole. "He was trying to get Murran, too, when Blackie Stenlo shot *him*."

"It was horrible," repeated Belle. She was silent for a moment. "Those awful things I heard. Pops wicked like Nat Murran — not my own father." Her whispering voice faltered. "Cole, he killed my father and mother, Nat Murran said."

Cole's arm went around the trembling girl. "Dacey didn't know there would be shooting. It was Murran's work; and listen, Belle, Dacey wasn't all bad. You were the one thing he loved and lived for. He was doing the best he knew to make up for what happened to your father and mother. It was for your sake he tried to kill Murran. He couldn't bear the thought of Murran's having you."

Belle relaxed against his arm. "He was always good to me." Her voice choked. "I — I loved my pops."

"Keep on loving the good you remember in him," urged Cole. "You were the one bright star that made life less dark for him."

"I've been a spoiled brat," she sobbed against his sleeve. "Oh, Cole, I'm so miserable. Take me away from this place."

"I'm taking you to the Bowmans," Cole told her. His arm slid from her waist. "We'll have to ride double, unless we can wangle a horse from the barn."

Belle was staring at an envelope crumpled in her hand. "The wind blew it through the window," she said. "I didn't know I was still holding it." She was suddenly thrusting it at him. "I think it is something Murran gave Pops to read."

Cole smoothed out the envelope, held it close to his eyes. "Can't read it," he said. "Too dark."

"Perhaps it's about Murran," suggested Belle. "I heard Pops say, *Didn't know your name is Fenn*. Perhaps the letter is important, Cole."

"It is, if it proves that Murran is Adna Fenn." Cole folded the letter, pushed it deep in a pocket. It would be burning a hole there until he could read it, satisfy himself that at last he had the proof that would put a rope around Adna Fenn's neck.

No more sounds came to them from the house. Only the wind in the trees. Cole looked worriedly at the girl standing close to him. She was safe for the moment. Murran, none of them, could know where she was. It was possible they would think she was in her bedroom, would leave her undisturbed until some plausible story had been concocted about Dacey's death and the two dead renegades removed from the office. Murran would do all he could to withhold the truth from her. No doubt the story would be suicide because of business worries.

"Where's your black colt?" he asked.

"In the barn," Belle told him. "His stall is next to the door that opens into the horse pasture. The supper bell rang just before it — it happened," she added. "Most of the men will be at supper."

Cole looked at her. She was still dressed as he had last seen her when her gun had saved him from Cherokee's bullet. Blue flannel shirt, jeans — even her hat.

She answered his unspoken questions. "I only got back a few minutes before Murran arrived." Her shoulders drooped. "I — I hated to come home, just mooned around down there like a silly cry-baby thinking about you — about *us*."

Cole said, harshly, "You're not silly."

"I've been worse than silly — a baby crying for the moon." Her chin lifted. "I'm years and years older than I was just a little while ago. I'm not the girl you met in Joe's blacksmith shop, Cole. I've had some sense beaten into me."

"They don't come finer than you, Belle," Cole said. "I'm thinking your parents were mighty nice people to have had a girl like you."

"You do like me, just a little, then?"

The humility in her touched him. He drew her close, kissed her. "I like you a lot, or I wouldn't be here."

There was no passion this time in the press of her soft lips. It was the kiss of a frightened little girl who wanted comfort, reassurance. The appeal, the trust in her eyes, touched him. He gave her an affectionate, brotherly grin, turned abruptly with a gesture for her to follow.

They found the opening in the cats-claw, crawled through and in a few minutes were down in the creek willows. Cole untied the buckskin horse, motioned for Belle to climb into the saddle.

She shook her head. "I want Diablo," she said. "The men will be at supper and now is a good time."

"We can't risk it," Cole argued.

"There won't be a soul in the barn," she persisted. "Perhaps old Sam, and he wouldn't stop me. Sam has known me ever since I could walk. He likes me and would want me to get away."

Cole reluctantly agreed to the plan. He knew the creek made a twisting course that cut across the horse pasture behind the barn. It was worth a try, only he was determined that he would be the one to take the risk of venturing into the barn.

Leading the buckskin, they followed the wash around to the rear of the barn, a slow walk of nearly half a mile. The wind was stronger, away from the trees, lifted sand in stinging flurries that drew gasps from the girl. It was easier when the creek made a sharp bend toward the barn, put the wind at their backs.

They reached an opening in the willows that Belle said was as close as they could get to the stable.

"You can wait here," she said.

"No." Cole shook his head. "I'm going up there for that horse."

"Diablo won't let a man touch him," she protested. "I've got to do it myself, Cole, and Sam might be there. He'll make trouble."

"Diablo let me touch him that day in the blacksmith shop," he reminded.

"Yes —" Her voice was faint, almost inaudible in the wind. "Diablo likes you, too, only Sam won't understand, and — and I couldn't bear it if anything happened to you — now."

Cole said nothing, made the buckskin fast to a willow stump.

"All right," Belle said. "We'll both go." There was a hint of the old arrogance in the way she spoke. "You'll have to tie me up, too, if you don't want me along." She patted the little gun in her holster. "You'll be needing me, maybe."

They went cautiously up the sandy slope. The barn loomed in front of them, hardly visible against the dark sky. Lamplight glimmered through the trees from the house, and another light up the yard sent a single gleam through the blanketing darkness. The men's bunkhouse, Belle told Cole.

They lay there below the edge of the creek bank, sand stinging their faces while they attempted to look and listen.

"Too dark," Cole muttered. "Can't see a thing beyond the corral. "We'll have to chance it."

He was on his feet, moving swiftly toward the barn. Belle followed. They did not worry about noise. The wind shrieking over the barn smothered any noise they made.

The big rear door was closed. Belle prayed the bar was not down. She waited, tense with anxiety while Cole gently pushed. The door moved, swung open and in another moment she was inside the big stall, speaking softly to the black colt.

Cole slid the saddle from its peg, eased it gently on the black's back while Belle slipped the tie rope loose. The bridle, slung over saddle horn, could wait until they had the horse down in the willow brakes.

Cole was reaching for the cinch when he heard the faint rustle of straw. He straightened up, gun in hand; and sensing his alarm, Belle stood rigid, halter rope clenched in her fingers.

The whispering of straw underfoot drew close. They heard a muttering voice. "I'm doggoned sure I left that door tight shut."

Belle was pushing past Cole. She peered into the runway. "Sam!"

There was a silence. Only the wind, tearing at the roof, the rattle of a tin can buffeted across the yard; and then a low, guarded voice.

"Was that you, Belle?"

"Sam! Come here." There was the old arrogant command in the girl's whisper.

"What you doin' back here?" Sam was close to the girl, head poked forward in a surprised look.

"I'm leaving here," Belle told him. "Don't you try to stop me, Sam."

Sam was gazing at her so intently he failed to notice Cole. "Ain't blamin' you none, now your dad is dead," he said.

"Pops wasn't my dad," Belle said. "That's why I'm leaving, Sam. I'm afraid to stay — afraid of Nat Murran."

"I've knowed a lot of years Jasper Dacey wasn't your dad." There was an odd wheeze in Sam's whispering voice. He was like a man struggling for breath. "It was me found you toddlin' down thar in the crik when the boys went to smokin' their guns."

"Oh, Sam! Were you one of them?"

Her anguish seemed to increase the old choreman's labored breathing. "I'm mebbe a lowdown cow-thief, but I ain't never been that kind of killin' wolf." Sam's hands came up, an imploring gesture. "It was Jasper Dacey sent me down thar to stop 'em. I was too late, Belle. My God! I ain't forgetting that night. Been hauntin' me ever since, same as Jasper Dacey. He never got over it, Belle — done his best to make things right for you."

Belle said, her voice hard, "You're a better man than he was, Sam."

"I wouldn't say that, Belle." Sorrow rasped the old cowboy's whisper. "Wasn't no time Jasper wouldn't have gone for his gun for you."

"He went for his gun too late," Belle said in the same hard voice. "It's finished now, Sam. I'm going — and going now."

"I ain't stoppin' you —" Sam's voice broke off and he turned his head in a startled look at Cole. "No call for you to stick your gun in my back," he complained. "I said I wasn't stoppin' her."

"We can't take chances," Cole told him. "I'll have to tie you up, Sam."

"I figgered to ride with you." There was mild reproach in Sam's voice. "Only me left now, to tell Belle things she'll be needin' to know about the ranch." He paused, hand pressed over his heart. "Get queer feelin's here once in a while. Kind of catches my wind."

Belle said worriedly, "Cole — let's take him with us. It's the best way, and — and he's the only friend I ever had here."

Cole holstered his gun. "All right, Sam. Get yourself a horse."

"I'm takin' old Sandy," Sam said. He snatched at a saddle, limped into the adjoining stall.

Cole gave Belle a look. She understood, led the black colt outside. "I'll be waiting," she whispered over her shoulder.

The moments dragged, Cole fretting, impatient, hardly daring to believe the good luck could hold. He fancied he heard sounds in the yard. The same tin can banging against the barn, the wind rattling a loose fence rail. He was not sure. The noises he heard might be the crunch of approaching boot heels.

Sam finally led his sorrel horse into the runway. He peered hard at Cole. "You're that young Thomason feller, ain't you?"

"That's right." Cole gestured at the open door. "Get moving, Sam."

"Wasn't seein' you good with no lamp here to show your face." Sam was fumbling inside a leather pouch tied under the cantle of his saddle. "I've got you sized up for a feller as would go to hell and back for Belle." He thrust a large, age-yellowed envelope at Cole. "Keep it safe, young feller. It's a gov'mint paper and shows that Belle's *real* dad homesteaded thisahere ranch. I filed in his name, after he was killed. Never told Dacey nor nobody, but I reckon that paper makes Belle sure enough owner of JD."

Despite his anxiety to get away, Cole could not resist the question that boiled up in his mind. "Hasn't Dacey filed in his own name?"

"Ain't nobody filed but me, for Belle's dad, name of Henderson. I've been watchin' careful."

"Murran?" suggested Cole. His ears were prickling now. Those sounds he was hearing were not made by the wind.

"Him!" Sam's whispering voice took on the thin, sharp edge of hate. "Murran never filed on nothin'. He sure despised puttin' his name on gov'mint paper. Thisahere home ranch is still in the name of Frank

Henderson, and he was Belle's dad. I've watched it close, paid all taxes private, and Dacey and Murran never knowed what I was doin'."

"You should have done something about it years ago," frowned Cole.

"Was scared to open my mouth." Sam picked up the sorrel's tie rope. "It's up to you, young feller. I'm sure glad to turn that gov'mint paper over to you. The way my heart's actin' I'm liable to cash in my chips most any day."

Cole was straining his ears against the screaming wind. Those sounds he heard were unmistakable. Somebody was approaching the barn. He crouched back in the stall, slid gun from holster. Sam obeyed his warning gesture, started for the door with the horse. A voice came from somewhere down the dark runway, challenging, suspicious.

Sam stopped. Cole guessed the old man was reluctant to let him face the crisis alone, or else feared a hastily-flung shot that would bring a half score or more men on the run.

"What you want?" There was surly impatience in Sam's voice. "The gal's black colt bust loose, went off in the pasture some place. I was just goin' after him."

The plausible explanation seemed to banish the newcomer's suspicions. "Leave the colt wait until you get Murran's team hitched. He's high-tailin' it back to town — him and Blackie Stenlo." The unseen speaker paused. "Here's Blackie now," he added. "Comin' on the run like he's some excited."

The pounding feet came up fast. Cole waited, heart-sick. The good luck had run out. Too late now, to make a dash for the door, already blocked by Sam and his horse.

The man spoke again, grumblingly. "Where's your lantern, Sam? Let's get some light here."

Blackie Stenlo's wheezy voice broke in excitedly. "Sam! Has the Dacey gal been in after her black colt?"

The other man saved Sam the trouble of thinking up an answer. "The colt got loose. Sam was just goin' to look for him in the horse pasture when I come in."

There was a silence, then Blackie's voice. "You won't find her bronc in the pasture. The gal is missin', too. She ain't 'round the house no place. I reckon she come and got the colt when Sam wasn't watchin' and high-tailed it away."

"Somethin' queer goin' on here," muttered the other man. "I'm bettin' Sam helped her make the getaway and was fixin' to follow her when I come in. He was lyin' about the colt bustin' loose."

Cole heard the scrape of guns jerked from holsters, a vicious snarl from Blackie Stenlo. "Get your hands up, Sam. I reckon Murran will be wantin' to make talk with you."

Sam dropped the sorrel's tie rope, lifted his hands. There was nothing else he could do. He was trapped, framed in the open doorway against the outside night, an easy target for their guns.

Straw rustled. Cole waited in the darkness of the stall, gun in lifted hand, his muscles like coiled springs.

He knew what he had to do. These men were ruthless killers. He would be as ruthless, show them no mercy.

Blackie Stenlo's bulky shape appeared. Cole let him pass. He had to get the other man first, before he could shoot. Fortunately, his intended victim was close on Blackie's heels. Cole clubbed him with the steel barrel of his gun.

The man's groan startled Blackie, and as he turned to look, old Sam leaped at him, snatched the gun from his momentarily lowered hand. The next moment Cole swung again, and the steel barrel of his Colt .45 caught Blackie flush on the temple. The big man was as strong as a bull. He lurched forward, hands reaching for the gun in Sam's clenched fist. Cole struck again. The big renegade's knees buckled, and suddenly he was down, sprawled across the legs of his senseless companion.

One look told Cole that both men would be unconscious for a long time. He stared down at their dark, still shapes, was suddenly aware of a third shape lying in the straw-littered runway. Old Sam, and there was something ominous in the way he lay there.

Cole bent over the choreman's prostrate body. Sam was dead. "*The way my heart's actin' I'm liable to cash in my chips most any day.*" Sam's last spoken words. Confessed cattle thief and outlaw, the smoldering spark of honest manhood in him had courageously flamed in defence of a deeply wronged young girl. In dying he had done much to brighten the dark pages of his life.

The minutes were precious. A moment's delay could bring disaster. Cole got the sorrel horse back in his stall, stripped off saddle and bridle, replaced them on the proper peg and went swiftly away from that dark scene of violence and death. There was nothing he could do for Sam, only make use of the few minutes the old man's flaming devotion had gained for Belle.

She was in her saddle, holding the buckskin horse ready for him. "Where's Sam?" She peered down at him, her face an indistinct blur in the sand-whipped night.

Cole's answer drew an anguished little cry from her. "Dead? Sam — *dead?*"

Cole stepped into his saddle. "I wouldn't be here if he hadn't jumped Blackie," he said. "Let's make the most of the chance he gave us."

They found a gate, rode steadily into the hills. Belle pressed her horse close to the buckskin. "Cole —" The wind almost smothered her words. "I heard Murran say that a lot of men were coming from town. He plans to raid the Bowman ranch — kill that — that girl and her father."

She wondered if he had heard her, turned her head in a quick look at him. The harsh profile etched against the darkness was answer enough. She swung her quirt, sent the black colt into a run. "Come on, Cole! Let's ride it fast!"

CHAPTER EIGHTEEN

It seemed to Jane Bowman that even the sky had a savage, foreboding look. The mountains were lost to view behind a menacing brown murk that she guessed was sand blowing from vast desert wastes. Fitful gusts of wind moaned through the trees.

She came down the kitchen steps, paused, wondering at the unnatural quiet in the yard. The cattle were drifting up the slope beyond the big pond, spreading out and contentedly grazing. Their bawls had subsided to an occasional bellow of a herd bull.

The stillness in the yard affected her unpleasantly. Something was wrong. Where were the vaqueros and their recently arrived women and children? She should be hearing voices happily chattering in Spanish, the excited shrieks of little *muchachos* and *muchachas* inspecting their new home. The strange silence was ominous, increased uneasy apprehensions that had been mounting from the moment Cole had left for the Dacey ranch. She knew he had made the right decision, but the thought of his danger appalled her. His attempt to get Belle Dacey away from the ranch could easily end in disaster.

Fear constricted Jane's heart as she stood there. She might never see Cole Thomason again. She looked up at the sinister brown murk billowing over the heavens, felt horribly alone and helpless in a dark and ugly world.

She shook her head, suddenly impatient with herself. She was letting fear get her down, behaving like a cringing little coward. She was a Bowman, and Bowmans kept their chins up, no matter what happened. She was also the granddaughter of Juanita Rivera, the beloved señorita of the forebears of those vaqueros now so mysteriously silent in the yard beyond the trees.

She reached the edge of the grove, stopped again, wide-eyed gaze on the Mexicans grouped around the wagons drawn up in a clearing the vaqueros had chopped free of brush. Beyond the clearing were a number of ancient adobe cabins, a double row with a narrow street between. They had not been occupied since Don Francisco Rivera had abandoned the rancho to the *Yanqui* conquerors. Jane knew it was Tranquilo Baca's plan to repair the crumbling walls, make the little rancho village come alive again.

It was plain that some calamity had befallen these kindly people Tranquilo had brought from below the border to help revive the ancient glories of *El Rancho Rivera*. Their dark faces were sullen masks of grief and smoldering anger. Some of the women were weeping softly, frightened children clinging to their skirts. Tranquilo was there, and her father, and she could hear the big chief of vaqueros' deep-throated voice, stern, admonishing.

Jane was suddenly remembering something odd she had seen just before Cole had ridden away on the dangerous mission that was taking him back to the Dacey ranch. A slow-moving wagon entering the yard, two solemn-faced vaqueros following close behind, flat-brimmed hats in their hands. She had been too worried about Cole to understand the significance of that little procession. She knew now it could have meant only one thing. *Death*.

She was remembering something else. The blond young cowboy, stumbling along at the end of Julio's rope. The vaqueros would have no mercy on the gringo who had slain one of their comrades. No wonder he had looked so frightened.

Her father saw her watching. He said something to Tranquilo and hurried toward her.

"It's bad business." His tone was grave. "Ramon's little brother was killed during the raid. A stray bullet, but the vaqueros are very angry. They want to hang the young JD man Tranquilo captured."

"I guessed as much." Jane gazed worriedly at the men across the yard. "We've got to stop them."

"I told Tranquilo I won't allow a lynching on this ranch," Lewis Bowman said. "He's doing his best to talk them out of it." He shook his head gloomily. "I don't know. They're in an ugly mood."

"Tranquilo is coming over now." Jane spoke hopefully. "I think it's going to be all right, Father. The men are beginning to unload the wagons."

The chief of vaqueros gave the girl a grave smile, answered the question in her eyes. "There will be no trouble," he reassured. "They have agreed to turn the gringo over to Señor Thomason who is a United States Deputy Marshal."

"It is a sad home-coming for them," Jane said sorrowfully.

"Many of us lie in the old graveyard yonder." Tranquilo gestured at a grove of trees. "Benito rides to Boca Grande for the padre, and soon there will be another grave."

A shout came faintly from the arroyo.

"Julio!" Tranquilo exclaimed. "Somebody comes." Astonishment deepened his voice. "*Por Dios!* Mateo Cota, and he rides the pinto horse."

Jane and her father exchanged startled looks, waited in silence for the old Mexican to approach. He slid from his saddle, respectfully removed his hat.

"*Si* —" He looked at Bowman. "It is the pinto horse ridden by the man who tried to kill you, señor."

"Where did you find him?" Bowman asked.

"The horse was left in the barn for the town marshal, Señor Turlo, to take into the chaparral and kill," explained the Mexican. "Señor Murran was very angry with Stinger for riding the pinto into the yard. He did not want it known that Stinger worked for him in secret to kill you, señor."

Bowman nodded, his face grim. "It proves that Murran is Adna Fenn," he said to Jane. "Only Adna Fenn has reason for wanting me dead."

"Señor Murran was very frightened when he heard that friends have come to fight for you." Mateo gave them a brief account of what he had overheard. "He has learned the truth about Señor Thomason and has gone to the Dacey ranch with Yuma and Stinger to catch him."

"Cole won't know!" Jane gave her father a despairing look. "He'll be trapped!"

Bowman, his face grave, made an attempt to comfort her. "Cole is no tenderfoot," he reminded. "He's got a nose for danger."

Tranquilo was eyeing the pinto horse curiously. "You came fast from Boca Grande," he said to Mateo. "This horse must have wings."

"The caves," Mateo replied.

Tranquilo nodded. "An old Apache trail," he explained to the Bowmans. "Cuts the distance to less than half. Only a few of us Mexicans left who know the secret of the caves." He gave Mateo an approving smile. "You did well to bring the pinto. Señor Thomason will be pleased."

"I promised him to use my eyes and ears," Mateo said. He looked at Bowman. "There is more I have learned, señor. I heard Señor Murran order Sil Turlo to bring many bad men to the Dacey ranch. He plans a big raid that will destroy all of us."

There was a silence, broken by Bowman. "It's not safe for you here, Jane."

She gave him a faint smile. "I'm as safe here as anywhere."

"Tranquilo can take you across the border — to friends in Chihuahua," her father suggested.

"I'm not running away," Jane said.

Tranquilo nodded approvingly. "We will fight them, my señorita." His eyes gleamed. "Now that we are warned we will be ready."

"We won't know where to watch for them," worried Bowman.

Tranquilo's hand lifted in a contemptuous gesture. "They will come the easy way, down the Hang Tree trail and through the pass," he said. "They will be trapped, under our guns." His laugh came, deep-throated, confident. "It will be the finish of these gringo wolves."

"It sounds dreadful." Jane spoke unhappily. "I — I suppose it's the only way."

Her father said grimly. "It's their lives — or ours."

"Señorita —" Mateo Cota's worried look was on Jane. "There is something you should know about *El Rancho Rivera*."

"Yes, Mateo?" Jane sensed he was addressing her as the descendant of Don Francisco's daughter.

"Señor Thomason told me to keep eyes and ears sharp." Mateo looked at Tranquilo Baca. "It is possible you already know what my ears hear Señor Murran tell Señor Dacey."

"No." Tranquilo frowned. "What is this thing you heard?"

"There is silver in Cañon Agua Frio." Mateo hesitated. "It is one of the two reasons Señor Murran wants our señorita and her father to die very soon."

Amazement widened Tranquilo's eyes. "I was born on this rancho and have never heard this tale of silver in Cañon Agua Frio."

Bowman gave Jane a grim smile. "No wonder Murran wants to be rid of us."

"Where is Cañon Agua Frio?" Jane asked.

Tranquilo waved up the slope. "Above the big springs. The gringos call it Coldwater Canyon."

"Silver," muttered Bowman. His eyes took on a gleam. "Some news, eh, Jane?"

"I suppose so." Jane spoke wearily. "I don't see any good in it now. It only makes things worse — makes Nat Murran all the more dangerous."

Their undisguised elation depressed her. Mateo's talk of silver was more important than the new peril threatening Cole Thomason. The news that Nat Murran had left for the Dacey ranch frightened her, despite her father's confidence in Cole's ability to smell danger. Cole was unaware that Murran had learned he was the mysteriously missing man from Santa Fé and would be looking for him at the ranch.

She went slowly back to the house, her heart heavy with misgivings. She would have given the ranch, the cattle — the silver in Cañon Agua Frio, in exchange for Cole Thomason's safe return. A hopeless wish, she realized miserably. There could be no barter with Adna Fenn, alias Nat Murran.

The gusts of wind had become a steady gale that kept up a ceaseless roar through the trees. Jane made the rounds of the house, shut windows and doors, finally found her sewing basket and sat down to do some mending. It was no use. Her nerves were too jumpy. She pushed the basket aside, flung herself on the bed, was suddenly aware of a voice frantically calling her name.

She ran into the kitchen. Benito stood inside the door, hand beckoning urgently.

"Señorita!" The words tumbled from his lips. "Señorita — there is much trouble! Please come quick!"

Jane gazed at him, speechless. Something dreadful had happened to her father. She could think of no other reason that would explain the old Mexican's fright.

He interpreted her dismay, shook his head. "No, no — not *El Señor!* It is the young gringo. They have taken him from the *cárcel* and say they will hang him."

"The gringo?" Jane struggled out of her sickening panic. "Where is Tranquilo — my father? Why don't you tell them — instead of me?"

Benito gestured. "They are not here, señorita. They went to Cañon Agua Frio with Mateo. There is not time to send word to them."

"I don't know what *I* can do," Jane said a bit hysterically. The situation appalled her. She felt that her father and Tranquilo should not have gone off and left her alone at such a critical time. Of course they had not expected the vaqueros to get out of hand again, and it was apparent that Tranquilo was not particularly worried about Murran's plans to raid the ranch. Nevertheless she found herself resenting their absence. It was hardly possible she could persuade the enraged vaqueros to forego their dreadful purpose.

"They won't even listen to me." She was unaware she had given voice to her distress, was surprised at the curious glow her words put in Benito's eyes.

"You are our señorita," the old Mexican said with gentle emphasis. "When our señorita speaks, we obey. Her word is our law — not to be broken."

Jane gazed at him, but the face she saw was the proud and lovely face of the Señorita Juanita Rivera painted by Carter Ruffin in the long ago. Courage and resolve took fire in her. She was a Rivera, too, as well as a Bowman, a descendant of the hidalgos who for generations had been lords of the old rancho.

She said, almost fiercely, "Come! Take me to them!"

The vaqueros heard Benito's warning shout, waited in sullen silence as Jane swiftly approached the cottonwood tree where they stood with their prisoner.

She went directly to the young JD man, pulled the noose from his neck and flung the rope on the ground. Her chin high, she turned and faced the glowering men.

"Shame on you!" She spoke quietly, but the scorn in her clear voice was like the lash of a whip. "You would break the promise you gave Señor Baca."

"The gringo dog killed Ramon's little brother," one of the vaqueros said gruffly. "He must die."

"We have no proof the bullet came from his gun," argued Jane. She was finding it hard to keep fear from her voice.

"It is all the same," the vaquero answered. "He was one of them. He must die."

“Not by your hands,” Jane said. “Put him back in the *cárcel*. You have my promise he will be turned over to Señor Thomason who is a United States Deputy Marshal.”

“The gringo law will turn him loose,” grumbled another vaquero.

“I am your señorita,” reminded Jane coldly. “With you, my word is law. It is my command that you return this man to the *cárcel* and that you make no further attempt on his life.” She paused, studied their dark faces with stern eyes. “Manuelo — Domingo — I make you two responsible for his safety. Your lives will be forfeit for his.”

The vaqueros gazed at her, respect, awe, in their eyes. It was talk they understood. She was a Rivera whose word for generations had been the only law they knew.

Jane sensed their submission, gestured imperiously. “It is finished,” she said. “I have spoken.”

Manuelo and Domingo stepped forward, stood on either side of the prisoner.

Jane gazed at him curiously. He was hardly more than a boy. “What is your name?” she asked.

“Curly, ma’am.” The cowboy’s freckled face lifted in a grateful look. “I’m sure obliged to you, ma’am.”

Jane asked another question. “Did Mr. Dacey send your outfit to stampede our cattle?”

“No, ma’am. He wasn’t knowin’ about the cows. We was scoutin’ ’round over in Lost Horse Canyon when me and Ringo spotted the herd.” Curly glanced uneasily at the watchful, dark faces. “Lute Soler got awful excited, said the boss wouldn't want them cows on our JD range. He said for us to turn the herd back, and the wagons."

"This ranch is not JD range," Jane told him.

"I wasn't knowin', ma'am," Curly said. "I'm only a cowhand. Lute would hand me my time awful fast if I didn't do what he says."

"You're too young to be mixed up in such dreadful things," scolded Jane.

Curly shuffled his feet. "I'd sure like to get a long ways off from this Boca Grande country. Ain't stayin' because I want to."

"Do you mean you're hiding out from the law?" Jane asked.

"I reckon so, ma'am." Curly's face lifted again in a shame-faced look. "Was buildin' me a herd back in the Strip, and got to swingin' too wide a loop. Had to leave there on the jump and that's how come Nat Murran got me a job with Dacey's outfit."

Jane nodded, her eyes deeply pitying. "I think I understand." She frowned. "Your first mistake was in running away from Oklahoma."

"They hang cow-thieves, back in the Strip," Curly said.

His laconic statement appalled her. It was in her mind that the rough and ready justice of the border west was little less than murder. He had fled the Oklahoma Strip to escape a death similar to the one from which she had just saved him. She heard her voice, comforting, reassuring.

"You must tell Mr. Thomason all about it. He's a United States Deputy Marshal — the law, and its the *law's* justice you need." Jane wondered unhappily if she would ever see Cole again. More than Curly's life depended on Cole Thomason.

"Yes, ma'am." Curly spoke humbly. "I reckon you're talkin' good sense."

"I know I am," asserted Jane. She looked at Domingo and Manuelo. "Take him to the *cárcel*." Her eyes flashed, her voice hardened. "Remember what I told you. Keep him safe."

Their voices answered as one. "*Si señorita*."

Jane stood there, watching until the two Mexicans and their prisoner disappeared inside the squat adobe that was the ranch jail. It was an ancient building and for generations had represented the power and the law of the lords of the rancho. The thought stirred her and she was suddenly aware of a great pride in the hidalgo blood Juanita Rivera had given to the Bowmans.

Her look went to the group of silently watching vaqueros. Her smile came, lay warm on her face, put a glow in her dark eyes. She said, softly, "Thank you my good friends."

The wind was threshing the big cottonwood under which she stood, almost smothered her low-spoken words, but the vaqueros heard, and their voices lifted in a great answering shout, "*Viva La Señorita! Viva El Rancho!*"

CHAPTER NINETEEN

The fitful gusts came faster and harder, flung stinging flurries of sand that rattled like buckshot through the harsh chaparral. Belle's black colt was not liking it, began to sulk. She fought desperately to keep him in the trail.

"He won't face it!" she cried despairingly. "I can't hold him, Cole."

Cole swung his horse in close, seized the black's bridle. "We'll put him on a short lead-rope," he said.

Belle unfastened the rope tied to her saddle and in a few moments they were again moving along the trail, heads lowered against the stinging sand, the black colt snorting, reluctant, but unable to resist the pull of the rope firmly snubbed over the horn of Cole's saddle.

The darkness closed over them like a suffocating blanket. Cole could hardly see beyond the buckskin's flattened ears. Uneasiness grew in him. The sound of hoofs sucking in deep sand indicated they were off the trail, and he did not like the low, menacing roar that seemed to be coming closer every minute.

He drew his horse to a halt. "I'm afraid we're lost," he said to Belle. "I can't see a thing."

"I'm frightened." Her voice was panicky. "Listen to that wind."

"We're in for it," Cole decided. "Slide from your saddle and stick close to me. We've got to find some kind of shelter." He was down from his horse now, hand reaching for hers, and leading their horses they commenced what seemed like a hopeless search.

Something dark loomed in front of them, a low ridge of tumbled boulders at the base of a lone butte; and Cole guessed why the buckskin had pulled off the trail. The desert-wise horse wanted shelter, too, had instinctively headed for the protection of the giant upthrust of rock.

They were hardly behind the ramparting boulders when the sandstorm hit with all its force, blasting across desert dunes with a roar that deafened their ears. Sheets of sand swirled over the rocks, drew resentful snorts from the horses. Belle pressed close to Cole where they crouched under an overhanging ledge, tried to shield her eyes against his shoulder. She was trembling, little spasms that shook her from head to foot. She had been through too much horror. Cole's arm went around her, and presently the fit of shaking subsided.

"It's the worst I've ever seen." Her hand tightened over his fingers. "I hate these sandstorms. One of our line riders was caught in one. It was years before his body was found."

Cole had heard similar stories of men and horses trapped in the crawling dunes, and found later when some new storm uncovered their bleached bones.

"We're safe enough, here," he reassured.

"I'd rather be here, than back at the ranch," Belle said. "Cole — what will become of me?"

"You'll be taken care of," Cole said.

"I don't even know my real name."

Cole was remembering the age-yellowed envelope Sam had given him. *Name of Frank Henderson*. Almost the old cowboy's last words. He repeated them to Belle.

She was silent for a moment. "I don't know —" Her voice was troubled, doubtful. "Pops loved me a lot, even if he did do — wicked things." She faltered. "He was killed trying to save me. Perhaps I should keep his name."

"No," Cole said. "Your name is your real father's right to give. He was trying to make a home for you when he was murdered. His name and his land belong to you."

"Do you mean JD belongs to me?" There was genuine amazement in her voice.

"I'm going to make certain of it." Cole's arm tightened reassuringly. "One of the first things I'll do when we're out of this mess." He wondered grimly if they ever would be out of it, resolutely pushed doubts aside. The girl huddled against him was needing cheer. In one moment she had seen her world crumble to ashes, learned that the man she thought was her father was not her father, heard him admit complicity in an abhorrent crime.

He found himself again wondering about the man who had shot Yuma. He had arrived at the ranch with

Murran and the other two renegades. Belle had never seen Stinger before, so he was not a JD man. One fact was clear. He would have killed Murran but for Blackie Stenlo's quick shooting.

Cole stared thoughtfully at the dark shapes of their horses, crowding close to the base of the butte. There was a familiar sound to the dead man's name. Something Cherokee had said only that afternoon. "*You want to know about the feller that rides the pinto horse . . . It was Murran sent him to kill Bowman . . . Wears the name of Stinger . . . a tough hombre . . .*"

Realization of the slain renegade's identity increased Cole's mystification about the shooting scene in the ranch office. He could find only one possible answer that might explain why Stinger had shot Yuma and tried to kill Nat Murran. His failure to destroy Lewis Bowman must have enraged Murran who probably had said enough to arouse Stinger's suspicions. Men who failed, or displeased the deadly little liveryman, had a way of disappearing, and no questions asked.

It was a plausible explanation that satisfied Cole. The picture was beginning to make sense. When Jasper Dacey reached for the gun in his desk drawer, Stinger had made a last, desperate gamble — and lost.

Another stinging flurry of sand whirled over the ledge. Belle stirred restlessly in his arm. "My face feels like raw beef," she complained.

Cole pulled off his bandanna. She pushed it aside. "I want to talk." Her pliant young body turned, brought her face close to his. "Cole —" Her voice was earnest, demanding. "Do you like Jane Bowman?"

He thought it over, said simply, "Yes."

"I mean do you like her a lot?"

"Yes," he repeated. "I reckon I like her a lot, Belle. I haven't had much time to think about it."

"Does she like you a lot? I mean the same way you like her?"

Cole thought that one over, too. "I think she does, Belle." There was an odd surprise in his voice, as if he had just made a wonderful discovery.

"I'll bet she hates me, making all this trouble for you."

"She wanted me to come and get you." Cole was suddenly silent, recalling those last moments with Jane, the promise in her eyes. He said, softly, "She's that kind of girl, Belle. She's wonderful."

Something like a smothered giggle came from the lips pressed against his shoulder. "I'll bet she can't ride 'em wild the way I can. I'll bet she'd fall off the first buck."

"I'll bet she would," solemnly agreed Cole.

Belle twisted free of his arm, brushed sand from her eyes. "I'm going to be a lady, too," she declared. "I'm going to school in Santa Fé and learn to be a lady — like your Jane Bowman."

He thought to himself, "Half child, half woman." Aloud, he said, "Such talk. You're lady enough just as you are."

"No!" Belle spoke soberly. "I'm like a colt that's run wild too long on the range. I need halter-breaking — the burrs combed from my hair."

Cole felt there was nothing more to be said. Her candid self-appraisement impressed him. She had the game heart of a thoroughbred, honesty and shrewdness, virtues that would carry her a long way. No need of words from him. Belle was already set to blaze her own trail. He promised himself, though, to keep his word about securing her rights to the big cattle ranch Jasper Dacey had developed from her murdered father's homestead.

She spoke again, sleepily. "I wish this wind would stop. My ears are getting numb with all that battering noise."

He offered the bandanna again, and this time she made no protest, pulled the silk over eyes and face, leaned against his shoulder, was almost instantly asleep.

Cole wondered how she could do it, was aware of an odd, warming glow as he felt he had the answer. She had settled things in her own mind, knew what she was going to do. The rest of it she was leaving to him in childlike faith that he would keep her safe from harm.

The hours dragged, and of a sudden the hoarse voice of the storm seemed to vanish into the distance. The stillness almost hurt his ears, awoke the sleeping girl. She sat up with a start, snatched the bandanna from her face.

"It's over," Cole said. He got to his feet, stretched cramped legs. "Getting lighter." He peered around with red-rimmed eyes. "Dawn's coming fast. Let's get started."

Belle got up, shook sand from hat and clothes. "I'm a desert rat," she fumed. Her face, plainly visible in that gray dawn, lifted in a look at him. "Don't think I'm crying. It's the darn sand in my eyes." She looked away, added in a low voice, "I just want you to know I've had a lot of sense knocked into me, and — and if Jane Bowman isn't good to you she'll never be a friend of mine."

"I'll tell her." Cole grinned, reached for the black colt's tie rope.

Belle climbed into her saddle. "I'll tell her myself." Her chin lifted. "I'll tell her she's crazy if she doesn't know that Cole Thomason is a man to ride the river with."

She heard his startled exclamation, saw he was gazing intently at a low ridge that sloped down from the hills a good quarter of a mile away.

He said urgently, "Quick! Get down!"

Belle obediently slid from her saddle, stood by his side, peered over the ledge at the horsemen silhouetted against the paling sky. More riders appeared, dropped from sight below the ridge. She gave Cole an appalled look.

"Oh, Cole! We're too late! They're ahead of us!"

He nodded, his face troubled. "More than thirty of them," he said. "I counted."

Belle sank on a boulder, put her face in her hands. "I'm so frightened. We can't do anything now."

Cole nodded again. The more than thirty riders he had glimpsed indicated that Sil Turlo had wasted no time sending reinforcements out to JD. Apparently they planned a surprise attack and it looked bad for Tranquilo Baca's outnumbered vaqueros. He could only hope that Julio's sharp eyes and ears would discover the raiders in time to sound the alarm.

"Is there any other trail?" he asked Belle. "You know this country."

She shook her head. "I don't know any way down to the arroyo except the Hang Tree trail. They've got us stopped."

"Only thing we can do is follow them," Cole decided. He looked at her worriedly. "It's going to be dangerous. You don't need to come."

She was instantly scrambling into her saddle. "You're not leaving me here," she declared. "I'm going, too, and anyway I've no other place to go."

"You could go to Boca Grande, stay with Dr. Johnson," he suggested. "He'll take care of you."

"I'm going where you go," Belle said. "Anyway, Nat Murran is back in town by now. I'd run smack into him. I like Doc Johnson, but he couldn't do a thing against Nat Murran." She settled herself in the saddle. "Come on! Let's ride."

Cole knew she was right. He could not leave her to wander the desert trails alone. There was no place for her to hide from Nat Murran.

He got into his saddle, and they rode steadily, cautiously, through the ghostly dawn, came finally to the dead pine on the bluff that overlooked the arroyo.

They halted, and Cole got down from his saddle and crawled to an overhang of rock around the bend in the trail. Sounds reached him from the brush-chocked gorge below, the scrape of shod hoofs on flinty rock, the creak of saddle leather, men's voices. It was plain the raiders were making no effort to conceal their presence, were confident of their ability to wipe out the nesters they had been sent to ruthlessly destroy.

Hope flared through Cole. The vaqueros could not fail to hear and understand. The warning, though brief, would give them a fighting chance. He lay there, wondering desperately what he could do to help. To follow too closely now would be suicide, draw not only the raiders' fire, but invite bullets from the vaqueros.

He heard a faint shout from the opposite bank. Tranquilo Baca's voice, and almost instantly the crashing report of a rifle. A yell of pain floated up from the deeps of the arroyo, and of a sudden more rifles were spitting flame and smoke from the opposite slope, a crescendo of gunfire that beat like thunder against high, granite cliffs. Cole heard dismayed yells, the crash of plunging horses in the brush as the raiders fled from the deadly ambush.

He ran back to Belle, motioned her to get down and slide over the bluff. She obeyed, and after a breathless moment he found a place the horses were willing to attempt and led them to a thick clump of junipers below the trail. Belle's hasty descent had landed her on hand and knees. She picked herself up, hurried to him, crouched by his side behind the concealing junipers.

A lone rider spurred around the bend. A dangling arm told them he was wounded. Two horses followed, their saddles empty. More riders appeared. They poured up from the arroyo, spurring tired horses. Cole counted as they fled past the dead pine. Fifteen of them, and in full flight. Others were still below, dead, or seeking cover from the vaqueros' rifles.

He told Belle what must have happened. "Tranquilo trapped them in the narrow gorge, a bottle-neck, where the trail crosses to the other side. It was slaughter. Those men hadn't a chance."

"Who's Tranquilo?" wondered the girl.

"He's the vaqueros's boss, and the smartest Mexican I ever knew." Cole spoke softly, awe, a great thankfulness in his voice. "He's beaten off the raid. It's all over."

They waited, listening to the intermittent rifle shots. "Picking off the skulkers in the brush," Cole said. He wondered if Lute Soler was down there, perhaps dead. He had not recognized the JD foreman among the fleeing desperados.

Three more riders swarmed past, and another empty saddle. Cole turned his attention to the rugged slope below. He was anxious to get to the house.

"Too rough for riding," he said, "but we could lead the horses, do some scrambling." He looked at Belle. "Can you manage it?"

She understood his impatience, gave him a grave little nod. Jane Bowman would be a very worried girl right now, wondering about Cole Thomason, perhaps thinking he was dead. "Let's," she said. "I can stand a few tumbles."

They began the precarious descent, Cole leading the way with the horses . . .

The crash of gunfire awoke Jane. She lay rigid for a moment. She was having a bad dream, she thought, and then she heard her father's hurried movements in his room. He was dressing, stamping into his boots.

Jane sprang from the bed, hastily flung on some clothes, slipped into her shoes and ran into the hall in time to see her father slam through the kitchen door. He was carrying a rifle.

She resisted the impulse to run after him. He would only send her back. She stood there, feeling very small and very helpless in that ghostly gray dawn. Yells drifted up faintly from the big arroyo, pierced the thunderous crash of the rifles. She vaguely guessed what had happened. The raiders had ridden into the ambush Tranquilo Baca had promised he would have ready for them.

She found herself standing under the trees, the heart in her heavy as lead. Cole had not returned from the Dacey ranch. He was dead. She would never see him again. It was more than she could bear. Life would not mean much without Cole, and she had let him ride away to save the daughter of the man whose riders had come to kill her, kill her father and all the kindly Mexicans who had returned to the old ranch home of their ancestors.

She heard a stealthy footstep, a dark shape was suddenly by her side. A hand grasped her arm, fingers biting into the soft flesh.

Jane's head lifted in a horrified look at the big man bending over her.

"I'm needin' a bronc," Lute Soler said in a low, gasping whisper. "You're takin' me to the barn, savvy?" The gun in his other hand nudged her side. He was struggling for breath. "Climbin' out of that damn arroyo took my wind. Got to get a bronc awful quick and hightail it away from here while that Mex bunch is busy down there."

Jane moved along by his side, helpless in his grasp, an automaton, unable to think — to resist. The corral gate was open, the barn doorway a yawning blackness from which Soler hoped to snatch a horse.

Another shape materialized, came to a standstill, hardly visible in that dark stable entrance. Soler muttered an oath, lifted his gun, and Jane heard somebody speaking. "That's Curly." It was her own voice, and the sound of it cleared the numbness from her brain. "He must have escaped from the *cárcel* and wants a horse, too." She was cool, matter-of-fact.

Curly, peering from the dark doorway, had recognized Soler. He slid up cautiously, and Jane saw a big *machete* clenched in his hand. He must have found it in the *cárcel*, apparently left unguarded during the excitement in the arroyo.

Soler said in a relieved voice. "Sure is a lucky break, us meetin' here, Curly."

"What's all the shootin?" asked the young renegade.

"Them damn Mexicans was layin' for us," growled Soler. "You go throw on a couple of saddles. We're leavin' here fast."

"What you doin' with her?" Curly was looking uneasily at Jane. He saw now that Soler's hand was gripping her arm savagely. His *machete* flashed up. "Damn you, Lute! I ain't lettin' you harm her. Turn her loose."

Soler parried the knife thrust with the barrel of his gun. He was afraid to shoot, attract attention. He swung again. Jane heard a sickening crunch of bone, a groan from Curly as he fell almost at her feet. The young cowboy had repaid his debt to her, died better than he had lived.

Soler, breathing hard, started to drag her into the stable. A voice, sharp, deadly, spoke from somewhere behind them.

"Turn her loose, Soler!"

The big man whirled, and taking advantage of his momentary distraction, Jane twisted free from the clutching fingers.

"Cole!" she screamed. "Look out! He'll shoot!"

The two shots sounded like one. Soler staggered, fell on his side. He began to crawl toward his fallen gun, went suddenly limp. Even from where she stood, Jane knew he was dead.

Cole came pounding up. Jane was running, too, into his arms. They closed around her, held her tight. Words were not needed. She only knew that Cole was safe.

She became aware of a girl, standing midway in the corral. She was holding a black horse and looked very tired and dusty. Her expression showed deep interest, also satisfaction.

Jane drew back from Cole's arms, and the girl dropped the reins, ran toward her. "I'm Belle," she said, "and let me tell you something, Jane Bowman, or maybe you already know that Cole Thomason is a man to ride the river with."

"Yes," Jane said, a bit unsteadily. "I — I've known it for some time — ever since I met him."

"We're going to be good friends," declared Belle. Her voice choked, and she added simply, "I'm needing friends."

Jane kissed her. "I think we'd better go to the house," she said. "Come on, Belle, it's your house, too."

They heard Tranquilo Baca's deep-throated laugh in the distance. "It is finished!" he shouted. "The wolves will never return to *El Rancho Rivera. Viva El Rancho!*"

The vaqueros took up the shout. "*Viva El Rancho . . . Viva La Señorita!*"

Cole watched the two girls until the trees hid them. Tranquilo Baca was only partly right. It was not yet quite finished, not while he lacked the proof that Nat Murran was Adna Fenn. There could be no safety for the Bowmans while Murran continued to live a free man in Boca Grande.

He searched a pocket for tobacco and cigarette papers, felt his fingers close over a tightly wadded envelope. He drew it out. It was the envelope Belle had given him. "*The wind blew it through the window . . . Something Murran gave Pops to read.*"

Cole's pulse quickened as he gazed at the inscription. His name, and addressed to him at Boca Grande. Murran must have tricked the postmaster into giving it to him.

He extracted the single sheet of paper. The handwriting was familiar, and although there was no signature he knew the writer.

> . . . and the letter written some twenty years ago by your grandfather has only just been found in an old trunk. It confirms the rumor you picked up. Fenn was actually seen in Boca Grande by the man who carried the news to your grandfather, whose death soon afterwards put an end to the search. I believe that the man who recognized Fenn is also dead. His story indicates that Fenn was using the name of Nat Murran . . .

Cole slowly folded the letter, thrust it back in the envelope. Proof at last! Proof that Nat Murran was Adna Fenn!

He gazed with bleak, unseeing eyes at the two dead men sprawled near the barn door. His job was almost done. He would finish it in Boca Grande.

CHAPTER TWENTY

The puffs of dust south of the low ridge drew a relieved grunt from Nat Murran. He leaned the brass telescope against the bench, spoke softly to the apparently empty livery yard.

"I reckon we'll be getting news from JD right soon."

Blackie Stenlo's moon face peered from the bushes beyond the water-trough. "Somebody comin', boss?" His tone was surly. The mysterious attack in the Dacey barn had left him with a sore head. He was not liking the role of bodyguard inherited from the slain Yuma, yearned to be back at the hotel desk and reaching for the whiskey bottle he always kept in the drawer. "About time Lute showed up," he grumbled. "Must be close to noon and layin' here in the bushes is gettin' me cramped."

"It won't be long now," Murran said. "I'm just waiting for Lute to bring the good news. I reckon that's him coming down from JD now."

Sil Turlo rode into the yard, halted at the water-trough. He shook his head at the question in Murran's eyes. "Cain't pick up trace of the Dacey gal nowheres," he said. "I been all over town, talked to Doc

Johnson and Si Dunket. They ain't seen hide nor hair of her."

Murran scowled. Belle's mysterious disappearance worried him. He could think of only one answer. The girl was infatuated with Cole Thomason. She had fled with him. It explained the affair in the Dacey barn. It was Thomason who had left Blackie and the JD man lying senseless in the stable. Apparently old Sam would have gone, too, if he had not dropped dead from excitement.

Murran picked up his telescope, gazed morosely at the distant dust haze. He would soon know if Thomason had taken Belle to the Bowman ranch. He had told Lute Soler to watch out for her, bring her back to town.

"See 'em comin'?" asked the town marshal.

"It couldn't be anyone else, making that dust." Murran lowered the telescope, frowned. "Moving kind of slow. I told Lute to get here on the jump."

"I reckon the boys is some wore out," Turlo said. "It ain't reasonable to expect 'em to head for town on the jump after pullin' off a big raid like they done." He swung his horse from the trough. "Mighty queer where the Mex went with Stinger's paint horse. He sure ain't no place in this town."

"Keep on looking for him." Murran spoke viciously. "I'm nailing his ears to the barn."

The town marshal grinned. "I'll do the nailin'," he promised. "Like I told you, come dark I was over here to get the paint horse and take him out in the brush. The bronc was gone, and so was Mateo."

Blackie Stenlo spoke from the bushes. "I'm bettin' the Mex was listenin' back at the office just before we drove off to the Dacey ranch, boss. He heard you tell Sil to take the bronc out in the brush and shoot him."

"That's the answer," agreed Sil Turlo. "He's likely below the border by now — figgers to sell the bronc for some *dinero* to bet on a cock fight." The town marshal grinned knowingly. "Well, I'll get this horse over to the barn and head for the Chink's place. I'm cravin' a cup of coffee."

He disappeared inside the stable. Blackie said longingly, "I reckon I'll get myself a cup of coffee, too, boss."

"No," grunted Murran. "You're staying with me until Lute gets here." He looked up the street, drowsing under the midday sun. Fewer people than usual were astir under the wooden awnings that shaded the sidewalks. A dozen or more familiar saloon loafers were conspicuous by their absence. The telltale dust on the Dacey road indicated they would soon be back, eager to collect their pay from Sil Turlo for the night's work.

Murran smiled sourly. The time had come to be rid of them for keeps. He would have a house-cleaning, make Boca Grande a decent town. He was safe now, beyond any possible reach of the law's long arm. No more rustling, no more dealings with border desperados. He had money, range, cattle — a silver deposit in Cañon Agua Frio. Within the week he would start work on the great house that was to overlook his irrigated green meadows — the new hotel — the store and the bank. He would be the most powerful man in New

Mexico, might even get himself appointed governor of the Territory. A narrow escape, but the danger was past. Nothing more to fear from the Bowmans, from Cole Thomason. They were dead.

He thought glumly of Belle Dacey. He had set his heart on making her the mistress of his new house, lavishing on her the best that money could buy. Silks, jewels — all the luxuries due her beauty. He hoped Lute Soler was bringing her back. Too bad for Lute if harm had been done the girl during the raid.

His idling gaze saw Dunket appear in the doorway of his store. He seemed to be looking down the street in the direction of the livery yard.

Murran lifted the telescope, studied the storekeeper carefully. He was holding something in his hand, a large envelope. After a moment or two he disappeared inside his store.

A satisfied smile wiped the gloom from the fat little liveryman's face. His expected government papers that would give him legal title to the Rivera ranch. Evidently arrived on the morning stage, and Dunket was wondering why he hadn't been over for it. The storekeeper was probably curious, suspected the papers had something to do with the postmaster job he feared he was going to lose to the new store across the street. It would explain his impatience to deliver the letter.

Murran's smile widened. The letter could wait until after Lute Soler got in. He leveled the telescope again at the ridge, where the road forked west to the Dacey ranch. He muttered a startled ejaculation. The riders, half a score of them, were in plain view, only they were moving in the wrong direction, were unmistakably heading into the Hachita hills.

"Blackie!"

"What's wrong, boss?" The big renegade crashed through the bushes, hand jerking at his gun.

"Get hold of Sil Turlo quick," Murran said. "He's back in the barn some place."

"Was just wonderin' what's keepin' him in the barn so long." Blackie's hand came away from his gun. "What for you want him, boss?"

"Don't stand there asking fool questions," almost snarled Murran. He was gazing through the telescope again, and his face had taken on an odd grayness.

Blackie took a hasty look at the distant swirls of dust. Too far away for him to see what was worrying the boss. He set off at a lumbering run for the barn.

Murran continued to watch through the telescope. The glass was not deceiving him. He began to shake, lowered the telescope to his knees. Those fast disappearing riders meant the JD outfit, or what was left of it, was in panic-stricken flight. There could be no other answer. Lute Soler and his raiders had met with some appalling disaster. Sil Turlo would have to send somebody out to the ranch on the jump — find out what had happened. What was keeping Sil and Blackie at the barn so long, anyway?

The liveryman half rose from his bench, slumped down again as he heard the hurried tread of feet approaching from the barn behind him. He called out hoarsely, "Looks like there's something wrong out at

JD, Sil. The outfit's on the run. Just spotted a bunch of 'em making tracks for Hachita."

"That's right, Fenn. You've guessed it."

Horror froze Murran to the bench. Not the town marshal's familiar voice!

"Take it easy, Fenn," warned Cole Thomason. "Stand up, and keep your hands away from your pockets."

Murran got slowly to his feet, the brass telescope spilling from his knees. His dazed eyes glimpsed somebody coming down the street. The storekeeper, a large envelope in his hand.

Hands jerked his arms behind his back. He felt the bite of tough rawhide tighten over his wrists.

"It's the end of a long trail, Fenn," he heard Cole say.

He made a tremendous effort, shook off his paralyzing fright, turned and faced the man he had been thinking was dead. "You're crazy," he blustered. "My name isn't Fenn. I'll throw you in jail for this outrage."

"Your town marshal won't do the throwing," Cole said. "Mr. Turlo and Mr. Stenlo are both nicely tied up and headed for jail themselves. You look surprised," he added with a wintry smile.

Murran was gazing with bulging eyes across the yard at the group of armed Mexicans watching from the stable entrance. Mateo Cota was one of them.

"Yes," Cole drawled. "We got in the back way and have been watching you for the past few minutes while you were watching the Dacey road for Lute Soler." His voice hardened. "Soler is dead, Fenn, and a half score more of your hired killers."

"I'm not Adna Fenn," insisted the liveryman, his voice a mumble. Too late he realized his blunder, hung his head dejectedly.

Cole pounced. "I haven't said your name is Adna." He spoke softly. "I don't need to tell you, do I, Adna Fenn? You see, I already have the proof you're Adna Fenn, thief and murderer of Judge Spottisford." He touched his shirt pocket. "I have the letter you tricked from the postmaster. It was all I needed, Fenn, and you're going to hang."

"You can't prove it," muttered the liveryman. His bluster returned. "I've got money. I'll get lawyers, fight the case." He gave Cole a sly, speculative look. "I can make you a rich man, Thomason, if you'll forget this business."

Cole shook his head. "I'm interested in only one thing, Fenn — your neck in a noose for the murder of a fine old man who trusted you."

"It was a long time ago, more than twenty years," Adna Fenn reminded. "You can't prove I killed him."

"I don't need to," retorted Cole. "I'm arresting you for the murder of Jasper Dacey. I was outside the office and saw the shooting, and so did Belle."

"You can't arrest me," spluttered Fenn. "You don't wear a star." He broke off, appealed to the lanky storekeeper who was watching the scene with open-mouthed astonishment. "Dunket! This man's gone crazy. Round up some help quick!"

The storekeeper's worried look went to Cole. "Is your name Cole Thomason?" he asked.

"That's right," Cole answered. He asked a question of his own. "Did you give Murran a letter addressed to me?"

"I didn't want to." Dunket frowned. "He asked if there was mail for you, said you'd want him to take it to the Dacey ranch." His tone grew apologetic. "I like to run the post office right, but he was awful sure you'd want me to hand the letter over to him. Hope I didn't do wrong, Mr. Thomason."

"It turned out all right," reassured Cole with a grim smile.

Astonishment was again in the postmaster's eyes as he became aware of the liveryman's bound wrists. He gave Cole a doubtful look, hesitated, eyed the letter in his hand. "It's for you," he said. "Seemed important, so I thought Murran would want to send it out to you at the ranch." His look went to the liveryman, returned to the letter, and an odd elation wiped the doubt from his austere face. "From Washington," he told Cole, "and says here on the envelope you're a United States Deputy Marshal."

"That's right." Cole grinned, handed the storekeeper his gun. "I'm deputizing you to watch my prisoner while I read it."

"Nothing will give me more pleasure," Silas Dunket said with grim emphasis. "I always thought he was a low-down scoundrel."

Cole rapidly scanned the papers he extracted from the envelope. "These papers are for you," he informed Adna Fenn. "It seems you found out that the Rivera heirs never had title to the ranch confirmed after the Treaty of Hidalgo Guadalupe. These papers confirm your claim as owner under the name of Nat Murran."

"Forget this business and I'll give you a half interest in the ranch," Fenn said. He looked at the storekeeper. "I'll make a deal with you, too, Dunket. Deed over the new store, building and all."

Mr. Dunket spat disgustedly. "That's what I think of you," he growled.

Cole stuffed the papers back in the envelope, pushed the envelope in his pocket. "They were sent to me as a United States Deputy Marshal to hand over to you if my investigation proved you a bona fide claimant, Fenn." He gave the ashen-faced liveryman a satirical smile. "I can't approve, Fenn. You're a criminal and your true name is not Nat Murran."

Silas Dunket said nervously, "Here's the stage coming, Mr. Thomason. I've got to get back to the store, take care of the mail."

Cole relieved him of the gun. "I'm obliged for your help," he thanked.

"The pleasure," the lanky storekeeper assured him, "is all mine. I'm thinking this town will have a chance to be a decent place now you've scotched this rattlesnake." He turned on his heel.

Fenn's malignant gaze fastened on Cole. "You can't keep me in jail. I've friends in this town. They'll have me out just as quick as the news spreads. You're crazy, Thomason. Your Mexicans won't have a chance."

"I'll sneak you out the back way," smiled Cole. "An old Apache trail you and your friends never heard of."

His hand lifted in a beckoning gesture to the vaqueros watching from the barn door.

Tranquilo Baca swaggered up, his riders close on his jingling spurs. The big chief of vaqueros eyed the prisoner scornfully. "He does not look dangerous, this king wolf." His deep-throated laugh came. "An insect to be stepped on."

Cole was not listening. He was gazing incredulously at the passengers scrambling from the stage that had come to a sudden halt in front of the livery yard. Bill Hobson, foreman of his own hard-riding Diamond S outfit, and he had brought plenty of help with him. All of them wore guns and carried rifles. He could hardly believe his eyes.

The driver kicked off his brake and the big stage rolled up the street in a cloud of dust. The Diamond S cowboys followed Bill Hobson into the yard. The tall foreman wore a wide grin on his lean, hawk's face.

"Hi, there, Cole!" he yelled.

Cole came out of his daze. "Bill!" he yelled back. "For the love of pete! How come?"

"Well —" Bill Hobson's gaze slid past the Mexican vaqueros to the prisoner. His voice hardened. "We wasn't hearing from you like you promised. Seemed a smart idea for us to come and look you up."

"I'm mighty glad you did," Cole said. "I was wishing you boys were here."

"I figgered the quickest way to get here was to catch the stage out of Silver City," explained Bill. His keen look rested briefly on Adna Fenn. "Is he the feller?"

"That's right." Cole looked thoughtfully at the group of Diamond S riders. Hard-bitten, efficient men. He knew their capabilities. "I'm leaving it to you to keep an eye on things in town, Bill." He drew the foreman aside, spoke low, hurried words.

"I'll be back in the morning," he finished.

Bill Hobson nodded. "Come on," he said to the horrified prisoner. "I'm taking you to jail, mister."

Adna Fenn, alias Nat Murran, moved stumblingly away between two frosty-eyed Diamond S men. Cole hardly looked at him. It was long trail's end. His job was finished, and a great urge was in him to get back to Jane Bowman. The thought of Jane made him forget his weariness. She would be waiting for him.

He smiled at Tranquilo Baca. "Come, *amigo*," he said. "Let's ride."